T0274499

THE
HOLY GRAIL

A NOVEL

THE ZACH DORSEY SERIES: VOLUME TWO

MARC MOUTON

THE HOLY GRAIL

THE ZACH DORSEY SERIES:

VOLUME TWO

The cataloging-in-publication data™ is on file with the Library of Congress.

Copyright © 2023 by Marc Mouton

Print ISBN: 979-8-35092-923-2

eBook ISBN: 979-8-35092-924-9

To my family:
Cabell, Skyler, *and* **Sarah,**
for your love and devotion has inspired me.

To my fabulous editors Anne Evans, Arianna McCool,
and Roxanne Marchand, your contributions were
invaluable and appreciated.

And to all who have believed in me and my abilities,
whose trust and faith in me will be richly rewarded.

God's Hall of Fame

"Your name may not appear
in this world's Hall of Fame
in fact you may be so unknown
that no one knows your name.

The Oscar's and the praise of men
may never come your way
but don't forget God has rewards
that he'll hand out some day.

This crowd on Earth they will soon forget
when you are not at the top
they will cheer like mad until you fall
and their praise will stop - Not God.

He never does forget
and His Hall of Fame
by just believing in His Son
forever there's your name.

I tell you friend
I wouldn't trade my name however small
That's written there beyond the stars
In that celestial hall.

For all the famous names on Earth
or the glory that they share
I rather be an unknown here
and have my name up there."

Jim Caviezel

"In the End, the Truth will be told"

Jesus Christ

FACT

- "Then God said, let us make man in Our image, according to Our likeness; let them have dominion over this fish of the sea, over the birds of the air, and over the cattle, all the earth and over every creeping thing that creeps on the earth. So, God created man in His *own* image; in the image of God, He created him; male and female He created them. (Genesis 1:26-27)

- "Come Holy Dove, mother of two young twins; come Hidden Mother, revealed in deeds alone!" (The Acts of Thomas)

- The hill that Rome is situated on is now called the Vatican, it used to be called Vaticanus, which means, in Classical Latin, "The Place of Divination."

- The Vatican is a government with its own money, Secretary of State, and ambassadors. It is a recognized nation.

- The first Horseman in Revelation 6 is the White Rider on the white horse. He is the Antichrist and not Jesus Christ; he will be the counterfeit Christ. This white rider only has one crown (Rev.6:4-8). The papal dynasty had no natural line. When a man becomes a pope, he is not born into a royal dynasty. He is given a crown and a kingdom that are not his. All Catholics must provide their complete submission and obedience of will to the Roman Catholic Pontiff as God himself.

- In the 20th century, during World War II, Hitler, Mussolini, and Franco were each Roman Catholics who had given their allegiance to the Papacy. They each signed official contracts with the Vatican and were called concordats (a political and religious contract of mutual support). To Hitler, "Christianity" was Roman Catholicism. He served Pope Pious XII "And whatsoever ye shall ask in my Name, that will I do, that the All-Parent may be glorified in the Son and Daughter of Man. If ye shall ask anything in my Name, I will do it." (The Gospel of the Holy Twelve)

PROLOGUE

It has been two years since Zach and Sam Dorsey, together with Zach's sister, Dr. Sofia Boudreaux saved Pope Aloysious from the Holy Seer's vicious plan to usurp power, part of a centuries-long cover up by a secret society who has infiltrated the Vatican. With the help of his mentor, Brother Guiden a specialist in the Royal Blood descendants of Jesus and Mary Magdalene, Zach, Sam, and Sophia traveled New Orleans and the ancient cities of Alexandira and Rome to solve antiquated enigmas to find the Lost Gospels of Mary Magdalene and expose the cover up. Now, the Holy Seer has returned with new power backed by the Antichrist. Zach and Sam soon begin to unravel clues to prevent this new worldwide threat. Can they convince Sofia to join them on their new mission to understand how to redeem the women of the world and save the Blood Royal children? Will they be able to do so and still save what is most precious to them?

CHAPTER 1

August 23, 2023, 10:07 A.M - New York City

Looking out the windows of his father's six-million-dollar apartment, Jacan watched as the people of New York City bustled their way to their pointless jobs. Ultimately, none of it would matter, not to most of them anyway. They were like sardines smooshed together in a tin-can fighting for their way to be eaten first, the irony of it all.

Sitting on the ground outside Starbucks was a blind woman who often begged for money. Jacan especially liked to torment her. He would put Monopoly money in her cup instead of real money. Other times, he would put different kinds of bugs–dead or alive–in her cup: ants, cockroaches, spiders, whatever he could find to give her a jump scare. And it wasn't like he didn't have money to give; he was given a weekly allowance of five hundred dollars from his father, meager in his opinion, but it was better than what most other fourteen-year-olds were getting, if they even got an allowance.

Jacan was an only child and the heir to his parents' fortune–a diamond mine in South Africa. His father was Senator Robert Eisen, a charming man to the masses, but he ruled with an iron fist, both in politics and at home. His father was always on a crusade for something: stricter gun laws, abortion rights, or plastic use on the environment. When his father would come home drunk, he liked to smack Jacan around and "remind him" who paid the bills in the house.

There were many times Jacan had to lie to his teachers about the bruises on his arms or his face. He told them it was from playing street hockey with his friends. Some of his teachers believed him as he was tall and strong; he looked like an "athletic type of guy," but there was one teacher who did not believe him, calling his bluff on playing field hockey as he was a "loner type" who kept to himself. The guy wasn't wrong. Jacan wasn't one to "have friends," only people he would converse with from time to time. Jacan told this particular teacher that he got beat up by lower-class kids who stole his money. When his teacher wanted to talk to the principal and his parents about being bullied, Jacan made sure to have an "event" happen where the teacher was fired.

His mother, Helena, was a South African woman who met his father at a Safari hunt during the summer of Robert's sophomore year in college. Pictures of lions' heads as trophies were now locked away in a safe to secure Robert's status as Democratic Senator. His father was of Mayan American descent, and Jacan had inherited his high cheekbones, olive skin, brown hair and eyes, and sharp, distinctive nose. His mother was only forty years old but had already received seven plastic surgery operations in the past five years. Helena was always at some charity event, spa, or gallery opening. Jacan felt she had traded him in for exotic trips and paintings.

Jacan heard the front door open and close. He turned around to see a man's silhouette standing in the hallway.

"Are you ready?"

Jacan nodded.

"Good." The man walked over to Jacan and put his hand on his shoulder. "Lucifer is your father now, and he has chosen *you* personally for this mission. You will not fail him, I promise you. *You* were born for this."

"They will never accept me. I don't have any powers as they do," Jacan said bitterly. "I'll be caught in a day, Max."

"The Lord of darkness has a way to bypass all of that," Max said with a sinister smile. "Don't worry, my little dark lord in-training. All will be revealed. I will explain everything in the car."

Max took his hand off Jacan's shoulder, glancing at Jacan's black Louis Vuitton duffle bag on the dining room table. "You'll have to leave this bag with me after I drop you off. And no designer clothes going in. You'll need to blend in with the others."

Jacan sighed, shrugged, and crossed his arms all at the same time. "This blows."

"I know you like being rich, Jacan, but you can't show that there. If you're going to blend in and gain *their* trust, you *must* pretend to be like one of them," Max emphasized. "I know you can perform when needed. I've seen you do it a hundred times before to get what you want; the only difference is now you have the full Antichrist's attention. All eyes are on you." Max tapped Jacan's temple. "You are the key to making this whole thing work. Do you understand?"

"Yes…but why me? Why did he choose me?" Jacan implored. "There are so many more kids out there who have powers and can be damaging to others."

"He finds the Blood Royals who have powers repulsive. They represent the royal bloodline of Jesus, and he finds them all to be abhorrent, revolting, and deplorable. Our Lord wants nothing to do with them; he sees them as another subservient species."

"Like how Hitler viewed the Jews?"

"Precisely. In those days, the white race was the right race," Max checked his watch. "These days, the ones not born of the abominable Jesus blood are the right race."

"I understand the concept. But I still don't understand why he chose me over so many others."

"The dark lord sees many similar qualities of himself when he was your age inside of you," Max turned to face Jacan. "He picked you out of a hundred others to his eyes and ears on the ground. You should feel a sense of pride now after knowing this. You, Jacan, have what it takes to bring them all to their knees and get the necessary information. Don't be too friendly, but don't kill them off too quickly. I know how you can get on your… fixations. You're not there to make friends. You are there to gain information and execute the ones we do not need. Understand?"

Nodding his head, "Yes, uncle."

"Good. Now grab your bag, you've got a plane to catch, and I want you out of New York before the announcement airs."

Jacon tilted his head, "Which announcement, aren't there two?"

"Yes," he replied, "but the one I'm speaking of is detrimental to all mankind, and I need you on that plane just in case they shut down airports when the riots start."

CHAPTER 2

August 28th, 2023, 11:10 A.M. -New Orleans

Sitting on Zach's perfectly tidy desk was a stack of students' papers he needed to grade by next Thursday. Zach had become the youngest professor ever accepted at Tulane University and had even finished his Masters' Degree a year early. Tulane University was so pleased with his work on the Blood Royals that they offered him a part-time position as a professor teaching two classes: "*The New Testament*" and "*The Royal Bloodline of Jesus and Mary.*"

He had to admit that his class "*The Royal Bloodline of Jesus and Mary*" was "all the rage," as his students had put it anyway. *His* students. It was still an inexplicable concept to him when he was only twenty-three years old, teaching students who were just a few years younger than him–and sometimes, it had even put him in quite a predicament, educating mature adults in their thirties and forties who would argue with him at every chance they could or who tried to prove him wrong about the Royal Bloodline. It was truly exhausting. He didn't know how much longer he could put up with it.

Two years ago, if you had asked him if his dream job was to be a professor at Tulane University, he would, without a shadow of a doubt, say yes, but now he wasn't so sure. There was an emptiness starting to take hold of his soul that he could not shake. Like Indiana Jones, he wanted to do more, be more, and explore more. He was craving another adventure like the one he had two years ago, and even though it had almost cost him his life, he had never felt more alive in his life until those fateful days. It was almost as if the culmination of his life rested on that one adventure. No matter how much research he did or what he had accomplished for the new sect of Christianology, nothing would ever top the feeling of traveling the world looking for lost relics by way of riddles and clues.

"Professor Dorsey."

Zach looked up to see his teaching assistant Clara Dahle. A woman who, quite honestly, caught him off guard regarding her teaching tactics. She could command a room with just one glance and have the room laughing in a fit of tears. She was twenty-five years old and on the fast track to becoming a young professor. He thought she looked like a tall Nordic warrior princess, with her long blonde hair reaching the end of her back.

"It's time, professor. The others are waiting in the common area for you."

"Thank you, Clara. Why don't you go ahead, and I'll follow here in a moment."

"Of course," she nodded.

Clara did a roundabout turn and walked off as if she were a soldier in the Norwegian Army. Zach began gathering up the essays he needed to take home and grade. He knew it wouldn't take him long to grade the papers, but he was more interested in finding out more information on his recent project: The location of the Ark of the Covenant.

As he picked up the last essay, he noticed a red envelope underneath the stack of papers.

"*How odd…*" Zach thought as he quickly opened the red envelope to read the contents.

"You are cordially invited to the crowning of the Red Pope. We hope you join us in this beautiful celebration of the transference of spirit and blood. It is only by blood that a debt can be repaid, so rejoice! For the consummation will soon take place.
Location: The Vatican at 6:42 p.m."
This must be the acceptance of the Blood Royals! Brother Guiden had finally done it!

Zach thought to himself. Zach threw the envelope and the essays in his satchel and ran to the common room.

#

Jacan was the last person to step off Kieron's private plane, trailing behind Kieron's company, New Light Technologies, employees. Jacan took a deep breath and inhaled the pristine air; thankful it lacked the whiff of piss in New York. As Jacan watched the employees get into a waiting travel bus, he looked around for his promised instructions.

Soon, a non-disclosed black limo pulled up and stopped a few feet in front of Jacan. The window rolled down, and a light brown hand with silver painted nails extended through the opening, waving at him to come inside. Jacan grabbed his luggage, opened the car door, and sat inside next to an attractive woman who looked like the creole women of New Orleans. Her beauty almost took the edge off his anger, but not quite.

"I don't do well with being ushered with a hand wave," he carped. "I'm not some bum off the street, you know. The Antichrist chose *me*. I'm the one for the mission, and I demand a little respect from you," he looked her up and down, "whoever you are."

Zara cocked her head to the side and smirked. She had to give it to him, he may be a pompous ass kid, but he had that defiant courage that Kieron needed. Zara uncrossed her long legs and slid closer over to him. He could smell her jasmine perfume. She leaned in close and whispered in his ear, "This will hurt slightly."

Confused, Jacan opened his mouth to call her a dirty name before he felt the sharp sting of a needle going into his left arm.

"What the hell was that!?"

"That, Jacan, is your microchip. It will give you powers like the other Blood Royal kids, so they don't suspect you." She sat back and crossed her legs, looking at him askance. "You may call me Zara."

"And you may call me Jacan," he mimicked, sarcastically.

"Now listen up, kid, we have a lot to review before you get to the compound…but before we do, you may want to brace yourself…" Zara warned.

"Huh? What do you mean by *brace* myself?" But before he could finish his sentence, Jacan felt electric sensations pulsing through his body. He rubbed his shoulder, and his eyes rolled to the back of his head. It felt like every cell in his body was being set on fire. He screamed in agony and fell to the floor of the limousine, crumpled in pain. Sweat poured off his body.

"The microchip is changing your cells to give you superhuman strength," Zara explained. "What other gifts you may be bestowed, I don't know. Scientists are still working out the kinks." She paused as he writhed on the floor. "You have some cajónes, kid, telling me off like that. I'll give you that, but I am a Punarjanam, a trained assassin, and I *don't* do well with demands. I'm the one who makes demands." She looked out the window and drummed her silver painted nails on the windowsill. "The only person who can command me is Kieron, our Lord and Savior of mankind. Not even the Holy Seer himself can command me."

Jacan's eyes rolled out from the back of his head to normal view; he stretched and straightened his body out from being crumpled on the floor, and slowly climbed back up on the limousine seat. He shook his head to clear his mind. Jacan felt more alive than he had ever felt in his entire life, like he could lift an elephant off the ground with one hand.

"So, I'll only tell you this once," Zara looked Jacan in the eyes. "Do not smart mouth me again, or I will make sure you experience this ordeal again."

Jacan met her gaze and nodded. He felt amazing, but he certainly didn't want to have to go through that pain again.

"Good. Now let's get started. We have a few hours for me to give you all the compound's details and everything it entails. There are a few Blood Royals I've had my eye on, but I need more information that I can't get, and that's where you come in."

CHAPTER 3

August 28th, 2023, 1:15 P.M – New York City

High above the clouds in a Penthouse Suite off 5th Avenue, a man dressed in a long black robe was reading a parchment of paper wedged between two protective pieces of glass. A lean young man shrouded in the darkness sat in a 17th Century chair; he cleared his throat and tightened his grip on the armrest.

A servant girl, no more than twelve years old, walked over to the bar, grabbed a bottle of Macallan 50-year-old Malt Scotch Whiskey, and poured two shots into the tumbler. She opened the freezer, dropped two gigantic ice cubes in the glass, walked over to the man shrouded in darkness, and handed it to him, her face slightly turned to the right to not stare at him directly.

The man swiveled the tumbler glass in his hand in a circular motion before taking a sip. He closed his eyes and relished the smooth liquor going down his body. 117,438 dollars for one bottle of Macallan liquor. No price was too high to pay when he wanted something.

"And what exactly do these parchments reveal, Cardinal? Are they of any significance to me?"

The man in the black robe cleared his throat and turned around. It was the Ex-Holy Seer Cardinal Villere; he glanced down at the parchments encased between glass lying on the intricate mahogany table before him. He picked them up, studying them one last time before speaking.

"The parchments reveal that she will be shrouded in darkness, only made known by being in the true presence of the Son of God, who is the light, sound, and Word of God."

The Holy Seer stopped speaking.

"I know there is more, Cardinal. Spit it out."

"She will have the power to heal and bring back the dead as the first Christ had done, but she will also be able to bring people to repentance by the light of her soul and the sound of her voice. She will bring knowledge of a person's sin to the forefront of their mind and bring them to their knees as they repent. How this all correlates to Zach Dorsey and his twin Sofia, I don't yet know."

The man in darkness threw the tumbler glass of Macallan whiskey at the wall. Seeing only his silhouette, his hands smoothed back his hair and ushered the twelve-year-old girl to pour him another drink.

"Where did you acquire these parchments, and why was I not told of this sooner?"

Cardinal Villere bowed his head and postulated himself towards the man. "My Lord, we only acquired the parchments last night. After studying them, I came immediately to tell you that they are real pieces of the Lost Gospel of the Divine Feminine. Zara's associate acquired them from a drugged-out American Archaeologist working in Turkey. She's working with two other Archaeologists on the project, although I am positive, she is the one who found the parchments and sold it under their noses."

"I want you to send a message to this American archaeologist. Tell her I want a meeting with her. Tell her I will make her rich beyond her wildest dreams."

"Yes, my Lord."

The young man shrouded in darkness got up; he had a thick cloud of darkness covering him as he walked over to a golden chest and opened the top drawer. He pulled out a small silver remote and turned it on; a light started to blink red.

"What is our status with finding the new incarnated Jesus? Are there any rumors of miracles or him waking up to the reality of his second incarnation yet?"

The Holy Seer shook his head no.

"I see."

The Holy Seer grabbed his upside-down golden cross and opened it to reveal a small knife. He lifted the robe from his arm and sliced his arm with the knife; blood started pouring out of his arm onto the black granite floor. "My Lord," he begged, "please accept this small sacrifice as a token of my dedication to you. My men have been searching day and night to find him, but so far, all we hear are whispers. There were a couple of men we thought could be The Christ, but they were only half-bloods. They could only show part of the abilities of his first incarnation."

The darkness that shrouded the man came off him and moved outwards to encroach the whole room. The man's eyes began to glow red, and he spoke in a language the Holy Seer couldn't understand. The darkness penetrated the Holy Seer, piercing him with fear so unbearable that the Holy Seer fell to the floor screaming as visions of demons gnawed on his flesh and ate his organs, smiling and laughing as they did.

The Holy Seer screamed again, "Please, master! Please give me one more chance, and I promise I will not fail you again!"

The man, still shrouded in darkness with only a silhouette, watched him wither in pain for a few more moments before calling back the darkness onto himself. "Fail me again, and I will make that vision come to pass in real-time."

"Yes… my lord," The Holy Seer trembled in fear, still bleeding, and picking himself up. He tore a piece of his robe and wrapped his arm to stop his arm from bleeding out.

The man walked over to him and put his hand over his arm, speaking in an unknown language. He removed the torn robe over his arm to reveal that The Holy Seers' cut was healed. "Blood Royals are not the only ones who can heal, Cardinal; I care for my wolves. You care for the sheep."

"What about Sofia?" The Holy Seer asked while rubbing his arm in disbelief.

"Leave her be for now. I want to see how this hospital trial plays out for her. I need to know what people think of her before I make my next move. Then I will come for her. What's the status of the Blood Royal children?"

"Most of the children are in Ireland with a few teenage stragglers making their way now by plane."

"And Jacan?"

"Jacan is on a plane and will meet with Zara to get microchipped when he lands. His uncle informed me that he understands the seriousness of the matter and insists that he will not fail you."

"I have a feeling Jacan will do very well with the others," he mused with a wry smile.

"What do you want me to do in the meantime?"

"Let Zara handle things for the next few days with the kids. I need you for a week or two here; then, I will switch you and Zara out. And then, Cardinal, you can have your playtime with the children."

The Holy Seer smiled sheepishly. "The sound of Blood Royal children's curdling screams is orgasmic, to say the least, as I'm sure you would agree," he proposed with a grin.

The man encased in darkness walked gracefully out of the shadows. The darkness that had once encroached on him dissipated. The man's face and body shined in a soft white glow; his icy blue eyes glued to the Holy Seer. The Holy Seer beheld the young man in all his glory. Seventeen-year-old Kieron Gederon stood six feet tall; his stature was commanding yet subtle, and his icy blue eyes radiated seduction and charm.

"There is nothing more satisfying than watching a child scream in agony, begging for their mother to save them, but what is more satisfying, Cardinal, is when the children's screams are coming from the bloodline of Christ himself," he smiled with absolute evil in his eyes. "However, I must attend to a more imperative matter." Kieron smiled nonchalantly and pressed the gold button on the silver remote he had held for minutes. "Let the hysteria commence, and my reign of power and authority rise out of the chaos."

CHAPTER 4

August 28th, 2023, 6:20 P.M. – Tulane University

Making his way through the vast hallways of Tulane, Zach made his way to the common area. Today was the third most important date of Brother Guiden's life. Since their last adventure, Brother Guiden had taken up residence in Rome as Pope Aloysius's confidant; he was trying to put together a new *"Council of Nicea,"* so to speak. Christianology was making waves in the news, but lately, not in a good way. Many priests, bishops, and deacons from the Roman Catholic Church made it hard for Brother Guiden to unite the two faiths. Some had even started smear campaigns on social media and news outlets, demonizing and pitting him against the Pope.

Zach knew Brother Guiden was *more* than qualified to become the next Archbishop of the Catholic Church. It was now down to him and three other men. Zach was apprehensive about whether certain members of the Catholic faith would turn fanatical and hurt Brother Guiden in the process.

"The television is on, guys; let's all settle down. It looks like it's about to start!" A young fiery red-headed teaching assistant spoke. Zach gathered around with his colleagues as they found the channel streaming the news live from Rome.

The feed showed hundreds of thousands of people assembled at the Vatican for the announcement from Pope Aloysius. Zach could pick up many voices chanting for the man they wanted as the pope's right-hand man, the new Archbishop to replace Cardinal Villere, or, as we all knew him, the Holy Seer. Pope Aloysius came out of the Vatican with his hands raised, waving to the masses of devoted Catholics. The masses continued to cheer for another minute before the crowd's cries died down.

"Two and a half years ago, the Holy Catholic Church and the world came to terms with factual evidence that people could no longer deny: evidence that the Roman Catholic Church covered up for two millennia–the holy and sacred bloodline of Jesus of Nazareth and Mary of Magdalene. The Catholic Church has for too long buried its head in the sand when we should have been shouting this news from the rooftops. Not only is this man the one who discovered the secret bloodline, but he and his trusted companions also exposed Cardinal Villere and his killing sprees of the Blood Royals. I am honored to present your next Holy Seer of Rome, Brother Jeremiah Guiden of New Orleans, Louisiana in the United States."

The crowd cheered as Brother Guiden made his way out onto the balcony of the Vatican. Brother Guiden embraced the

Pope with open arms. Zach could see a tear forming in Brother Guiden's eye as the camera panned his face.

Brother Guiden wiped the tear away and started to speak, "Thank you, dear friend for your kind words," he addressed Pope Aloysisus. "The honor is all mine; I can assure you. Placing me as your right-hand man, well, it's a dream come true, truth be told. I can only imagine the great insights I will glean from a man of God like yourself." He turned to address the masses, "together, we will show the world how powerful and magical the bloodline of Jesus and Mary truly is."

Brother Guiden smiled at Pope Aloysius. Pope Aloysius pushed the side of his robe to show the *fleur-de-lis* mark on his chest. The camera panned to the pope's chest and then to the crowd. Hundreds of thousands of mouths went agape. The pope of the Roman Catholic Church for twenty years was a Blood Royal, and no one was none the wiser. Zach knew, of course, but he didn't know how the people of the world would take it.

"Well, I'll be a monkey's uncle," Professor Wright remarked. "I always knew there was something special about him," he laughed.

All the professors and teaching assistants started to come up to Zach to ask him questions about the Blood Royal lineage and the powers they possessed.

"What do you think about–"

Zach saw something on the camera flying toward Pope Aloysius and Brother Guiden at a constant speed. As the item moved closer to the Pope and Brother Guiden, Zach could see a drone with a red crown lying on top of it. The drone came face to face with them both; the red crown started to hover and flew up to land on Pope Aloysius' head. Zach looked down at his watch. It was exactly 6:42 p.m. at the Vatican. Zach looked back at the TV staring at the red crown. The pope's face seemed...surprised... like he didn't understand what was happening.

A look of terror filled Pope Aloysius's eyes as he started to walk towards the balcony. He wanted to speak but could not. His eyes only showed terror and confusion. Brother Guiden sprinted towards the pope as he hopped onto the balcony railing and jumped off St. Peter's Basilica. Brother Guiden went over to the ledge to see Pope Aloysius' body crumpled to the floor, blood spilling on the ground and around his *fleur-de-lis*, his red crown still attached to his head. Guards quickly surrounded Brother Guiden and rushed him inside the Vatican. The people of Rome screamed in terror and cried hysterically, filled with complete disillusionment that the pope of the Holy Roman Catholic Church just committed suicide on national television.

CHAPTER 5

August 29th, 12:30 P.M, 2023, 12:16 P.M – Istanbul, Turkey

Deep in the throng of the masses, Lennox Gold, a young American archeologist, maneuvered her way, weaving in and out of the bustling flea market of Istanbul. Her light green eyes darted left and right in her freckled face. Every now and then, she glanced over her shoulder, looking out for a fellow she needed to avoid because she owed him money. Making a right on a narrow alleyway, she smelled vanilla and wood incense from a meat market vendor twenty feet away. She brushed her light brown hair away from her forehead and breathed in the familiar smell that signaled relief. She had become accustomed to the smell on her wayward path of destruction, a path she never thought she would go down but nonetheless found herself.

Passing the meat vendor, Lennox headed towards an elderly blind woman begging for money. Lennox bent down to kiss the old woman's head, dropped a few lira notes in her woven coin purse, and sat beside her. Lennox found it astounding that her friend could knit even though she was blind in both eyes. She had made Lennox a woven beanie to wear in winter. The blind woman smiled and grabbed her hand to kiss it.

"Is that you, Lennox?" The blind woman asked peacefully.

"The one and only," Lennox denoted with a smirk.

They had had the same routine for four months straight now. Three days a week, Lennox would meet the woman in the alleyway, kiss her on top of her head, drop some lira in her woven coin purse, and sit down next to her; and each time, the woman would ask if she was Lennox and kiss her hand once, Lennox answered yes. The routine never changed, nor would anyone else kiss the woman on top of her head like she did, which made it even funnier to Lennox; it made her laugh during this period of her dark night of the soul.

When first getting to know the blind woman, Lennox would ask her about her life growing up in Turkey, savory foods to try, and places where the locals congregated. After coming to see her a few times a week, putting change in her purse, and giving her food to eat, six weeks later, the blind woman started to tell her grandiose stories about her life. Stories of how she grew up poor on a farm but was whisked away by a sultan of many riches. The sultan declared his love for her in front of the kingdom: she was the most beautiful woman in all the land. And she was still beautiful, even with two blind eyes, and nearly seventy years old. The blind woman had a youthfulness and glow about her that Lennox couldn't explain.

They had a lavish wedding ten days later, and she moved into his exuberant palace where every want and need was met even before she asked. After bearing him two daughters but no sons in six years, in a fit of rage, the sultan blinded both of her eyes with hot coals and exiled her outside the palace to beg for the rest of her life. Her baby daughters were slain, one torn limb to limb, and the other was thrown into a fire pit and burned alive. The sultan remarried a princess who bore him three sons and a daughter. Lennox thought the blind woman was a master story-teller….or, she was just starting to lose her marbles.

Only three weeks ago, the woman mentioned that her ex-husband, the sultan, used to take her to a secret room filled with ancient scrolls and gospels beneath the mosque of Hagia Sophia. Lennox's ears pricked up. The woman didn't tell her anything more about the scrolls beneath Hagia Sophia. Still, she did tell her about another lost gospel in a ruin outside the city in a heavily forested area.

Lennox had heard rumors here and there of lost gospels, but nothing like this one, a gospel written by the divine feminine part of God, that was written by all female disciples. She knew this revelation would change mankind's history forever. Now, whether it would be for good or for worse, she didn't know, but she kept coming back to the blind woman hoping to find out more infor-mation. And to be honest, Lennox loved talking to her; there was something about her presence that soothed her soul. Maybe it was because the blind woman helped keep her grounded when all she wanted to do was wallow in her self-pity, misery, and pain.

"My sweet girl, have you found what you were looking for? It's been a month, and this old woman wants to know if you have found the mysteries you seek."

A wave of pain washed over Lennox's body. Her legs ached, and she started feeling nauseous. Closing her eyes, she tried to focus on anything but the withdrawals. Lennox thought of Jax's bright smile, how his warm brown eyes crinkled beneath his tortoise-shell glasses, and how he could make her laugh with her whole body. Lennox thought Jax was out of her league with his intelligence, tall and wiry good-looks, and easy-going, confident manner, not to mention his adorable British accent. He was the dig director of their excavation site, so she acted like one of the guys around him. She had put herself out there too many times and had been rejected too many times to count. She wasn't about to do that again to herself, especially when she and Jax had a good thing going with work. If that meant only having Jax as a kind and funny friend for the rest of her life, that was something she could accept.

She repositioned her body and cracked her neck, opening her eyes to see the woman's smile replaced with angst across her face. Lennox hated that she was lying to her friend. She had found the pieces of the lost gospel last week and sold them off to an unnamed bidder in the United States off the dark web. Lennox also hid the lost fragments from Jax and Loch, her other co-worker; she hated herself for it, but she didn't have the strength to stop what she was doing. Heroin had overtaken her life, and she would do almost anything to get her fix.

"We've only found pottery and some human remains. The parchments have yet to be found. But don't worry, Anne, there's always tomorrow, and I'm not giving up on finding it."

Anne took Lennox's hand and looked her in the eyes. Her once beautiful brown-honey eyes were now clouded and protruding out of her face, with rings of scarred red tissue circling both eyes. Since the woman would not reveal her real name to Lennox for fear of her life, Lennox had to get creative and pick a name for her. When she googled the Turkish name for man, the word "Anne" came up. Lennox found it ironic that their common name for "man" was a personal woman's name in other parts of the world.

"I believe in you, my child, and you *will* find what you have been seeking your whole life." Anne grabbed Lennox's hand and squeezed it. "I'm not just talking about the lost gospel. You will find peace and acceptance within yourself. You will find love and happiness and see the God of Abraham, Isaac, and Jacob work miracles in your life."

Anne knew that this would be her last conversation with Lennox and fought back her tears as she watched a vision pass through her mind's eye. It was a vision of Lennox slumped over with a needle in her arm, her face blue, the light in her green eyes going dark. There was only one way for this vision not to pass. Anne would gladly accept taking Lennox's place in death if it meant Lennox living and fulfilling her destiny. Anne prayed that her sacrifice would not be in vain, as she knew all too well that man had free will to do what they wanted. That was God's gift, after all, to mankind, and for better or worse, Lennox could still choose to go down the path of destruction.

"It's hard for me, Anne. I'm not like you. Your faith comes easily to you."

"But my life has not."

"So stupid," Lennox thought in her head. Lennox dropped her head in shame. "I'm sorry, Anne… I don't know why I said that. Sometimes, I say things without speaking. I know your life hasn't been easy. I could never have a smile on my face every day like you do, knowing that I was homeless."

"My dear Lennox, it is when you try to do life on your own and strive in your own power that you feel that way, but when you depend on Jesus and his peace and grace, you will see your life flourish in ways you never imagined. Jesus found me. He healed me. *And…* He told me about you ahead of time. I've had visions about you for the past two years. I knew one day I would meet you and pass on all my knowledge and the secrets I have kept for so long."

"What do you mean by that? How did Jesus heal you?" Lennox cried aloud, "You are the kindest and most courageous woman I have ever met, and if he is a God of miracles, then why hasn't he healed your blindness?"

"I see more now than I *ever* did with my natural eyes," Anne explained gently. "Jesus healed me of my anger and rejection of man."

Anne began to stroke Lennox's hair. "It's not up to us who God heals or doesn't heal. There are purposes God has that are beyond our understanding to comprehend. Most of the time, people do not come to God unless they are suffering; that was how I found Jesus; through my suffering, I began to drop the veils of hate and resentment from my eyes and focus on the God who heals from the inside out. God gave me a child to make up for the two that were stolen from me, and that child for the past four months has been you, Lennox. You have brought me so much joy these past four months, and I am proud to call you my *kiz*, my daughter in the Turkish language."

Anne started to feel waves of energy and pain bounce from Lennox's body to hers, pains of muscle soreness and a thick cloud of fog overtaking Lennox's mind. "I will tell you how to get to the secret room beneath Hagia Sophia, but you have to promise me one thing," Anne continued.

Lennox's face was flushed with beads of sweat pouring down her forehead, her stomach queasy and nauseous; Lennox bent over in agony. She had stayed too long talking to Anne and was about to throw up if she didn't get her drugs quickly.

"Yes… I promise," Lennox whispered, "whatever you ask, I will do."

"My real name is Emira. Now that you know my real name, they will come after you. I'm telling you this information because you need to find Yousef and Raziah. You have to be the one to find the lost gospel of the divine feminine before he does."

"Before, who does?"

"Before the false light, or he will destroy the lost Gospel of the Feminine and all of mankind will be lost forever. You must find Yousef and Raziah, who will lead you to your destiny. I'm telling you this, Lennox, because there is power in a name. I need you to understand this concept; there is *power* and *authority* in a name. Now that you know my name, you have access to the real me, my real name. When you speak my name out loud in existence, as with any name, certain things must come to pass when you speak life or death with that name. Only use my name in dire situations. Otherwise, I'm just known as Anne. Now hurry and go find the couple of whom I speak. You haven't got much time before he makes his move and his presence known."

Lennox held her stomach as it rumbled. She stood up, still not understanding any of this but knowing she had to act fast, or she would pass out.

"And Lennox."

"Yeah?"

"The day you decide to put a needle in your arm is the day you will die. That's why I told you my real name. You are here for a reason. If God didn't tell me to do it, I wouldn't have, and you would have gone down that road and died, but at least now you have a choice. Will you choose drugs and death, or will you choose life and freedom? I leave that choice up to you, but know I love you and only want to see you succeed."

Lennox bent down to kiss Anne's forehead, and as she did, a single tear fell down her cheek. Lennox's phone beeped from a text message. It was from Jax and Loch telling her to meet them at their usual spot in twenty minutes.

"Emira is going to take getting used to, but for now, I just want to use the name I've known you by; I love you, Anne; so much," Lennox said. "Thank you for always looking out for me.

I gotta run and meet up with the boys at the dig site. I promise to find that couple and the lost gospel and tell you all about it!"

With that, Lennox ran off, dodging merchants and street kids selling bracelets to foreign travelers. Lennox took a sharp turn on an adjacent alleyway only to catch sight of the back of Loch's purple-dyed hair, as he spoke in an animated way with his tattoo-sleeved arms to, none other than, Jax. Jax was bent down lacing up his boot, so neither of them saw her as she pivoted and took another route. She wondered if they were discussing her tardiness. Lennox bit her lip in despair, knowing she could not go to the excavation in her state of mind. Her withdrawing body wouldn't allow it. Trembling, she grabbed her phone to text them in the group chat that she was on her way.

Lennox turned around to walk back to the half-point where she met Anne and looked for the run-down building that sold many things. Stepping inside, she was led by a small-statured woman further into the store, where customers were prohibited. Opening the door, she entered a room filled with burnt smoke, candles, and chanting. Some people were lying across the floor, passed out; others were getting their tools ready for a hit.

A man with pinpoint eyes walked up to her. "You've come back to chase the dragon, have ya? If you strap, you can feel the heroin one hundred times more. There's no greater feeling. I'll even let you try it for free."

Lennox avoided his gaze and turned her attention to some teenagers; they were strapping up a few adults in their mid-forties. She couldn't believe teenagers had a job to help strap and prepare drugs for adults. Remembering what Anne told her, she wasn't ready to leave Earth just yet.

"I'll take two grams."

"And?"

"And I'll stick to smoking and snorting it," Lennox asserted. "Thanks for the offer, but I'm good."

The beady-eyed man's smile went away. "Your loss." He reached into his pocket to give her a bag filled with brown powder. She gave him the money and walked over to an empty table. The man sat on the torn brown couch, putting his arm around a woman in her late twenties with bruises all over her arm.

Lennox shivered, shook her head, and sat down. She grabbed the tin foil and an unused straw left on the table. She put a line of heroin in the tin foil, grabbed a lighter out of her pocket, and lit the bottom of the tinfoil, using the straw to suck up the smoke. A warm fuzzy feeling came over her body, and the nausea started to disappear with just one hit. Lennox took out more of the heroin and put it on the table, this time to snort it. She put the straw up her nose and snorted a small line of heroin. She couldn't get high as the boys would know something was off with her. She just needed to take the edge off for now.

Putting the straw down, Lennox shrunk into the chair and closed her eyes; everything and everyone faded away. She couldn't hear the chatter of people talking or the visions or prophecies of Anne running through her mind. All Lennox could feel was the warmth radiating through her body. All she could see was the blackness beneath her eyelids.

CHAPTER 6

August 28th, 6:43 P.M – New Orleans

The letter that Zach had received had come true. The Pope had died wearing a red crown, his white robe stained with blood as he lay in the street. A sacrifice was made, but to whom? He knew by the look of terror on his face that he didn't jump to his death; the crown had made him do so. This was an attack on the bloodline of Jesus and Mary, and Zach knew only one person who would make this assault, the excommunicated Holy Seer Cardinal Villere.

"Professor Dorsey…" the red-haired assistant squeaked. Zach looked away from the TV to notice that all eyes were on him.

"Aren't you a Blood Royal…are they going to come after you next? You know…since you saved Pope Aloysius two and a half years ago?"

"That is not the right question, Pip," Clara interrupted. Pip raised an eyebrow. "The right question would be, do you think Brother Guiden had the pope killed to take his place? To become the next Pope of the Roman Catholic Church?" Clara demanded with seedy eyes.

Zach had never seen Clara act like this before, she could be stern at times, but this was out of her nature. And then the thought hit him like a ton of bricks: Zach could see where this was all going. The Holy Seer wanted to blame Brother Guiden for taking up his old role. He wanted him arrested and put on trial for the murder of Pope Aloysius by way of technology. If he had to guess, nanobot technology was placed inside the crown and sent electrical impulses to the pope's frontal lobe cortex to control his impulses.

"No, Clara, I do *not* think it was Brother Guiden, but I have a pretty good idea who it was."

CHAPTER 7
August 28th, 2023, 1:45 P.M – Istanbul

Jax must have looked at his phone a hundred times, checking for any missed calls or messages from Lennox. She was forty-five minutes late to the dig site and was nowhere in sight. Jax's jaw began to clench with worry, Lennox seemed to be off her game lately, and he didn't know why.

"Why does it feel like we're being stood up?" He turned to Loch.

"Cause we are, mate."

Jax checked his phone again and then shoved it into his pocket. He put a hand through his dark brown hair, which seemed to be turning into a soft black. Winter was coming, and his hair always turned darker in the winter months.

"You think it's over a lad?" Loch asked, "She's been acting a little ditzy at the site. If her head weren't attached to her head, I would think she would have lost that too."

"So you know."

"Oh, I know," Loch nodded. "I can always tell when a lass has taken a shine to somebody." He tilted his head towards a figure sprinting their way.

Lennox ran up to Loch and Jax, huffing and puffing. Dirt covered her face and body; a purple bruise blossomed on the right cheek of her face.

"Bloody hell! Lennox, are you okay?" Jax asked with terror in his eyes. He reached out to brush the hair out of her eyes, but she brushed him away.

"I'm fine, guys, really." She ducked her head and began to brush the dirt off her clothes and then took her phone out to reveal a big crack on her screen.

"You guys know I'm clumsy. I got a phone call from my brother about our dad. I didn't realize how much time had passed until after I got off the phone with him. When I realized the time, I was texting and running and ran into a peddler pushing a cart of roasted corn and kebabs. My cheek hit the pole of the cart."

"Did the gadgie smack you, Lennox?" Loch asked. "Cause if he did, I'd rip in a new arsehole!"

"That's sweet of you, Loch, but it was my fault. You should have seen the cart afterward. It was a total disaster. I knocked everything over. He probably would have beaten me up if I didn't shove a week's wages in his hands. That made up for the day's waste, plus six more days of corn and kebabs. Safe to say, he ended up giving me his number in case I wanted to run into him again for another week of wages. I can promise y'all he made out like a bandit. Now let's get to the truck. We have a site to dig up."

For once, Lennox didn't lie to them about why she was late. She really did run into a vendor. The problem was she was high, not texting while running. That was the problem.

Lennox jogged ahead and climbed into the truck. Loch leaned in and whispered to Jax, "You believe the lass?"

Jax thought about all the times Lennox had dropped stuff even before the last few months of her starting to act weird. She was dropping things and misplacing things all the time. "I do believe her."

"And the parchments, lad? What happened to those? One of the locals said she found something after we left base camp. When he asked her what she found, she turned bright red and pretended to get a phone call and run off. There is something really off with the lass, and it breaks my heart."

"I didn't know you had a heart, Loch."

"Tell anyone, and I'll break your bones." Loch hit his fist into the palm of this hand.

Loch winked at Jax and took off to catch up with Lennox. Before getting to the site, Jax didn't know how to address the situation. He was sure the local would have said something to the manager on duty about it. He would have to think of a delicate way to bring this up. Jax thought it had something to do with her father. He had lung cancer and wasn't doing so well, and her mom was working three jobs just to help cover the medical bills. Lennox probably sold the parchments to help get her father cancer treatment. If she did, he couldn't blame her. He probably would have done the same if it was his father.

#

Lennox stuck her hand out the window as Jax drove them to the dig site. They had been driving for an hour and had twenty minutes to go before they arrived at the site. If he was going to say something, it was now or never.

"Lennox."

Lennox closed her eyes as she weaved her hand up and down in a wave motion outside the car window.

"Yes, Jax?" she replied, her eyes still closed with a slight smile. She pulled her hand inside and sat up to face forward.

"Is everything okay…with your dad?"

Lennox scrunched her shoulders.

"I'm just worried about you, er, we're worried about you." Jax thumbed to Loch in the backseat.

Lennox turned around to see that Loch's eyes were closed, his head leaned back, and he was snoring. Lennox sighed and bit her lip. "Not really. No."

"Lennox, we love you like a sister, so whatever it is, you can tell us. Loch is snoring like a gorilla, so if you would feel more comfortable telling me, I'm all ears."

And there it was. Jax told her she was like a sister to him. His words had stung more than what Anne had said to her about a needle in her arm and death knocking at her door. *Why did this feel worse than thinking about her death,* she thought. Lennox picked the dirt out of her fingernails; she tried to focus on something other than the feelings of rejection Jax's words brought.

"He's in stage three… it's not looking good, Jax. They're giving him a year to live."

"Oh god, Lennox… You must feel gutted. I… I can't even comprehend what you're going through. If there is anything I can do… Please don't hesitate to ask. Ok?"

"There's nothing you can do, Jax."

"I can pray. God is always listening; you and I both know that."

Lennox didn't know how much faith she had in God to cure her father's cancer. It was his own fault from all the drinking he had done over the years. Sometimes she wondered how much God would help those who had addiction problems. Being an addict herself, she thought God wouldn't help much, especially her.

"God helps those who help themselves, and I don't think God is going to help my dad when he did it to himself," Lennox said weakly.

"All you need is a mustard seed of faith, Len." Jax smiled and tried to catch her eye. "God will take care of the rest."

Lennox pushed her lip to the side, thinking, "Yeah," she said, shaking her head, "I can do that."

Jax leaned back as he turned into the dig site. He would need to find the manager on site and see if any of the locals had said anything about the parchments. If so, he'd have to explain the situation and hopefully Lennox wouldn't be tried and put in prison. She had too much going on to let this one decision let her ruin her life forever.

CHAPTER 8

August 30th, 6:26 A.M. - The Vatican, Italy

Brother Guiden finished his morning ablutions and slipped into his cassock. He pondered the problem of the guard outside, and how he'd been stripped of his technology. This abundance of caution for his safety was truly out of hand. He desperately needed to contact Zach and Sofia to tell him what he knew, what he suspected, to caution them of the danger they were in, and to guide them in their next steps. All signs led to the rise of the antichrist, but that also meant there was a solution, an equally strong force…a message from the divine would make itself known to one of them soon, he could feel it. But both Zach and Sofia were heads down busy in their work…Zach with his research and caring for Chritianlology, and Sofia with her trial against Dr. Wooldridge and the British hospital system…would they even know how to make themselves present to receive the signs or a direct message?

Their Royal Blood fleur de lis birthmarks should alert them with pain or burning, but sometimes the person needed to be ready to receive the message, or they might not feel it at all. Brother Guiden had to make contact today.

He slowly opened his chamber door, crossing his fingers that the guard might be asleep, or better yet, have taken a bathroom break, but no such luck. The young guard looked up earnestly and grinned.

"Good morning, Brother."

"Good morning! Might I ask the time?"

The young man pulled out his phone, "Almost 6:30 a.m., sir."

"Thank you, kindly. And may I ask another favor?"

"Yes sir?"

"I need to contact my um, niece and nephew, just to let them know I'm all right. Until I get security clearance, I can't use any of my own devices. But I don't see how using your device could possibly be a security problem, do you?"

"Umm…." the guard hesitated. "I don't know about that. My order are to…"

"Oh orders, yes, you're very right to follow them for everyone's safety," Brother Guiden interrupted, reaching out and taking the young man's phone. "It'll just be a second. You may stand here and watch and listen."

The young man was so taken off guard by Brother Guiden's swiftness that he stood befuddled as Brother Guiden quickly shot off a few text messages to Sofia. He just called Zach's number, when another, older guard rounded the corner with his breakfast and a change in shift.

Brother Guiden hung up the phone and gave it back to the guard. He went inside to receive his breakfast and ponder his next move.

CHAPTER 9

August 30th, 9:33 A.M – Dublin, Ireland

Jacan had spent a week in Dublin learning about the Elite Blood Royals in the compound. He had to admit he had his work cut out for him. After seven days of memorizing the elite Blood Royals' names, where they were from, abilities, strengths, and weaknesses, as well as Zara training him on how to use the super strength abilities that the microchip gave him, Zara gave him the okay to immerse himself in the compound. Unlike the other kids in the compound, the Elite Blood Royals had extraordinary powers. Their abilities were prized above all others.

"Now, when we get there, I will have to blindfold and drug you. Don't worry; the effects will only last a few hours, and you'll wake up with a headache, nothing more. You have to blend in as much as possible. Understand?"

"Understood."

"Good." Zara stuck Jacan with another needle in his arm. His eyes felt heavy, like they weighed one hundred pounds of gold. Jacan closed his eyes and drifted off to a deep sleep.

#

Jacan woke up to the sounds of children screaming and crying, his head pounding from whatever drug Zara had given him. She wasn't kidding about the splitting headache.

"On your feet, you filthy Blood Royal."

A tall menacing man standing six feet and four inches towered above him.

Jacan's body was lying on the grass, the smell of the ocean rising in his nostrils. Jacan couldn't see Zara anywhere in sight, but he knew she must be somewhere around the premises.

"I said get on your feet, you filthy piece of shit," the menacing man commanded. "Do *not* make me ask you again, or you will go into the fighting pits tonight. And believe me, on your first night, that is *not* where you want to go."

Feeling his blood boil and clenching his fists, Jacan stood up and punched the 6'4" man in the stomach, knocking him back twenty feet before landing on the ground. One by one, the crying children stopped their insufferable wailing and turned to look at him. Many children and teens looked at him wide-eyed as if he were the answer to their prayers. Three guards ran up to him and tackled him to the ground. One put him in a headlock while the other put on a special restraint restricting his superhuman abilities.

As the guards walked him over to an undisclosed area, Jacan noticed a few kids and teenagers that Zara had described facially. A Russian male was being pitted against a Turkish girl. He caught the Russian boy's eye who let his guard down for just a moment. The Turkish girl shot red light energy from her hands at the Russian, knocking him off his feet onto the ground. The Turkish girl smiled. The tall man finally caught his breath, ran over to Jacan and the guards, and stopped them.

"You see that lot over there, tough guy? They're going to tear you to shreds in the arena. You just wait." He smacked Jacan so hard across the face that he fell, leaving a red imprint on his cheek.

"Now, get up and follow me. We have some initial testing for you to do. Then in a few days' time, you'll be in the arena, and I, for one, can't wait to see your ass being kicked."

Jacan got up off the grass and followed the guards into a pyramid building made of black glass. He darted his eyes one last time outside to see hundreds of kids fighting, boxing, and using their powers on one another. He saw a young boy with red hair and freckles wave to him. Jacan gave him a slight smile and walked into the pyramid building. Phase One was complete. He had gained the attention of the Blood Royals with his superhuman strength. It was time for Phase Two, working on sleeping in the same quarters with the most potent Blood Royals.

#

Two days had passed at the dig site without a word about Lennox stealing the parchments. If anything, the crew had their arms wide open to their team, which Jax found strange. The local who had found Lennox taking the parchment was nowhere in sight and, in fact, went home on a family emergency. He couldn't understand why he didn't tell anyone but was glad he didn't. He couldn't stand thinking of Lennox being imprisoned for the rest of her life.

Now, all he and Loch had to devise was a plan to make it stay that way. He hated the idea of making a forgery, but he didn't want to lose Lennox. It would take a miracle to get her out of this, one he hoped was moral. He didn't know what else to do.

Jax walked over to the area of the Belgrade Forest away from the site where he couldn't be seen by the others and prayed out loud, "God, if you can find it in your heart to forgive Lennox and help us out of this mess, I swear on my life I will dedicate my life to you."

A middle-aged Turkish man and woman he had never seen before walked over and stood on both sides of him. They were silent but smiling, both radiating in appearance. The man was athletic and still fit for his age, with broad shoulders and strong muscular legs that looked like he hiked at least five miles a day. The woman wore a long skirt and blue hijab that covered her dark hair; her kind brown eyes were flecked with amber, and when she looked at Jax, he was filled with a deep sense of peace and trust. Without a word, the woman handed Jax a black leather binder. Jax was about to open his mouth and ask what it was, but something told him not to. He opened the bag; inside were three parchments, exactly like the ones they were looking for.

"How…who…," but Jax couldn't finish his sentence. He was speechless.

"They are forgeries, of course," the man said.

"But flawless," the woman spoke confidently, "I assure you."

"We've been looking for you for a long time," the man continued.

"Who are you," Jax asked in unbelief, and how did you know I needed this?"

"We gave the local enough money to pay his rent for a year. He is no longer an issue. And who we are," the man smiled, "are the people who will help you change the course of destiny." The man stuck out his hand for a handshake, "I'm Yousef, and this is Raziah."

"How did you know we were here?" Jax asked. "How did you get here?"

Raziah smiled, "By teleportation, of course."

CHAPTER 10

September 4th, 7:49 P.M, 2023 – New Orleans

A week had passed, and all Zach could replay over and over in his head was Pope Aloysius falling to his death. He had received the letter ahead of time but didn't put it together until it was too late. He felt responsible for the death of Pope Aloysius. He hadn't been honest with Sam with his remorse. She didn't need that kind of pressure, especially when she had been feeling ill lately.

He wasn't allowed to contact Brother Guiden until the Italian Secret Service deemed it was safe for him to receive phone calls. Zach had received only one encoded text from an unfamiliar number that he believed to be Brother Guiden. If he'd deciphered the cryptic text correctly, Brother Guiden had sent him a warning: the Holy Seer was active again, and both he and Sofia were in danger. They needed to be alert to their fleurs de lis. They also needed to look for messages coming from unlikely people, while at the same time not to trust too readily as the Holy Seer was employing secret agents. Zach walked around campus wary of all he encountered - students and faculty. He combed his notes for any sign of how to take action against the rise of the antichrist. He called Sofia, but his rings only ended in voicemails.

#

After Lennox, Jax, and Loch met Raziah and Yousef, four days passed; the archeologists didn't know how to quite handle the situation. On the one hand, Lennox was grateful that they had supplied them with a forgery, so she wouldn't go to prison; on the other hand, this teleportation business was too much for all of them to handle. Lennox didn't know if she wanted to be in awe or cower away from the happy couple. It was just too much for her to think about at the moment.

"So, you're telling me you can teleport anywhere you want, even inside a bank," Loch asked.

"I can go anywhere as long as I have a picture of the place I want to go inside my head," Raziah smiled, "but I do not use this gift to steal."

"How did you know we were at this exact spot?" Lennox asked.

"Honey, it doesn't take much to ask the locals where three foreign archeologists are digging. We teleported to Istanbul and asked around."

"Well, I'll be damned," Loch spoke. "I guess we are fish out of water here."

"I know this is a lot to ask…" Reziah looked from one face to the other, "but we need you all to teleport with us to Istanbul. We don't have any time to waste."

"The hell we will, we don't know a single thing about you guys, nor do we know what kind of physical ailments we will get from teleporting," Lennox said. "I'd rather take the jeep back."

"Unfortunately, that will take hours, and we need to get to Istanbul asap," Yousef said as a matter of fact.

"I'm with Lennox," Jax agreed. "In four days, all you lot have spoken about is some quest, but nothing entailing any details. Once you let us in on what you want us to do, we'll help," he nodded to Lennox and Loch. "Otherwise, it's a hard pass from all of us."

Yousef and Raziah looked at each other with solemn faces. It would be harder to get them to come than they thought.

"Let's talk about it all over dinner tomorrow night," Raziah suggested. "You guys should get some rest. We have a lot to go over, and we want to be fully prepared to give every answer we can."

Lennox was thankful. She didn't want to spend another minute here with the supernatural couple… she was starting to feel nauseous and needed to get her fix before she threw up. It had been twenty-four hours since she had her last dose. She only had enough to snort two more lines before she ran out. Maybe teleporting back to Istanbul wasn't a bad idea; after all, she could get a hold of her drugs sooner.

CHAPTER 11

September 5th, 2023, 1:06 P.M – Undisclosed part of Ireland

Jacan spotted the familiar boy with red hair and freckles who had waved to him a few days earlier. Older Blood Royals kids were picking on him in the corner of the field. One blond kid held him by the collar, while another kid gave him a rug burn on his arm.

"Your arm's as red as your hair now," the blond boy jeered.

Jacan would have done exactly the same thing as them if he wasn't on a mission. He was a bully, after all, but he needed to get on the elite Blood Royals' good side so that his idol and master, Kieron, would reward him in the age to come.

"Why don't you pick on someone your own size, coward?" Jacan tapped the large blond boy on his shoulder. "Or are you to chicken shit to fight anyone your own age?"

"Why don't you get the hell out of my face?" the boy said, still turned away from Jacan. The boy spoke with a heavy German accent, "Or, I'll give you something to–." The German boy turned to face Jacan which caused him to pause. The boy shrank in Jacan's piercing stare and broad stance.

"Ya, you know that 6'4 man I knocked out with one punch?" asked Jacan. "I'll knock all your teeth out with just my pinky finger, so if I were you, I would get the hell away from the red-haired kid. And if I ever see you bullying him again, you will eat pudding and applesauce for the rest of your life. And that's a promise."

The boy dropped his hands from the collar of the shirt of the red-haired boy and briskly walked away with two other Blood Royals teenagers.

"Thank you…" the boy said as he wiped away tears from his face, "I'm Rowan."

"How old are you?" Jacan asked.

"Eight," Rowan replied.

"Where are you from?"

"Dublin," he squeaked out in a fine Irish brogue.

"Jacan, American. Fourteen years old." Jacan held out his hand and Rowan shook it.

"Not big on words, are you, Jacan?" Rowan mimicked an older person, standing up straighter in an effort to compose himself.

"Depends on the situation and the person." Jacan paused to look at his surroundings. "Why are there no kids past those poles over there? This area is big, but I never see anyone go past those poles, not even the guards."

The Turkish girl, who'd been watching the scene with interest, walked up, and stood next to Jacan with her arms crossed.

"That's because an electromagnetic barrier emits off those poles. If you walk past them, you're electrocuted on the spot."

"You're burnt to a crisp and turned into a pile of black ashes," Rowan added.

"I was trying to be delicate." She flashed her dark eyes at Rowan.

"Delicacy is not my forte," Rowan said, still mimicking someone older.

"No shit." The Turkish girl reached out and messed his red hair.

"I'm guessing you've both seen this with your own eyes?" Jacan asked with as much sincerity as he could muster without sounding like a phony.

The Turkish girl nodded and flipped her long brown braid over her shoulder. Jacan stuck out his hand, "I'm Jacan, and you are?"

With her arms still crossed, she eyed his hand and looked out into the distance. Jacan noticed lighter amber flakes in her dark eyes. "Rune."

Without shaking his hand or saying another word, Rune walked off to another part of the quadrant and approached one of the guards. Jacan couldn't make out what she was saying, but the guard nodded and took her to another part of the perimeter, where he saw Zara for the first time in days. She spoke in a hushed tone with a man with olive skin in a white doctor's coat. Noticing Rune walking up, she sent away the man in the white lab coat. Jacan needed to act fast to catch this conversation, so he took

Rowan's hand and moved closer to a tree to catch the exchange between Rune and Zara.

"What are we doing?" Rowan asked.

"Shh, kid, I'll tell you afterward. Just sit down at this tree and pretend you have a bad headache."

Jacan eyed Rune and Zara intently as he touched Rowan's head, pretending to comfort him.

"Rune. What a pleasant surprise."

"Pleasant is not the word I would use."

Zara let out a slight laugh. "You were always one to never beat around the bush."

"Well, I learned it from someone I know. Kinda hard to undo what's been done."

Zara nodded but didn't say a word. "What can I do for you?"

"I want to take Rowan's place in the arena tonight. He's not ready; he shouldn't be going up against someone twice his size."

"Nobody said life was fair, Rune."

"Clearly. I'm living in a death arena, being poked, prodded, and disfigured daily because I have this royal bloodline's lineage that gives me special powers." Rune was about to say something else but shut her mouth. She eyed Zara so hard Jacan thought she would kill her with that stare.

Zara's face turned from a slight smile to a grim one. "I will let you take his place, but he must go in at some point, Rune. You can't protect him forever; you can't protect *them* forever."

"Someone has to because clearly, *you* won't."

Rune gave an empty stare to Zara and walked off with the guard to the black pyramid building.

"What's that all about?"

"Who, Rune or Zara?" Rowan asked.

"Both."

Rowan puckered his lips and let out a sigh. "Rune is Zara's little sister. Rune is a Blood Royal, but Zara isn't."

"How can that be?" Jacan turned to face Rowan. Rowan shrugged his shoulders, "I don't know, maybe ask her yourself? Wait, actually, I don't think I was supposed to let anyone know that…."

Jacan scratched his neck and then folded his arms, deep in thought. Maybe being a Blood Royal was a recessive gene. "How do you know for sure they're sisters?"

"I accidentally overheard them arguing once about their parents when I was playing with Mei and Albie."

"They know this too?"

Rowan nodded. "Yes, but we all swore to keep it a secret. Please, Jacan, you can't tell any of the guards, especially him… they'll kill her."

If Zara ever did him wrong, he now had ammo against her. But what he wanted to know was if Kieron knew this information. He had to get the message to Kieron somehow. How that would be, he didn't have a clue.

"Don't worry, Rowan," Jacan smiled looking into the distance, "your secret is safe with me."

#

Lennox took her last bump of heroin before walking into the tent to meet the others. It was barely enough to take the edge off, knowing she would have to deal with the consequences in hours if she didn't get more drugs. She was scared to teleport and go on a quest with strangers, but she didn't know how she could ride in a car for hours without drugs in her system.

"Okay, let's get this party started," Loch said, flashing his wide grin. "Tell us what you know and what you want us to do."

Putting his salad down, Yousef opened a map and pointed to different locations. "All around the world, Blood Royals are being kidnapped, adults, teenagers, and children. Our child is one of those that was taken. We want to find her and get her back, but we can't do that until we help someone else first. We have no idea where she is or where she might have gone."

"But this is what we do know," Raziah said thoughtfully, "We were told by the Divine mother to find you three and bring you to Zach and Sam Dorsey. Zach is a Blood Royal and is on a quest to find the Holy Grail, David's harp, the Speaking Stone of Destiny, and the Crown of Thorns. We know the Crown of Thorns is at the Louvre Museum, which we can borrow because of my… capabilities," she smiled.

"Lennox, we need you to tell us what was written on those parchments," Jax said.

"We made a forgery but had to make up what was written on them," Yousef explained. "We need to know the next step to determine where the other relics could be."

"To be honest, there wasn't much written on them," Lennox replied. "Just weird metaphors and sayings." She wrapped her arms around herself as if she were cold. Jax thought she looked like she might be getting sick.

"Please, anything will help," Raziah cried.

"Okay, okay, I think the parchments read something like

'Shrouded in darkness, she will come,
Only made known by the Son of God,
Blood, light, sound, and water will have their part,
But not before life imitating art,

She will bring back the dead and bring them to their knees,
Only by repentance and the rule of threes,
What is to come has come before,
Make sure you don't open the wrong door.'

"What the heck does that mean?" Jax asked.

"We think we have an idea, but don't understand it completely," Yousef said. "That's where Zach Dorsey comes in. He may be only twenty-three, but he is an expert in this field. He studied under Brother Guiden, the priest who discovered the truth of Mary Magdalene and Jesus Christ's marriage and their secret child. He and Zach Dorsey were the ones who found out that the Catholic Church had known this secret for millennia and hid it. Certain members of the Church even went to wage wars and crusades against Blood Royals, trying to destroy their very existence."

"What we do know is this: Eve is to be incarnated again to redeem her sins for mankind," Raziah added. "That's all we truly know—everything else Mr. Dorsey will need to explain. We're supposed to bring the knowledge of the parchments to him so that he can get to the relics before the Antichrist does, or else all hell will break out on Earth, literally…." Razia paused and took a deep breath. She looked Jax in the eye, "Do you understand why we must take you to Zach and Sam Dorsey now? We want our child back," Raziah spoke softly but intently.

"The future of mankind is in your hands," Yousef said. "It's up to you as a group to make this decision."

Loch, Jax, and Lennox huddled in the corner to weigh their options and discuss the matter. After a short deliberation, they came back to Raziah and Yousef.

"We will help you with your quest," Jax said with determination, "but we have one request."

"What's that?"

"Lennox will teleport with you, and Loch and I will drive the jeep back; it's a rental, and we can't afford to not return it. The salary of an Archeologist is non-existent, to say the least," Jax laughed.

"You have yourself a deal," Yousef grinned.

CHAPTER 12

September 6th, 2023, 3:33 A.M. - New Orleans

Waking up from his slumber, Zach became aware that he was not in New Orleans anymore. He was surrounded by desert and bones everywhere he looked, with no living thing in sight. Taking his surroundings in more detail, he noticed the sky was a dusty red, with thick, darkened gray clouds blocking the sun. He was alone in a barren desert, devoid of buildings, plants, animals, people, or vegetation. Every way he looked, he saw bones piled up in heaps or laid across the sand.

"*Where am I?*" Zach said aloud as he puckered his lips. His lips were dry and cracked, he was boiling, and he couldn't see any water in sight. His Fleur de lis birthmark on his chest started to throb and he rubbed it, trying to soothe the pain.

"*And how the heck did I get here*?" He asked himself as if speaking out loud would invoke the answer. He knew he needed to get to fresh water and fast, or else he could die from dehydration in a matter of hours. Zach walked over to a pile of bones and picked one up. After examining the bone, he detected it was a human femur. He looked out and stared off into the distance. He saw thousands of human skulls scattered across the wasteland of the desert.

"What happened here? Where am I?" Zach asked, his voice cracking. *"God, why am I seeing this? What happened to these people?"* Zach tried speaking some more, but it was of no use. After saying those twelve words, he couldn't speak anymore. His voice was done without water. Zach dropped to his knees and fell into the sand.

Sam's face enveloped Zach's mind. He smiled as he thought about their wedding day. Thinking about how beautiful she was in her wedding dress, a vision of their wedding opened up to him in a panoramic 4D view. He was at their wedding in Lake Tahoe but was still stuck here in the desert, existing in both places simultaneously. Zach watched as the memory unfolded right before his eyes in real life. He took Sam's hand and walked out onto the dance floor; they were having their first dance as husband and wife. She wore a simple but elegant white wedding dress that trailed a few feet behind her. Her dress was spaghetti strapped, laced with delicate flowers. She took his breath away as he held her close for their first dance.

Their first dance, which was meant to be a slow dance, somehow turned into him twirling her around like a ballerina, and Sam doing the moonwalk and then the funky chicken. Zach shook his head in laughter and awe at his bride and looked at all their friends' and family's faces. They laughed, clapped their hands, and joined the funky chicken dance. Zack clenched his fists, grabbing two handfuls of sand, jolting him back into reality and ending the vision.

He was dying of thirst. Even just one drop of water would soothe his soul. Feeling a slight breeze, he meditated on what to do next. There was no damp ground, vegetation, or evidence of parched riverbeds. Without that, he wouldn't be able to locate fresh water. Out of the right corner of his eye, he saw a flicker of orange light. Squinching his eyes, he realized it was a tree on fire. He ran towards the tree and stopped in his tracks.

The tree was on fire but was not being consumed by the fire. A small circular mote of water surrounded it. Zach saw three pieces of worn-out parchment floating in the tree. He walked over, stepped over the mote of water, and reached out to grab the first parchment. It was in an ancient Hebrew text that Zach couldn't read. The sky opened inward upon itself and protruded out a black hole. Out of the black hole came glimmering lights, stars no bigger than Zach's fist descended about him. The reddened sky was now completely dark and filled with stars. A feminine voice from the black hole spoke. Her voice was tender as gentle rain and emoted love, peace, and tranquility.

"The Holy Grail that you seek,
Is not one that is always meek,
Cast down from the ineffable light,
Drink from the cup; don't put up a fight.

For the two to become one,
Remembrance and repentance must be done,
By blood, you have been redeemed; holy blood, you have
been saved,
It is now your turn to go into the grave.

The Father of Light died for your sins,
The Mother of Life wishes to live again,
For all of this to come to be true,
Look inside yourselves; what will you do?

The act of the transgressor is "The Soul,"
Those who seek will find redemption by not denying
the whole,
The "Self-Perfected Mind" has come forth to live once more,
The Holy Grail must be transformed to be restored.

How this is done, is by gathering the four,
The Holy Grail, the stone, the harp, and the thorns,
Put them all together with the Son of Man,
Then the two will become one and be united again."

Zach contemplated for a few moments before responding
to the divine.

"You are the divine aspect of God."

"I am." She replied.

"What am I doing here? How did I get here?"

"You are in the spiritual realm."

"So, I'm asleep?"

The Divine Feminine gave out a small laugh. "You are with me here, body, soul, and spirit."

"Why am I surrounded by millions of bones in a barren desert?"

"This is a possibility of the future, of what is to come to all of mankind if they do not wake up to the reality of who God is."

"So, what must I do to stop this from happening?"

"You must speak to the dry bones and tell them to live. God is male and female in the spirit, but we are not both genders; we transcend gender. We are the embodiments of all aspects of the masculine and feminine. The people must come back to the full truth of who God is. To deny us is to deny themselves. How can they see males mating with females in all aspects of creation and then deny that there is a female aspect of God? To deny the feminine aspect of God is to deny yourselves. Ironically, people see the female image every day in people, animals, and even in fruit and plants, yet deny that there is a female aspect of God. It hurts me deeply when my children think I do not exist when they see me in every aspect of life. Every day people see me in their mothers, sisters and aunts, co-workers, and friends, and yet they do not believe in me, and in fact, they blaspheme me to say that I am only male. Males and females are made in the image and likeness of God. It takes both the male and female images to complete the Godhead."

Zach thought about Sam and Sofia: the unconditional love Sam gave Zach every day; no matter how many times he messed up with her, Sam always forgave him. Zach thought of how Sofia would help care for the sick and the suffering, giving herself away no matter the cost to others.

Zach held the parchments of paper up to the sky to the female voice. "What am I supposed to do with these?"

"They are parchments from a lost gospel, the Gospel of the Divine Feminine of God. You must go to the Hagia Sophia Mosque in Turkey. You will find others looking for the same parchments, some to use for good, some to use for evil. You must find these lost objects, Jesus, who has been reborn, and my daughter Wisdom Sophia who has incarnated. She is God's divine feminine aspect and Christ's spiritual wife. The two must become One. Just as Jesus had Mary, Christ has Sophia. The barren desert filled with dry bones represents the House of Israel and the Gentiles. They all must come to accept Jesus and Sophia, the male, and the female aspects of God. The Antichrist will devour the world and lay waste leaving nothing but bones in the midst if he gets these items before you do."

Putting away the parchments in his pockets, Zach saw a faint red light rupturing in the night sky. The blackness of the sky imploded back into the black hole, taking back the glimmering stars to go with it. The sky turned back into a dusty red. Zach began to levitate upwards, then his body shot into the sky at lightning speed toward the black hole. Zach's eyes and heart filled with terror as he remembered what he read about what happens to a human even before they enter the event horizon of a black hole. The person's body would be stretched, and every single particle, atom, and molecule would be "spaghettified," the body stretched and destroyed by the warping of space and radiation surrounding the event horizon.

The Divine Mother began to soothe Zach's heart, not to be afraid, reminding him that God can do the impossible, even letting a human being experience the majesty, wonder, and awesome terror of a black hole.

"Every single hair on your hair is numbered and will not be touched; therefore, you shall not be afraid, for you are loved and more treasured than a multitude of sparrows."

The Divine Mother had spoken Luke 1:27 to him, giving Zach a divine sense of peace and trust that surpassed all understanding. As he flew towards the event horizon of the black hole, a red comet appeared in the sky, seemingly out of nowhere. Trailing behind the red comet was a rider on a white horse, carrying a bow with a crown of gold on his head.

CHAPTER 13

September 6th, 2033, 9:47 A.M. –New Orleans

Sam stared at her sparkling diamond wedding ring, highlighting Bible verses in Matthew 24, wondering where Zach had run off. He wasn't in the apartment and had left his cell phone on the nightstand, still charging from last night. Zach had never *once* left his cell phone behind, which made her worry even more that something had happened to him or, worse, a possible repeat of the events from two years ago.

She was not opposed to another adventure if God willed and desired, but she had grown accustomed to the two and a half years of peace in their life. No one had not heard a peep about the ex-holy seer of Rome, Cardinal Villere. They knew he was in hiding, and after what happened with Pope Aloysius, they all suspected Zach and Sofia were next in some way.

What was strange was that the Holy Seer had been in hiding for three years. If she were to consider the amount of time the Holy Seer needed to plan whatever he was planning, it made Sam feel uneasy even more so. She didn't need that kind of stress, especially after what she learned last night.

Sam reached over and dialed Brother Guiden's number, hoping he would be able to answer after the chaos that ensued just a week prior. The phone rang seven times before Brother Guiden answered. Sam began unloading all her worries about Zach to Brother Guiden when she felt a blast of wind coming from above her. She glanced up to see a portal three feet wide and two feet in height, encased in darkness, swirling above her.

Zach came shooting out of the portal headfirst, landing on his stomach on their queen size bed. Sam's body violently bounced a foot and a half above their bed. Sam screamed and dropped her Bible in the process; her eyes filled with confusion and dismay, wondering how Zach came out of a space-time portal as she landed with a thud back down on the bed. Sam glared at Zach as she saw her Bible crumpled on the floor.

"Zachary Dorsey! I swear if I didn't love you so much, I would kick your butt to Timbuktu!"

Raising his hands in protest, "Hey now, don't shoot the messenger! And boy, oh boy, a message do I have." Zach said, making a case with his eyes and stance to Sam. Sam never could stay mad at Zach when he gave her those puppy dog pleading eyes.

Sam rolled her eyes, "Geez, the things I do for love."

Sam got off the bed to gather her Bible, yellow highlighter, and phone off the floor and plopped down next to Zach.

"Hello...hello, anybody? What in God's name is going on over there!"

Sam's phone was still on the speaker; she had forgotten all about her phone call with Brother Guiden. Settling on the bed and catching her breath, she responded to Brother Guiden's worried hello.

"Zach just fell out of a portal from the ceiling in our bedroom. Turning to Zach, "Which, by the way, you were gone for HOURS; what in the heck is going on? Where did you go? I need an explanation, and now would suffice; thank you."

Brother Guiden could be heard ruffling through papers but stayed quiet, waiting for a response from Zach while he gently nudged a couple of guards who were pestering him to whom he was talking on the phone.

"Brother Guiden, I received that message you told me to look out for!" Zach said excitedly. He flipped over and put his hands in his pockets. He laid out the bed with three pieces of old worn-out parchments. "I received three parchments. I was taken to a desert filled with bones. In this place was a tree set on fire, but it was not consumed by the fire. A small mote of water surrounded it, and there wasn't a living thing in sight, and the sky was dusky red. Suddenly, a portal, or a black hole, opened. The black hole swallowed up the red sky, and the night sky came out with stars shooting out of it."

"I get dreams like that when I eat pizza before bed" Sam mused.

"You're forgetting me coming out of a portal from our ceiling, Sam."

"Oh yeah... right," Sam blushed. "Forgot that already."

Zach shook his head in laughter.

"As I was saying," he said with a smirk, "I heard the divine voice of God speak to me, but it was the feminine aspect of God!" Zach quickly explained all that the Divine Feminine had revealed. "These parchments are only a few pieces of a lost Gospel of the Divine Feminine that we must find before the Antichrist does. She told me that we must go to the Hagia Sophia Mosque in Turkey to find the other missing pieces of the gospel and that she would send us people to help us on our journey. The lost gospel will lead us to four things to help defeat the Antichrist."

"What are the four items, my son?" Brother Guiden asked, still rifling through papers.

"David's harp, Jesus' Crown of Thorns, the Speaking Stone of Destiny and the Holy Grail."

"So, impossible items to find. Or get, for that matter," Sam rolled her eyes, but her tone was business as usual. "Sounds like a great start to the journey."

"Aw, come on, Sam, don't think like that! The divine feminine gave us this task because she knows we can do it! We can succeed!"

Brother Guiden interjected on Sam's speaker phone, "The Stone of Destiny, also known as the *Speaking Stone of Destiny* or *Stone of Scone*, was a place for kings to be crowned. According to lore, the Stone of Destiny would speak or roar joyfully when the rightful king sat upon it."

"Okay... so we need to find a yelling stone."

"Speaking stone, my dear."

"And where would this Speaking Stone of Destiny be?"

"Some say it's still in hiding; some say Ireland, some say Scotland. There are many folklores and legends to the Stone of Destiny."

"So, I'm guessing we need to bring all these items to the Stone of Destiny?" Using her fingers to count, "David's harp, the Holy Grail, and the Crown of Thorns to defeat the Antichrist. But it also sounds like we're supposed to... crown somebody?" Sam asked, befuddled. "But who?"

Zach smiled and grabbed Sam's hand. "Not who but whom. We need to crown the new incarnated Jesus and his feminine counterpart, the divine feminine part of God, Wisdom, also known as Sophia."

"Sofia...like your twin sister Sofia...?"

"I'm not sure if she's *The* Sophia we're looking for, but she does come from the Royal Bloodline of Jesus and Mary: she can heal the sick and bring people and animals back from the dead. Her name *is* Sofia, just spelled differently, so I think she's the strongest candidate we have so far."

"Looks like the gang is getting back together for another adventure," Brother Guiden chimed in, "and you *all* know how I love a good mystery. What do you need from me, my son?"

"Well, we still don't have proof that a chalice exists. We only know a secret divine bloodline of Jesus and Mary. Can you do some digging in the Vatican and find out everything you can about the Holy Grail? Find out if there is an actual chalice or if it means something else besides the offspring of the Royal Bloodline. Also, see what you can learn about David's harp and any associated legends or myths. It shouldn't be too much of a problem for you, you know…since you're technically the Holy Pope of the world now."

Sam elbowed Zach on his ribcage.

"What I meant to say is that you're going to be a phenomenal Holy Pope. The people love you already; I've seen them gathering around you to support you on social media."

"He's right, you know, Brother Guiden." Sam agreed. "Amidst it all, if Pope Aloysius could have picked anyone to replace him, it would have been you. You stand up for the truth and love people fiercely. There's nothing you won't do to protect people and guide them to the truth."

After a few moments of silence, Brother Guiden responded. "Thank you both for your touching words. It means a lot to this old man."

"You're not old," Zach and Sam both responded simultaneously.

"Getting back to the mission at hand," Zach said, "the Crown of Thorns is locked up in the Louvre Museum in Paris, so we'll need to find a way to get a closer look at it and, umm… borrow it."

Raising her eyebrow, "You mean steal it."

Zach coughed and grabbed a water bottle on his nightstand to take a drink. "We'll ask politely, and if they don't let us borrow it, we will borrow it on our own accord and give it back when the mission is finished. But before we go to Paris, we have to go to the Hagia Sophia Mosque in Turkey. That's where the parchments are hiding, underneath the mosque, so we'll need to find a way to get in there, too."

She raised her eyebrows, "I better not have married a con in the making."

Zach let out a boyish laugh, "Of course not! You married a Robin Hood; I give back to the poor what the rich have stolen. All I'm doing is giving people back the knowledge hidden from them for millennia. Secret societies, cults, and religions who hide the truth of our reality and the nature of God."

"I couldn't agree more," Brother Guiden said. "So, what's our first move, my son?"

"There was… one thing that disturbed me in the vision."

Sam could see Zach's face had turned pale.

"We can only tackle this mission head-on with all of the information," Guiden spoke serenely.

"I saw the White Rider of the Four Horsemen from Revelation riding with a bow and a crown on his head. There was a red comet trailing behind him. I don't know if it's symbolic or literal."

The room fell dead silent. After some time, Brother Guiden broke the silence with caution in his words.

"The tree that was burning but could not be burnt is the divine male aspect of God, while the mote of water around the tree is the water of life, the womb; it represents the divine female aspect of God. The red hue in the sky is a warning of the red comet before it comes. The desert represents the world or the lack of the true word of God on earth. This is why you did not see a living soul or any life. The lack of knowledge and nature of God has been depleted. Water always represents the Holy Spirit and the word of God."

"It all sounds so dire, Brother Guiden."

"Yes, Sam, it does, however," Guiden said with a hopeful tone, "In Zach's vision, before he saw the white horseman, he saw the red sky swallowed up and the night sky come out with stars surrounding him. I interpret this vision as other Blood Royals who will be a part of the end-times battle. They will come forth from the Divine Mother to help us on our quest before the comet appears," Brother Guiden paused to let this information sink in.

"Well, that's good news at least," Sam said.

"But I fear that there is no stopping the Antichrist, at least for now, as there are still some things that need to come to pass that are written in Revelation," Brother Guiden continued. "We need to focus on the tasks given to us by the divine Mother and trust that God is guiding us every step towards salvation for mankind."

Zach and Sam nodded in unison, agreeing with Brother Guiden. "For all mankind," Zach exclaimed.

"Zach, call Sofia and let her in on everything you told Sam and me. She may have some information on the matter. If not, then it's best to leave her be for now, but warn her that she may be in danger. She has a lot going on in her life, and I'm not sure she's up for this adventure…."

"Sofia? She wouldn't miss this for the world, Brother Guiden. She's addicted to traveling as much as I am. We are twins, after all."

Brother Guiden shook his head and sighed, knowing full well Zach could not see the emotions written across his face.

"Pack your bags and get to the Lakefront airport. You both are flying on the Concorde 2 jet to Istanbul. You both need to find those fragments. They may just be the key to discovering The Holy Grail's identity. I'll research what I can find out about David's harp and the Stone of Destiny."

"And the Crown of Thorns?"

"Go to Turkey first and find the parchments. We'll worry about the Crown of Thorns later. Maybe Sofia has contacts in France that can help us to "borrow it," as you say.

"Right," Zach sheepishly smiled.

They all said their goodbyes and hung up the phone. Brother Guiden put down his cell phone and rubbed his temples with his fingers. He had been having headaches for the past few weeks, which seemed to worsen daily. He had also been having dreams of the future. Dreams about Zach and Sam, Sofia and a mystery man, and new friends about to enter their lives. Brother Guiden was told by an angel the exact time and place of his death. He couldn't tell Zach as he didn't want to deter him from his mission to help the incarnation of Jesus and Wisdom Sophia save humanity from the Antichrists' total annihilation. God help them all.

CHAPTER 14

September 6th, 12:00 P.M, 2023, 6:23 P.M. - New York City

Tom watched Delaney pacing back and forth by a picnic bench, her face draining from color by the second. Smoothing his chestnut brown hair behind his ear, he grabbed his Starbucks coffee and took a swig before returning to set up the camera in front of Delaney.

"You're on in five minutes, and I need you to get your shit together. You're a reporter, for God's sake."

Delaney stopped dead in her tracks and squinched her shoulders. "I…I…" But Delaney had no words. For the first time in her life, she was speechless. She felt completely helpless as a journalist, as a reporter, and as a human being. If what this professor is saying is true, Earth, as they knew it, would never be the same.

Tom eyed Delaney as she smoothed her black slacks and her curly auburn hair. She cupped a silver heart locket around her neck, closed her green eyes, and mouthed words inaudible for Tom to hear. After a minute of praying, Delaney put an earpiece in her ear and lined up in front of the camera.

Tom grabbed the mic and tossed it to Delaney. "Look, kid, just report the facts as you've always done, keep an even tone, and don't show emotion." He focused the camera as he spoke. "You don't want to freak out these people even more by having a breakdown on national television."

Giving him a side-eye, Delaney said, "I'm not going to have a breakdown on national television, Tom, but I think the people of the world have already started having breakdowns themselves. After the attack on Israel that Russia and China executed, the people of America think the United States is next."

"All hearsay, don't believe the rumors, and besides, America is the safest place to be," Tom reassured her.

"You have read the statement NBC issued me, right?" Delaney asked.

"I have."

"And?"

"And I think it's your job to report the news, and it's my job to film you."

"That's it, that's all you have to say?"

Tom nodded and gave Delaney her thirty-second mark before going live on air. For the first time in her life, Delaney was terrified of reporting the news live on air. It was hard to make her nervous, most things didn't scare her, but this news scared the living crap out of her.

"We'll talk about this later, red." Tom held up his fingers, giving Delaney her cue after her ten seconds were up. She was now live on air.

"A record-breaking comet, a hundred thousand times more massive than a typical comet around the sun, has been discovered by Ethan Levitt, a Planetary Science and Astronomy professor at the University of California," Delaney began her newscast. "The comet is the largest body identified to date, with its nucleus measuring eighty miles across. It is sixty-six times bigger than the heart of most comets. Astrophysicists have named the comet Rubrum Draconis, Latin for The Red Dragon, as the comet's tail has been identified as having a red tail instead of the typical blue or green tail, which has never been seen on Earth. Professor Levitt stated that the red gases are very faint and short-lived. They are produced by a type of emission that is close to red, called "forbidden oxygen," which occurs when atoms make a rare energy transition between states of "excitement." But it's very faint and short-lived. Comet dust often actually does "redden" sunlight. However, this comet is fast approaching Earth and will have a deep red color and a composition that could have carbon monoxide and carbon dioxide. Mr. Levitt discovered the comet at 2:37 this morning and stated that the mega comet is headed to impact Earth in March or April 2027. Mr. Levitt has also stated that the United States government has known about the comet for years but has hidden this knowledge from the people."

Tom could see that Delaney's hands were shaking, her voice quivering. Her body began to give off a low red hue. Delaney continued with her segment, having no idea what was going on with her body.

"Professor Levitt stated that without government assistance, he cannot know for sure what the impact of the comet will entail for humanity. He has stated on his podcast that people should start preparing by stocking dry, canned goods, clothes, medicines, and anything else that one would need to live off for years deep in caves or an underground bunker if the comet poisons our waters or changes the atmosphere. A seventeen-year-old boy genius and tech guru of New Light Technologies, Kieron Gederon, has issued a statement on Twitter fully supporting Mr. Levitt and will give him full access to his company's resources. Kieron Gederon has stated that he has developed an energy field that can destroy the comet if it gets too close to New York, but that at this time, he will need more funding to expand the energy field to encompass the whole earth. Neither the President of the United States nor NASA has commented on Professor Levitt's accusations about the foreknowledge of the comet, nor have they replied to Mr. Gederon's statement for funding. Professor Levitt's tweets have gone viral, and thousands of people all over the country have surrounded the White House, NASA headquarters in Washington D.C, and both NASA space centers of Houston and Merritt Island of Florida. Police in these areas have issued statements asking the protesters to return home, keep the peace, and wait for a statement from the White House. This is Delaney Woods reporting from NBC News."

Tom quickly turned off the camera and grabbed his phone to message his superior.

"Did you see what I saw on national TV?" Tom texted.

"Yes."

Delaney's phone started to ring; it was the network calling. Off at a distance, people started to rush up to Delaney and bombard her with questions.

"How did you do that?" An Emo girl asked.

"What are you? Some kind of a witch or something?" A Southern woman demanded.

"No, she's one of those Blood Royal freaks! I've heard about them all over the news in

the United Kingdom. They're a wicked species, I tell you. It's just not natural!"

"Blood Royal, what is that?" Delaney thought.

"Hey! Can you glow red again? It would look really cool on my Insta stories if you could glow red like that!"

"Umm…what?" Delaney spoke.

Delaney watched in horror as more and more people bombarded her with questions or demanded answers. She was completely baffled by the madness that encircled her.

"What are you all talking about? Have you all gone mad? Has the news of the red comet made you all go insane already?"

More people came, pulling out their cell phones to record Delaney. Delaney, not understanding what was happening, was beginning to feel a burning sensation rise deep inside her, her anger rising each moment as people sneered, called her names, shouted obscenities, or just wanted a picture or video of her.

Her body once again started to give off a red glow, and a surge of energy came through her, expanding toward the people surrounding her. People around her began falling to their knees, placing their hands on their faces and crying, rocking themselves back and forth, only saying one phrase, "Forgive me, Mother."

Delaney's eyes widened as she saw a man running at her with a pocketknife.

"Die, you filthy Blood Royal!"

Tom ran to block the man, grabbing Delaney's body to place in front of his; a surge of energy pulsated off her body as Tom's hands touched her shoulder. Tom shot backward, landing on top of the man with the knife, and by some miracle, unbeknownst to him, the knife didn't pierce his back. When Tom touched Delaney, it caused him to glimpse what the people saw in their minds. He gathered himself and knocked the man running at her with a microphone to his head. The man dropped instantly to the ground and lay unconscious.

"We have to go!" He told Delaney.

Delaney gave Tom a puzzled look. "We? You don't even like me."

Tom pointed to Delaney's tires on her silver Ford truck. Two of her tires were slit.

"It doesn't matter if I like you or not. We have to get you out of here, NOW! Unless you feel like becoming target practice again."

Delaney looked up to see a mob of people coming towards them, hatred on their faces with murder in their veins.

"Where?"

"A hotel, my uncle's hotel."

"Which hotel?"

"The Draconian."

"Of course. How the irony continues."

"Come on, your highness, we haven't got all day."

Tom gave a slightly curved smile at Delaney. His eyes were smiling oddly, making her feel very uneasy, but she would rather be in the presence of a mean millennial than a New York lunatic.

"Let's go," Delaney yelled. Running to Tom's black Mercedes Benz, Tom and Delaney hopped in the car and sped off.

#

Meanwhile, back in the coveted forest, Lennox held her breath, counted to ten, and closed her eyes. Since this was her first-time teleporting, she figured she might throw up, if not from the teleportation, then from being in withdrawal. She really needed to mind her p's and q's around Raziah and Yousef. Raziah would look at her strangely during the past few days as if she knew she was hiding something…as long as she didn't figure it out and tell Jax, all would be fine. She couldn't bear to have him find out; he would never look at her the same.

"Okay, Lennox, we'll see you in about six hours."

Jax went in to hug Lennox and lingered a few more moments than he should have as a friend, but Lennox was so caught up and worried about the teleportation and not getting sick that she didn't notice. Taking the hint, Jax quickly pulled away and stood beside Loch. Loch walked over to Lennox and gave her a bear hug.

"See you soon, lass. Stay outta trouble, you hear?"

"I hear you, big guy," Lennox said as she grabbed and squeezed his tattooed triceps. "You're getting really buff; you know that?"

"It is my best asset."

Lennox gulped to keep down the sickness. She turned to Raziah and Yousef, "I'm ready."

Raziah grabbed Yosef's and Lennox's hands. Raziah closed her eyes and smiled, "May the Lord take us to the exact place we need to be. By blood, we have been made; by blood, we are saved."

A strong gust of wind encircled Lennox, Raziah, and Yousef. Jax was about to yell out "Be careful" to Lennox, but in the blink of an eye, she was gone.

Loch turned to face Jax, "You know there are these things that pass messages from one end of the world to the other? It's called a cell phone."

Jax punched Loch in the shoulder. "Ouch!"

Loch shot Jax a devilish grin, "Hurts, don't it."

CHAPTER 15

September 6th, 2023, 9:00 P.M – London

Drinking chamomile tea on her new mahogany couch, Sofia was reviewing her notes to testify in her court case against the hospital. It had been two years in the making, and she was ready to bring down Dr. Wooldridge and the London Royal Hospital for covering up his actions toward the hospital's nurses.

In the two years since she first discovered his antics towards the nurses, Sofia had discovered even more damning information to blow up the hospital to smithereens. With the help of a few Blood Royals, she discovered that the hospital was refusing medical treatment for Blood Royals. They were also funding money for two secret programs by the British government: one was for keeping doctors on even though they had multiple malpractice cases. If the doctor in question made the hospital a lot of money, the government would sweep the case under the rug and threaten the family in question with prison time.

The second program, the more damning one in her opinion, was that the British government was kidnapping adult Blood Royals to run tests on them as well as do unspeakable things to their bodies in a secret underground base. She finally had enough evidence to not only put Dr. Wooldridge and multiple board members behind bars for life, but she could ask the United Nations for the first-ever international court case against a whole government. Sofia suspected these same atrocities were happening all around the world by other governments.

A loud knocking at her door interrupted her thoughts. She looked at her phone to see it was almost one in the morning. Putting down her teacup and grabbing her pepper spray, she rushed to the door and looked out the peephole. Unlocking the door, Sam rushed in and gave Sofia a bearhug, followed by Zach.

"You had us worried sick, Sof!" Zach said, embracing both Sam and Sofia. "You weren't answering your phone or responding to our messages, so we decided to swing by to ensure you were alright." He dropped the embrace and began inspecting her apartment for intruders.

"You know, usually when people don't answer, it's because they're asleep, busy, or working." Sofia followed Zach with her eyes as he checked her bathroom and closets. "My phone has been on airplane mode all day," she called to his back. "I didn't want any distractions."

"We know you've been busy," Sam said.

"Don't you think you're overreacting just a wee bit coming all the way over here just because I didn't answer my phone?"

"Not with this news," Zach said, wildly moving about the flat.

"What news?" Sofia asked.

After Zach had thoroughly checked every nook and cranny, he told Sofia about his encounter with the Divine Feminine and everything he had seen in the vision.

"So, you see, Sofia, we can't let you be alone right now," Zach said, approaching her. "You could be the incarnation of the Divine Feminine herself! The Bride of Christ, Wisdom Sophia herself! Literally!"

"Hardly!" Sofia scoffed.

"If the Holy Seer..." Zach shook his head, ".... Cardinal Villere is still alive and well, then he and the Antichrist will be looking for you." He searched her eyes to see if she was taking him seriously. "And we don't know if that means killing you or using your gifts and abilities against people somehow." He took hold of her hand. "You must come with us to Turkey or go to Rome and stay with Brother Guiden at the Vatican. We must protect you and keep you safe until we learn more about what all this means."

Sofia was flabbergasted. She took her hand away, pepper spray on the kitchen counter, and stared at Zach. "Look around you, Zach," she motioned to the boxes that filled her living room.

Zach noted the ten or eleven boxes filled with papers. "What's all this?"

"This, Zach, has been my life for the past two and a half years, remember?"

"Of course, yes. Yes, I remember. How could I not?"

"I gave up *everything* for this, Zach, *everything*. I gave up pursuing my Doctorate. I gave up having a social life and stepped down as a Cardinal for Christianology for this, not just for Blood Royals who want to be known and found, but for all of us, Blood Royals and Non-Blood Royals. We have a systematic problem in our world, Zach; one of those is our political systems. We must start implementing change now."

"All those people can wait, Sofia; you can set another court date, but we have to leave, and we have to leave now."

"Please, Sofia," Sam pleaded, "we don't want to lose you."

Zach approached Sofia again, but she put her hand up to stop in his tracks.

"Listen, I love you both more than life itself, but if you think I'm throwing away this court date because you believe I am the literal incarnation of the female aspect of God herself, you are both bat shit crazy! You have known me for two years, Zach. You have seen me mess up, miss the mark, and sin. If the old Jesus never sinned, not even once, then don't you think this Wisdom Sophia will not sin either? That's not me, and you know it."

"But Sofia–" Zach protested.

"But nothing, Zach! Maybe you've forgotten what it's like to be a Blood Royal these past two and half years, but I haven't. We're fighting for the right to exist, Zach! Have you been watching the news about what's going on over here?"

"Yes, well….a little," he admitted.

"They've started segregating Blood Royals from Non-Blood Royals in schools and universities across the U.K., just like in the U.S. when blacks were segregated from whites. Some hospitals deny Blood Royals proper medical treatment and even experiment on us in secret underground labs sponsored by the British government. But you don't have a CLUE as to what's going on because you're so wrapped up in your perfect life back in New Orleans."

Zach's face was stunned in place. "What...? I'm actually speechless, Sofia, that you would think that of me."

"We haven't had a proper conversation on the phone in four months, Zach, and before that, every time I talked to you, you only talked about yourself, your research, your job, and your role in Christianology. You've become so self-absorbed in your work that you've forgotten what all of this is about...." Sofia motioned to the many boxes in the room. "This isn't just a research project to study; real people's lives are at stake. Witch hunts are going on everywhere to exterminate us one by one. Blood Royal children and teenagers are going missing daily here in the UK; my theory is that the Holy Seer has something to do with it."

Sam darted her eyes back and forth from Zach to Sofia as their argument escalated.

"You know what, Sofia, I came here to help you, to save YOU from a possible assassination," Zach pointed at her. "But if you're so hell-bent on dying, go right ahead. And you're absolutely right. There's no *possible* way you could be the incarnation of the Divine Feminine. You push everyone away. You think you're better than everyone else because of how you grew up, Prada this, Prada that." Zach mimicked a model walking on a runway. "You spend all the money you have on clothes, shoes, purses, and fancy watches from the salary you made as Cardinal of Christianology Church, that is, before you left. The Divine Feminine would never be as stuck up as you are."

"Yes, giving up my life for two and a half years for the good of the Blood Royals is self-centered," Sofia replied sarcastically. She put her hands on her hips and emphasized each word, "And BY THE WAY, it is not a sin to want nice things, Zach. It's only a sin if you make Mammon your god. You don't give a damn about the REAL issues."

"All I've been doing, Sofia, is finding evidence to help Blood Royals."

"No. All you've been doing is researching to get a Nobel Prize, have a book written about you, or try to go on another adventure like Indiana Jones. I'm the one that's doing all the leg work, trying to make a difference. You're delusional, Zach! You need to wake up and get your head out of your ass. If you can't even see what's happening right under your nose, I don't want ANY part of your little charade." She crossed her arms with finality.

"You got it." Zach stormed out of Sofia's flat and headed back to the driver, who was waiting for them parked outside. Sofia gave Sam a "get-out look." But instead, Sam walked over to Sofia and took her hand.

"Sofia, I'm sorry you've felt all alone. I know it was never Zach's intention to hurt you or not be there for you."

Sofia looked away, but let Sam hold her hand.

"He's just been so busy gathering money for the new building of the Christianology church and his research…" Sam continued, "to give the Blood Royals a place to call home.".

"Funding a building and doing research….how is that important when there are lives at stake? They want what's in our blood, Sam, and *no* school nor *any* research is more important than actually saving the lives of the people he claims to have so much love and respect for. It's just not."

Sofia let go of Sam's hand and opened the door for her.

"Now, if you can, please leave; I need to review the rest of my notes to be fully prepared for tomorrow's trial. Thousands of Non-Blood Royals and Blood Royals will be there, lining up the streets each day. It'll be on TV and shown worldwide, but have I heard from either of you in the past month leading up to it? No. I've been left to do all this work with my lawyer, Agnes, a few Blood Royals, and Brother Guiden."

Sam nodded, hesitating in the doorway.

"HE has still made time to help me. He's been "borrowing" guards' phones just to check in with me while he's being watched like a hawk, but my own brother doesn't call to ask how I'm doing. Now, if you'll excuse me, I have important matters to attend to."

Sam rummaged through her purse for a few seconds before finding what she wanted to leave for Sofia. She placed something in one of the boxes filled with paperwork and gave Sofia one last look before walking out the door. Sofia shut the door behind her without caring what Sam left behind in the box.

CHAPTER 16

September 7th, 2023 – 6:00 A.M- London

Sofia awoke to her phone ringing and the smell of rich Brazilian coffee permeating her nostrils. Opening her eyes, she realized she had once again fallen asleep on the couch. She wasn't surprised. Her living room had turned into her new living quarters. She often fell asleep on the couch after a long night of researching. She felt around the coffee table for her phone.

"Hello?"

"Sophia! I don't have much time."

"Hi, Brother Guiden. How are you?"

"Fine, dear, fine," Brother Guiden rushed. "Listen, I just wanted to send you my thoughts and prayers. I know today is a big day for you."

"Thank you."

"And Sofia, please be careful. I've had my ear to the ground recently, and some people who mean you harm, might take today's publicity to act."

"I know that's a possibility."

"I would be there with you if I could," Brother Guiden said.

"I know."

"Take care of yourself. I'm with you in spirit."

"Thank you, Brother Guiden."

"I must go now, Goodbye."

"Goodbye." Although anxious about the trial, Sofia felt calmed and inspired by Brother Guiden's support. His deep faith in her and in God's will was contagious. She walked into the kitchen to fetch a cup of coffee.

She had to hand it to the Americans by coming up with the idea of an automatic coffee maker. She liked the idea of saving time and money, and although the thought of an automatic coffee maker sent shivers down her spine at first, she came around to the gadget. Sam had a way of convincing her to try American things she usually wouldn't even take a second look at. Hearing a knock at the door, Sofia walked over and opened the door to a friendly face she had grown to love more and more.

"How are you doing, hun?"

"I woke up feeling like I'd been hit by a double-decker bus. But a friend called, and I'm feeling better now."

Agnes scooted into Sofia's flat, holding a small yellow box. Eyeing the box, Sofia shut the door and went to the kitchen to pour Agnes a cup of coffee. Adding two sugars and a bit of cream,

Sofia set the cup of coffee before Agnes. Agnes took a sip of her coffee, set it down, and straightened herself up.

"Are you ready for today?"

"I slept in my clothes from yesterday, Ag, so that's a big no," Sofia laughed.

"I just want you to be fully prepared for however the trial pans out. Whether we win or lose, you should be proud of your accomplishments. Every nurse I know stands behind *you* because they know what you stand for. People are tired of the corrupted system, not just the NHS workers but our fellow man. You're helping to bring these issues to light so that changes can be made in the system."

Sofia took a deep breath and collected her thoughts. She didn't know how she felt about having the trial televised; it *would* bring more exposure to the corrupt systems of the NHS and private hospitals, but Sofia had this nagging feeling that putting the trial online and, on the news, would cause more harm than good. Social media had a way of canceling you before you could mutter a word.

"I'm ready to take them down, Agnes. Dr. Wooldridge doesn't scare me; the London Royal Hospital doesn't scare me; NHS doesn't scare me. However, social media *does* scare me, and how the news portrays people scares me. They can make or break people at the drop of a hat. I can handle being put under scrutiny. It's the lies they make about someone I can't handle. It's the news creating a whole concoction of attitudes and beliefs in people that even the strongest minds will bend to," Sofia paused and took a sip of coffee. "Herd mentality is a real thing–where the herd goes is usually where the winner lies."

Agnes was quiet for a moment. Sofia's words sank in like a ton of bricks falling in quicksand. She hadn't given too much thought to the press or social media; she always considered Sofia a capable lass who could fend for herself.

"You're absolutely right, Sofia, and I'm sorry I didn't look at it that way. I guess this old bird needs to get with the times more. After working for thirty years, you would think I've seen it all, and let me tell you…I have, but sometimes I forget how much social media's power affects people, especially the younger generations."

Agnes pulled out a yellow box, "Before I forget, I got you a little something for your first day at the trial."

"Oh, Agnes, you really shouldn't have. I possibly couldn't accept…."

"You can't refuse me; I'm a Northerner." Agnes said with the biggest smile. "I'll just force it on you if I have to,"

"Okay, okay, you win."

Agnes handed Sofia the pale-yellow box, anxiously awaiting her response. Sofia opened the yellow box and gasped.

"There are many things I can't explain about you, but what I do know is that you are something special," Agnes said. "You've taught me more about healing and the love of God these past two in half years than I ever have by a Baptist preacher. So, when I saw this in the bookstore window, I immediately thought of you. It was like a force compelled me to buy it for you. It was the strangest feeling…but honestly, I don't question these things anymore,

I'm just doing what the spirit moves me to do, and the spirit of God wanted me to give you this."

Laying in the box was a simple wooden cross. Sofia must have seen the cross a thousand times inside the windowsill of the bookstore hidden deep in an alleyway of Camden Town. While researching the trial at the bookstore, she asked the bookstore owner if she could get a closer look at it. The man who owned the bookstore looked like he was a character in a Disney film, he always had a twinkle in his eye and a squirrel who would come into his bookstore and eat nuts right out of his hand.

On the back of the cross was an Aramaic phrase. When she asked the bookstore owner what the meaning was, he said he didn't have a clue but that he had bought it from a man who bought it from a young man who looked middle eastern. This man, as crazy as it sounds, he said, claimed he was given the cross by a man who could make the blind see, make the deaf hear, make the cripple walk, and even make people invisible. The bookstore owner said when he wore it, his eyesight was healed, and he no longer needed to wear glasses, but he could never walk through walls. Sofia told the book owner the man sounded like he was talking about Jesus, to which the owner replied that's exactly what the man said.

"Agnes, I have looked at this cross a thousand times inside the windowsill of the bookstore and tried buying it from the bookstore owner, but I could never afford the price he was asking. He said the wooden cross had special powers from a man who had been given the cross from Jesus Christ himself."

"Jesus of Nazareth, the man who came over 2,000 years ago, that same Jesus?" Asked Agnes, puzzled.

"The one and the same. He has incarnated again."

Sofia thought of Zach and how he would love to know this new information. She would tell him–eventually. But that day was not today. She had bigger fish to fry.

#

Lennox barely landed on her feet, wobbling left and right before crashing down on her left side toward the ground. Her head throbbed in pain. She sat up and rubbed her leg. Raziah helped her up to her feet while she brushed the dirt off her pants. Baffled by the scenery, Raziah, and Yousef stepped back to take in their surroundings.

"Where are we?"

"Well, we're not in Istanbul!" Lennox cried out.

Raziah and Yousef looked around their surroundings, but they couldn't place where they were. They could see green grass, the ocean, and cliffs until the end of time.

"Wherever we are, it's where God wants us. It's where he wants you, Lennox. If he wanted Jax and Loch, the Divine Feminine would have had them here with us, but she didn't, so there must be some reason why we're here before we return to Istanbul."

"We need to go back. Now!"

Lennox grabbed her stomach and fell to the floor, throwing up all over the ground. She wiped her mouth and started to cry.

Raziah bent down and brushed Lennox's hair out of her face. She grabbed the hem of her dress and wiped the sickness off her chin.

Raziah looked deep into Lennox's eyes. "Lennox, you must stop this; this is why the Divine Feminine wants you here. You are on a sabbatical to get well. We are here to help you transition back to how you were before."

"The first few days will be miserable; it will be hell, you will cry and beg to die, but then you will feel better and become stronger from it," Yousef added.

"I don't want to quit! I'm not ready to quit…and you can't make me quit!" Lennox yelled.

Raziah sighed, "You're right. We can't make you do anything you don't want to. We had a son, you know, he was about your age, we lost to this godforsaken drug years ago. This isn't a game, Lennox; you can kill yourself over it. Is this drug really worth risking your life?"

Lennox thought back to Anne and what she said to her. There was power in a name; at this point, she was too sick to care whether she lived or died. She just needed to get her fix. "Send me back to Istanbul, or you're on your own."

"We're not returning to Istanbul to get you drugs, Lennox," Yousef said. "You're going to have to do this cold turkey. I'm sorry."

"By the way, I know *exactly* where we are."

They both stayed silent but were intrigued.

"I know Emira."

"What did you say?" Asked Yousef.

"I said, I know Emira. She told me there's power in a name. You know her; I know her, and I'm telling you, I know exactly where we are. You have to grant my wish; that's what Emira was trying to tell me. And my wish is to get drugs so that I'm not sick. If you want my help, and if you're supposed to obey Emira like I think you are, then you will help me, and I will help you. That's the deal, take it or leave it."

Yousef cracked his neck and rubbed it. He didn't think he would hear that name ever again. But it was–Emira. The famous Emira, the woman who's visions always came to pass. She may be blind, but she was not someone to mess with. He understood that very well. She was well protected on the other side. He never had any qualms with her. Quite the opposite. He had deep respect and admiration for her after everything she had been through; it was truly amazing all the feats she had accomplished.

"Where are we?" Yousef asked.

"I told you I'm not helping you until I score. So, unless you have pain pills or know where to get opiates in Ireland, we're going back to Istanbul."

"Do you have any heroin left at all?"

"Why?" Lennox asked suspiciously, thinking they would take the last of her drugs away from her.

Yousef sighed, "Because I have the power to multiply any item, which would include substances… that is what the Lord gave me when I found out I was a Blood Royal. Raziah can teleport, and I can multiply any object or item."

Scrunching her eyes, Lennox pulled out a clear bag with a tiny amount of brown powder in the small baggy. Yousef eyed Raziah who nodded. He grabbed the bag, closed his eyes, and placed the bag in between both hands. "God, I know using drugs is not your will, but please multiply this substance so we may continue this journey and find our daughter. Keep Lennox safe and on the straight and narrow path. I know you have us here for a purpose, and one of those purposes is for Lennox to be with us when we find our daughter. Help us complete the mission so we may bring our daughter back home."

Yousef opened his hand to reveal the bag of heroin was full to the brim with powder.

"There must be ten grams in there!" Lennox exclaimed excitedly.

Lennox was about to grab the bag out of his hand when Yousef moved his hand. "Where are we exactly?"

"The cliffs of Moher in Ireland."

"She's here, Yousef," Raziah said, "I can feel it deep within my bones."

Yousef handed Lennox the bag of drugs. Like a mad dog, Lennox opened the bag and poured some brown substance onto her hand. She closed one nostril and snorted the substance. A warm sensation ran through her body; Raziah and Yousef could see her eyes had become pinpoint. Lennox looked at them both, "What about Jax and Loch?"

"We'll take care of it. Right now, what we need to do is start walking," said Raziah. "The Lord will lead us the way to her."

"What's your daughter's name?"

Lennox could see they both became tight-lipped, "You know what, never mind, don't tell me; probably best if we keep it simple between us. And look...I'm sorry about not wanting to help you until I got my drugs; I just... I'm just not ready to quit. I can't do it," Lennox said as she held her arm.

Yousef nodded understanding, "I know that deep down, you are a good person. I can sense that you have great qualities about you. You're just...clouded by this drug. It turns you into a person that is not you. One day you will see."

Raziah stayed quiet, walking over to give her a hug. "We all have demons, Lennox. Just don't let this demon suck the life out of you."

Lennox nodded with a tear coming down her cheek. She wiped it off, put the bag of heroin in her pocket, and began to walk south of the cliffs.

Raziah waited until Lennox was out of earshot to speak. "Do you think she'll make it?"

"Only by the grace of God," Yousef replied. "I don't know if she is strong enough to kick this habit."

"What do we do about Jax and Loch?"

"I'll message them that the Divine Feminine has us on a detour. They need to find Zach and Sam; that's their most important task. They know what the parchments say. We need to find our daughter. We need to get Rune back. She's our only fighting chance to help win the war against the Antichrist."

CHAPTER 17

September 7th, 2023, 10:43 A.M –Vatican City

Finally given his access to technology back, Brother Guiden scored through his old files searching for any information that might help Zach and Sam find David's harp or the Stone of Destiny. He was reading up on the Mosaics of the Hagia Sophia when guards burst through his door and told him they must go to the Bunker below. Israel had just been bombed.

Brother Guiden grabbed his laptop and allowed the guards to escort him down the long hall with portraits of all the previous popes. He knew some had been corrupt, while others had been very wise. He sucked in his breath and felt tears fill his eyes as they passed the most recently deceased pope - his friend, Pope Aloysius. He fought down his complicated emotions. He and Pope Aloysius had been on the verge of bringing more truth to light regarding the Blood Royals and where they fit into God's will. He'd loved his friend and missed him deeply, their long intellectual conversations on matters of theology, their mutual hopes for the future of the Church. These feelings fought with the bitterness of his loss mixed with the regret he felt about not having prevented it. He should have suspected The Holy Seer and the Antichrist would try an assassination that day. He shook his head in shame.

After the hall of portraits, the guards led Brother Guiden down many secret stairs to the secure bunker beneath the Vatican. Once settled below, he was briefed on the news. Russia and China had bombed Israel, in effect beginning World War III. Also, a red comet had been discovered that scientists calculated would strike the East Coast in six years. Mysterious earthquakes - in places where there were no meeting of tectonic plates were also occurring across the globe.

Brother Guiden quickly relayed this information to Zach, but he got no response. He knew Zach and Sam were currently on the Concorde jet, but he was almost certain that jet had Wi-Fi.

As the acting Pope, he reached out to Israel to see how he could be of assistance. He knew the dire warning of these signs. He needed to minister to people everywhere. Between calls to political leaders, cardinals, and bishops, he sent Zach information about the Hagia Sophi that might be helpful. He texted him to look for clues in the mosaics and the pillars. He paced back and forth in the bunker, waiting to hear more news.

#

Sam thought she could cut the silence with a knife on the Concorde jet. She had not seen Zach in such a state of anger since his fight with Brother Guiden two years ago. That fight was over Brother Guiden keeping secret from Zach that he was a Blood Royal. She could do nothing to help soothe his soul from Sofia's words. All she could do was hold his hand to let him know she was there for him–when he wasn't pacing the aisle. She desperately needed to tell him something, but she didn't know when a good time for this information would be. It's better late than never...

"Zach?"

Zach looked over at her.

"Remember when you said–"

Just then, they both heard the intercom with an announcement from the pilot:

"We'll be landing in Istanbul in approximately thirty-six minutes. The weather is seventy-four degrees and should remain nice for the rest of your time in Istanbul. If you need anything else, please don't hesitate to ask the Stewardess, Cassandra."

"What were you saying?"

But Sam didn't have the strength to tell him. Not now, not yet anyway.

"Just that you had agreed to take me out to get a falafel when we got to Istanbul, and Lord knows I'm starving."

Zach showed a slight smile. "Of course, let's drop off our stuff at the hotel, grab something to eat, and then make our way towards Hagia Sophia. I have no idea how we're going to find this married couple. The Divine Feminine never gave me a location to meet them. All she said was to find them, but I don't know how...."

"I know how," Sam gave a wide grin.

"How?" Zach asked, perplexed.

"By this." Sam put her hand on Zach's chest. His *Sangreal* birthmark began to heat up, with warmth radiating through his body. Zach brushed a hair out of Sam's face.

"How could I ever forget," Zach laughed. "I'm sorry for being so angry; I just don't know what to think or how to handle the Sofia situation."

"Just give her time; she does have a lot going on. We'll pray about it and ask God for clarity on how to handle the situation."

"I can feel in my bones, Sam, that Sofia does have a part in all this… I'm not sure exactly what it is, and it makes me sad and upset that she can't see it."

"All in God's timing, my love. Let's just focus on using your visions and your *Sangreal* birthmark to lead us the way to Raziah and Yousef. We'll focus on Sofia later down the road when God tells you more about the Divine Feminine. Capisce?"

Zach smiled, "Capisce."

#

"When is he getting there? Kieron asked as he went up the stairs towards the

low-lit conference room.

"He and Samantha are headed towards Hagia Sophia as we speak," the Holy

Seer remarked.

"Good. It's time for Zach Dorsey to know who's in charge around here."

Kieron grinned at the Holy Seer but quickly changed his stance to a solemn face as he walked into the room to shake the hand of the Prime Minister of Israel.

#

The Hagia Sophia was breathtaking, Sam thought. She had never seen such beautiful architecture in her whole life; it was the way the domes and spires played off each other in space that appealed to her aesthetic.

"Why can't our churches look like this? This mosque is stunning."

"Not as stunning as you."

"Now you're just being a kiss-ass," Sam smirked.

"Maybe both are true," Zach joked.

"Uh-huh."

"So, Brother Guiden emailed me some research on the Hagia Sophia," Zach pulled out his phone and began reading, "It was built as a Christian church under the direction of Byzantine emperor Justinian I in the 6th century. In subsequent centuries it became a mosque, a museum, and now is a mosque again. It is made up of 104 columns, mainly of marble from Ephesus. The main dome rises one hundred and eighty feet above the ground. The Hagia Sophia is the second-largest pendentive dome in the world after St. Peter's Basilica in Rome. There are two semi-domes on either side, one at the altar and the other at the main entrance, with four minarets to protect the building against collapsing onto itself."

"Do you think there is any significance to the number of columns or minarets? 104 and 4?" Sam asked.

"I'm not sure. Let's look inside and see if we find anything that can lead us to the lost Gospel of the Divine Feminine."

Just then, both Zach's and Sam's phones began to have multiple texts and notifications of missed calls hit their phone.

"What in the world," exclaimed Zach, "We must have just gotten cell service!"

Sam closed her eyes and said a quick prayer, preparing for the worst; she opened her eyes and read her phone.

"Oh, my God," Sam spoke loudly, her eyes wide in terror, her breath becoming shallow.

Zach scrolled on his phone to see about forty notifications of missed calls from Brother Guiden, members of the Church of Christianology, and friends he had in the political and governmental spheres.

His worst nightmare had come true. The start of the tribulation was upon them. The red comet Zach had seen in the vision would hit New York City and the East Coast in six years. The nation of Israel was bombed yesterday when they were on the Concorde jet to Istanbul. Zach suspected the Holy Seer had somehow messed with their Wi-Fi so they could not receive messages or news from the outside world. *How on earth could he do that?"* Zach thought.

Russia and China had been the ones to bomb Israel, as predicted in the Book of Revelation. It was the start of World War III, and Zach was no closer to finding out who could be the Antichrist, the incarnated Jesus, or wisdom Sophia.

#

Loch raised an eyebrow as Jax threw his phone on the ground. They were back in Istanbul, but Lennox, Raziah, and Yousef were not in sight. He thought his cell phone would shatter into a million pieces, but for some reason, it stayed fully intact, which Loch found strange considering how hard he threw his phone.

"You okay, lad?"

"No, Loch. I'm not. Raziah and Yousef basically kidnapped Lennox. They're on some divine mission from the goddess herself."

"She's not a goddess, Jax. It's two aspects of one God." Loch held out one hand then the other. "The masculine and the feminine." He clasped his hands together to demonstrate.

"Since when did you become an expert on God?"

"I just listen to the information given to me," Loch touched his head and heart as he spoke. "Something you used to do before your head and your heart went to shite." He grinned.

"She drives me crazy, Loch, she really does," Jax shook his head. "We must go after her. She's going through so much; we can't just leave her with them."

Loch didn't think it was the right time to tell Jax what he had stumbled onto. It would break his heart. He had seen Lennox take a bump of a brown substance out in the forest while she thought no one was around. He happened to be at the right place at the right time to witness it. She sold the parchments to send money back home to her dying father, as well as to buy drugs to help her cope with the fact of knowing her father was dying. It wasn't his place to tell Jax; it was Lennox's business, and he had no place in revealing something that would destroy Jax's heart even more so.

"What did they tell you?"

"To keep with the mission and find Zach and Sam Dorsey."

"Then that's what we need to do, Jax. Lennox is perfectly safe with Raziah and Yousef. He used to be an Iman priest; for God's sake, if we can't trust a priest, then who can we trust? You need to let Lennox make her own decisions, and we need to keep track of what we're supposed to do. Now come on, we've got to figure out where these two are and give them the revelation on the parchments. Then we'll have done our job, and we can get Lennox. Deal?"

Jax thought about everything that had happened between him and Lennox. He needed to be her friend first and foremost. He needed to let her walk her own path, even if that meant that path didn't include him.

"You're right, Loch. You seem to be right a lot lately," Jax smiled.

Loch smiled and shrugged, "Just looking out for my mates, that's all it is."

"Okay, so how do we find the Dorsey's?"

"Trial and error, mate, trial and error."

CHAPTER 18

September 7th, 2023, 10:00 A.M. –London

A man with fierce eyes and salt-and-pepper hair walked over to Dr. Wooldridge and whispered something Sofia could not make out in his ear. Dr. Wooldridge was pompous as ever; his eyes widened, and a smirk filled his face. He nodded, saying he understood whatever the Royal London Hospital's lawyer had just told him. A policeman walked up to Sofia, holding a Bible in both hands; raising his right hand, he asked Sofia to place her hand on the Bible and raise her right hand.

"Do you swear to tell the whole truth and nothing but the truth, so help you, God?"

"I do," Sofia responded with determination and honor.

"You may sit," the policeman responded back.

The salt-and-pepper-haired lawyer took center stage and started his attack.

"Miss Boudreaux, how long were you a resident presiding at the Royal London Hospital?"

"I was a resident at the Royal London Hospital for three years."

"And how would you describe your time at the hospital?"

"It was some of the best times of my life. I love being able to help someone in need. But that all changed after nurse Agnes informed me of the bullying between Dr. Wooldridge and the nurses. After I found that out, I did some digging and found out the hospital was covering up deaths from prominent doctors at the hospital."

The court spectators started to gasp at Sofia's revelation. Reporters could be seen scribbling fast on their notebooks while two cameramen had their cameras facing toward Sofia.

"I loved all the nurses and the doctors; it was only–"

"So, you loved working under Dr. Wooldridge?"

Sophia opened her mouth and then shut it. She knew she had to choose her words carefully. "At one point, yes, until I didn't."

"I see. Did Dr. Wooldridge ever help you in any manner or fashion that went above and beyond?"

Sofia could see where this was going but knew she had to answer truthfully.

"He did, yes, but he was a complete jerk to the nursing staff."

"What did Dr. Wooldridge help you with?

Sofia bit the inside of her cheek, "He gave me extra lessons outside of class so that I could be at the top of my class."

"So, Dr. Wooldridge helped you outside the classroom, teaching you and taking hours out of his own time to help you with your schooling. It seems you are saying that he was a mentor to you."

"In a manner of speaking, yes. But he was wretched to everyone else. It wasn't until after I had heard the rumors about him, did I start looking at his character beyond myself and the realm of doctors. I had no idea how he treated the nursing staff and everyone else."

"But never to you, isn't that correct?"

"Well…no, never to me."

"What else did Dr. Wooldridge help you with?"

Sofia sighed, "He helped me get into Harvard University. He sent a letter of recommendation and put in a good word for me to the Dean of Admissions and the president of Harvard University. I was going to move to America, finish my residency, and get my Ph.D. in Boston."

"So, if it weren't for Dr. Wooldridge, you never would have gotten into Harvard, even with your impeccable GPA."

"That is correct."

"So, one could say that Dr. Wooldridge went above and beyond with you. He recognized your talent and molded you into the doctor you are today."

"He helped me in many aspects of performing surgeries to expertise. I have no issues with his surgical skills, but there are doctors who are household names in London who should have been fired years ago. It's not the doctors or soon-to-be doctors Dr. Wooldridge had a problem with. It was everyone else on staff at the hospital; he thought he was better than everyone else."

The lawyer smiled, knowing that Sofia had just walked into his trap.

"Isn't it true that you think that you are better than everyone else?"

Sofia let out a small, cute snort and gave the lawyer a bewildered look. "I think everyone is equal and should be treated equally."

"But you are not equal. You are more than the average human being."

Sofia's *fleur-de-lis* birthmark started to tingle, a warm sensation on her chest. Sofia put her hand over her birthmark and gently rubbed it. "You and I both know that's not true."

"Objection, your honor, this has nothing to do with the case at hand," Mr. Hughes stated.

"Overruled; I want to see where this is going. Get to the point, Mr. Peabody."

"Of course, your honor. The defense would like to present the exhibit "Q" to the court, your honor."

Mr. Hughes searched his files but could not find any document listed as Q.

"Your honor, this must be a new piece of evidence because I do not have a document lettered "Q" in my possession."

"We just found this piece of evidence a few hours ago, your honor, and I thought it would be best to start with this information."

"Oh, come off it, Peabody; you've had this information all along, haven't you?"

"I most certainly have not. You can check the date on my computer when the file was sent if you'd like."

"I need both counselors to approach the bench," commanded the judge. "Now."

Judge Steele put his hand over the microphone as he talked to both solicitors.

The courtroom went silent. Everyone in the courtroom leaned in to try and make out the contents of the conversation, but it was of no avail. They couldn't make out the travesty that was blooming before them.

"But your honor! This is despicable! How could you!?"

People from all around started to whisper and shout out questions to Judge Steele.

"What is the damning evidence, your honor!" A bulky reporter asked intently.

Judge Steele pounded his hammer, "Order! Order in my court! The next person who shouts out or even so much as a peep will be removed from my court."

The people began to quiet down; Sofia could tell none wanted to be removed. The show must go on.

"I will allow this piece of evidence, Mr. Hughes. Please wait until it's your turn to cross-examine your witness."

Sofia looked at Mr. Hughes, wondering what piece of evidence had him so riled up; the look in his eyes told her everything. It was damning to her case. Sofia closed her eyes and started to pray while circling the *fleur-de-lis* over her silky cream blouse.

The policeman walked over to gather Mr. Peabody's evidence. It was a USB. The policeman dragged his feet as he walked over and plugged the USB into a laptop. As he did, a video of Sophia appeared on the screen. Sophia opened her eyes to expect the worst.

The first video played was a clip of Sofia as one of the leaders of the Christianology Church, started for Blood Royals. She was walking into the first built Christianology Church that opened in Rome two and a half years ago. The second clip was of Sophia and Zack bringing the late Pope Aloysius from death back to life, as well as clips of Sofia healing and bringing back animals from the dead. The third clip was of her being on talk shows about the Church of Chrostianology. The last and final clip was something she told no one, not even Zach. "*She was so careful. How the hell did anyone catch this on camera,*" she thought?"

She never revealed to the world that she was also a Blood Royal. The cat was out of the bag.

Sofia darted her eyes toward the crowd and the jury. Their mouths were agape, their eyes widening.

Sofia saw a handsome young man sitting in the first row; she had never noticed him before until now. Sofia took in all his features; he had raven-black hair, ivory-white skin, and emerald-green eyes. He was wearing a black Armani suit that fit him to a tee. They made eye contact, Sofia smiled with her eyes at him, but he did not reciprocate. He looked at his watch as if he was in a hurry to be somewhere.

"So, as you can see, this is no ordinary woman; she's a real-life Superwoman in the flesh. The power to heal, bring back the dead to life, and can fly… She boasts about her religion while not telling the world she is a Blood Royal. She talks about Mr. Wooldridge being a bully when she is a liar. She keeps secrets from her own people! How can we trust *anything* she says in this court if she is not honest with her own people?"

The handsome young man started to mouth Sofia, "Get down and cover your head."

Sofia looked at the handsome man strangely but proceeded to give an answer to the commotion that had erupted in the court.

"Your honor, if I may, it's no one's business if I am a Blood Royal, and if anything, this PROVES my next point. I discovered that the British government has an underground lab where they experiment on Blood Royals. Many are dying, and schools and universities are being segregated from Blood Royals to Non-Blood Royals. How can we stand by our own government kidnapping, testing, and killing people for the sake of scientific purposes?"

Judge Steele slammed his mallet.

"Order in the court! I, Judge Steele, order Sofia Boudreaux to be arrested immediately for nondisclosure of being Blood. She lied under oath, and I will not have any liars in my court," Judge Steele smiled slightly.

He was working for him. Of course he was, Sofia thought.

The court started to shake. Blood-curdling screams came from every direction; Sofia remembered what the handsome man had mouthed to her and got down under the podium and covered her head.

CHAPTER 19

September 7th, 2023, 11:14 A.M. – Istanbul

It wasn't like Zach to lose his bearing, but he was about to do just that if he didn't get inside the Hagia Sophia mosque. Zach looked at the line to the mosque. It would take them over an hour just to get inside.

"Not on my watch; come on, Sam!"

Zach took Sam's hand and made their way to the front of the line. A couple was about to protest when Zach slipped a fifty-dollar bill into the lanky man's hand.

"For your troubles."

The young man took a step back and let Zach and Sam pass. Making their way past a frenzy of American tourists, Zach and Sam settled in the middle of the mosque and looked around for clues. Zach took the parchments out of his pocket and read the sayings out loud of *The Lost Gospel of the Divine Feminine*.

'The Holy Grail that you seek,
Is not one that is always meek,
Cast down from the ineffable light,
 Drink from the cup; don't put up a fight.

For the two to become back one,
Remembrance and repentance must be done,
By blood, you have been redeemed; holy blood, you have
been saved,
It is now your turn to go into the grave.

The Father of Light died for your sins,
The Mother of Life wishes to live again,
For all of this to come to be true,
Look inside yourselves; what will you do?

The act of the transgressor is "The Soul,"
Those who seek will find redemption by not denying
the whole,
The "Self-Perfected Mind" has come forth to live once more,
The Holy Grail must be transformed to be restored.

How this is done, is by gathering the four,
The Holy Grail, the stone, the harp, and the thorns,
Put them all together with the Son of Man,
Then the two will become one and be united again.'

"Are you okay, Zach? You seem a bit shaken up."

"Yeah, I'll be fine."

"After hearing about the bombings, the revealing of the red comet, and everything that happened with Sofia, it's a lot to take in. It's okay not to be okay."

"And that's precisely why we must figure out what this means. There's no time to waste. Brother Guiden texted to look for clues in the mosaics."

Zach let go of Sam's hand and looked at a mosaic hanging on the north side of the wall. Sam's eyes filled with sadness; Zach looked like he had been hit by a double-decker bus; he had dark circles under his eyes and had barely eaten anything in the last week. Sam thought there was no better time than now to tell Zach what she had found out two weeks ago. With everything going on, there wasn't a right time to tell him.

Sam walked over and stood next to Zach. He was staring intently at a mosaic of Jesus sitting on a bejeweled throne, holding up a book with a cross on it while making a hand gesture. Next to him was a knight with a bag of gold and a king holding a scroll.

"Look, Sam, this king is holding a scroll. I bet if we go look at the other mosaics, it will tell us the story of what we're looking for."

The next mosaic they saw was of Mary holding up Jesus as a baby, this time with a Queen holding a scroll and a knight holding a bag of money.

"In both of these mosaics, a king and a queen are holding a scroll."

"So, you think the Gospel of the Divine Feminine was passed down a royal bloodline?"

"I think it's someone of importance who's lineage of one of the tribes of Israel. It could be distant, which may be why Israel was bombed. The Holy Seer may be trying to either destroy the evidence or smoke them out to find it. But it could also be a British lineage, or the Stone of Destiny is involved. I know that history portrays the king as Emperor Constantine, but I think that's a façade to the real meaning behind the mosaics."

Sam looked at Mary holding up the baby Jesus and smiled; she took Zach's hand and placed it in hers. "We're about to have a little king of our own."

Zach tilted his head in confusion. Sam placed his hand over her stomach.

"Oh my God, Sam! Really?"

Sam nodded and smiled.

"I can't believe it! I'm really going to be a dad?"

"Yes, and you will be the best dad ever."

Zack kissed Sam passionately while still holding onto Sam's stomach. He never knew how much he wanted to be a dad until this moment in time. He had thoughts off and on about having kids, but they had never really talked about having kids this early in their marriage.

"This kid will have the best parents ever, with you being the best of us, Sam.

Sam blushed and laughed, "I'll take this one for the team."

They embraced a moment longer, basking in their joy.

"I needed you to know," she said. "I couldn't hold it in any longer," she smiled. They kissed again. Zach pulled away and beamed.

"But," Sam reminded him, "we have a job to get back to."

"Right. Okay. It's just a lot to process! I'm thrilled, truly," Zach gave her final squeeze before returning to the riddle at hand. "So, the Holy Grail is someone who is not meek, she fell from grace, and she has to remember her past and make amends…. Like how Eve was the first to sin compared to Adam."

"It's a tale as old as time, the journey of the dark night of the soul," Sam added.

"Eve is Sophia, and I think she represents mankind as a whole." Zach said thoughtfully. "One of Brother Guiden's texts he sent while we were on the plane said, "We are the new Eve," Zach continued. "I didn't know what he meant until now - I think this riddle is saying that a single woman must bear the sins of all mankind, just as Jesus, the male figure, died for our sins; the feminine aspect of God must die for her sins, for all our sins. The process is not complete until she does. That's why the whore of Babylon rides a beast in Revelation, and the woman with twelve stars over her head represents a woman from the twelve tribes of Israel," Zach's voice increased as he unraveled the mystery. "There will be a counterfeit to the real Eve, an imposter Eve and the real Eve!"

"You got all that from looking at two mosaics?" Sam asked, dumbfounded.

Zach laughed, "No, the Gospel of the Divine Feminine is most likely a branch from the Gospel of The Sophia of Jesus

Christ; the gospel was found in the Nag Hammadi Library. It narrates how wisdom Sophia fell from grace by creating the material world with a consort that was not with Jesus, an angry Arch-Begetter who is called "Yaldabaoth," an imposter god who thought he was the only god and the real god of creation."

"Sounds like another variation of Satan wanting to be god over all things," Sam chimed in.

"Exactly! I believe the gospel we seek will give new revelation to what we are looking for in the Holy Grail as a human being, a more detailed revelation about the divine human being herself. I think the Gospel of The Sophia of Jesus Christ was tempered by followers of Satan. It is Yahweh who created the universe, not this Yaldabaoth character."

"Okay, so we got most of the Holy Grail figured out. Can anything else lead us to the other three relics?" Sam asked.

"Only one way to find out," Zach grinned. "Let's split up to cover more ground. You take the back, and I'll take the front."

Zach and Sam looked around the mosque for over an hour, but they couldn't find anything pointing them in the right direction of the other three relics. Making their way out of the mosque, Zach took one last look inside the top of the dome.

"The mosque's interior is adorned with gold, but the original design showed Christ holding a book with a cross behind him, which I'm positive would lead us to the lost Gospel of the Divine Feminine."

Sam was starting to get tired and leaned on one of the pillars to rest, but before she did, she noticed some small gold writing with two trinity symbols above and below the writing.

"Zach! Look at this!"

Zach studied the writing for a long time, trying to decipher what the riddle could mean.

"What does it say?"

"The riddle says:

'As above, so below,
The connected ones will start the show,
If it is the harp that you seek,
Sound and vibration will start at the teeth
But first, blood and sweat must be unleashed.'

"What the heck does that mean?" asked Sam.

"I think we need to look for something in the mosque that can produce sound or looks like a mouth to get the next clue."

"Why was the writing on the one random pillar? Should we look at the other pillars too?"

"Doesn't hurt to try," Zach spoke softly.

After many minutes of looking at the pillars inside the mosque, they found no more golden writings that could give them more information about the dark saying.

"There must be a reason why the writing was only on that one pillar," Sam announced.

"I think you're right, Sam; let's go back and look at the mosque and see if we can find anything else."

CHAPTER 20

September 7th, 2023, 12:43 P.M– Jerusalem, Israel

Death and destruction were no strangers to Kieron. He had been torturing children since he was a child himself, bombing countries since he was eleven years old. It made him feel alive, feel powerful, feel…in control. He was his father's son, after all.

"Kieron, it is a miracle you were here in Jerusalem; if it weren't for you, we would have lost the whole city."

"If only you knew," Kieron thought.

"I don't believe in coincidences Prime Minister. Everything happens for a reason. What was a meeting with a friend turned into salvation for your people. And to think I almost didn't bring my microbots with me."

"I'm forever in your debt; my people and I owe you a great debt."

"Nonsense Prime Minister. After what you and you people have been through, I have a gift to give you. The technology is new, but rest assured, you will never be bombed again on my watch."

Prime Minister Yonatan Mizrahi looked at Kieron confused, "How is that possible?"

"By a force field that is impenetrable," Kieron said with confidence. "It's the same technology I hope to use worldwide to stop the comet. Of course, this will only happen if I get more funding."

"I will make sure of it," Yonatan remarked, "My people, and I support you 100%. Anything you ask of me is yours. I will petition the council for funds and request a meeting with the UN. Planet Earth cannot afford not to have this technology. You are truly a savior to the people."

"I'm going to protect the nation of Israel. This I swear to you."

His plan was formed to perfection. Now all he had to do was sit back and wait for the rest of the dominoes to fall into place. "But I'm no savior, Prime Minister. I'm just a kid who happens to be blessed with intelligence and understanding."

"I beg to differ, my friend, I beg to differ."

CHAPTER 21

September 7th, 1:00 P.M – Hagia Sophia Mosque, Istanbul Turkey

Back at the Hagia Sophia mosque, Sam and Zach studied the pillars and their positions. They could find nothing important in geometric positions, access points, or even longitude or latitude degrees of position.

"I wish the divine mother would give me another vision or speak to me in my mind." Zach said, "I really don't know where to go from here."

"Now, where would the fun be in that?" joked Sam.

Zach smiled at Sam's always undaunted spirit.

"Wait…Zach! When you took the front of the mosque, and I took the back, I saw a stone with a golden bronze halo attached to a pillar! It's called the wishing column or weeping column; it's rumored that the column performs miracles. You put your thumbs inside the hole and twist your hand 360 degrees. If you feel wet on your finger, it's said that your wish will come true. I did it and made a wish."

"What did you wish for?"

"To be fulfilled in all things and for direction to the next clue."

"Sam, you're a genius! Your wish guided you to the pillar with the hidden writing on that single column. We would have never found that writing if it weren't for your wish."

Zach kissed Sam gently, took her hand, and walked to the wishing column.

Zach recited the riddle once more.

'As above, so below,
The connected ones will start the show,
If it is the harp that you seek,
Sound and vibration will start at the teeth
But first, blood and sweat must be unleashed.'

"Okay, so we're the connected ones being husband and wife, as above symbolizes the masculine while the down below symbolizes the feminine."

Zach looked around to ensure no one was behind him and took out a small pocketknife. Holding his breath, Zach pricked his finger and put a few drops of blood in the hole. Zach put both thumbs in and turned his hand 360 degrees. He felt warm droplets hit his thumbs. Zach took out his thumbs, put his mouth to the opening, and closed his eyes. He spoke out loud to the wishing hole; according to the riddle, he figured it needed to hear the sound of his voice, with both sound and vibration, in order for him to attain the next clue to find David's harp.

"I, Zach Dorsey, a Blood Royal from the tribe of Judah and a descendant of Jesus Christ and Mary Magdalene, humbly ask the wishing column the whereabouts or next clue in finding the lost harp of David."

Something strange happened after Zack spoke his wish inside the hole of the wishing column. Zach's *fleur-de-lis* birthmark began to tingle, and a warm sensation pulsed throughout his chest. He heard harp music playing softly in his ears.

"Sam! Do you hear that!"

"Hear what?"

"The sound of angelic music coming from a harp?"

"No, I don't…" Sam said sadly. "Looks like only a Blood Royal can hear the sound to steer away from imposters, I bet," Sam remarked.

"I think you're right, Sam. Follow me."

Zach and Sam followed the sound of the harp playing music toward the back of the mosque. Zach followed as the music got louder to an old, blind woman sitting down drinking water with a coin purse.

"Come closer, Zach."

Zach was stunned, "How do you know my name?"

"An angel of the Lord told me. You must go down to the underground chambers of the Hagia Sophia, but you cannot do it alone. You must have another Blood Royal to open the seal to recover the Holy Grail."

"I'm confused…I'm looking for David's harp, and the Holy Grail is a specific woman, not a chalice."

"It is a specific woman," the blind woman said, "but there is a chalice that the Holy One must drink with wine purified from Jesus. She must drink this wine to represent his sinless blood."

The woman smiled, got up, and used her cane to go outside the mosque.

"I heard harp music playing, but Sam couldn't hear. Is David's harp down there as well?"

"This I do not know. It could be down there, or there could be another riddle in the crypt to show you the way to the harp. I'm sorry I cannot be of more help," said the old blind woman.

"Do we need Jesus to open the crypt for us to get the chalice?"

"We have yet to learn who he is. He hasn't made himself known to the world."

"Your sister holds the key to get inside the chamber."

"Is it a literal key?" Sam asked, confused.

The old blind woman smiled, "She wears a cross necklace made from the wood with which Jesus Christ was crucified. The wood is blessed by God, and only the cross can open the crypt to recover the chalice."

"Why did the wishing column take me to you?" Zach asked.

"I am a Blood Royal and come from the Royal line of David, Jesus, and Mary Magdalene. The Lord placed upon me a special gift, secrets of the unknown, and visions of the future. There are six people you will encounter who will help you on your mission, be wary of one of them. They are not what they seem. In the matter of the chalice and David's harp, the Lord prevented my mouth from uttering any word about the chalice until all steps were taken.

"What about the Stone of Destiny?"

"I know no matters of that relic. I'm sorry."

The blind woman made her way through the crowd of people and disappeared. Zach picked his phone out of his pocket and dialed Sofia's phone number.

"It went straight to voicemail," he reported to Sam. "She's probably still mad at me. I can understand why, Sam. I completely abandoned her in her greatest time of need. I need to make this up to her. I need to make it right. We can come back for the chalice. We won't get anywhere without the key she possesses.

CHAPTER 22

September 7th, 2023, 11:19 A.M. - London High Court House

Sofia didn't know how much more of the screaming she could take. She grabbed the wooden cross necklace around her neck and prayed, "Jesus, please keep me safe and put me somewhere safe from those who wish me harm."

Sofia felt a warm sensation pulse through her body as she held the cross. She opened her eyes and saw her boxes flung about, with half-burned papers scattered all over the floor. Something white and blue caught her attention on the ground. Across the way, three feet in front of her, lay a small stick on the ground; she scooted her way over and picked up the white stick. It was a pregnancy test. It must have been the item Sam placed in her box! She couldn't believe how mean she was to Sam and Zach. She was still mad as hell at Zach, but she should have looked in the box to see what Sam left her. She felt absolutely horrible as a friend, sister-in-law, and sister.

"You need to come with me," the young man said. "Now!"

Sofia was about to protest when she felt the ground shaking again. She looked up to see a small group of people joining in hands; they were mouthing words in Latin. They were the ones creating an earthquake. They were Blood Royals. She just knew it in her heart.

Sofia grabbed the young man's hand and ran towards the back door. They ran down the hall and opened a door that led to the stairs to the parking garage.

"Who the hell are you?" Sofia asked in confusion.

"Your knight in shining armor," he grinned slightly, showing pearly white straight teeth.

"Stop them!"

"Sofia and the unnamed man saw Judge Steele, the constable, and the four pack of Blood Royals run after them.

"We need to haul ass."

After running for what seemed like ages, they finally got to the parking lot, where a sleek black Dodge Viper was already waiting for them, running with the doors open.

"Subtle," mused Sofia.

"Always need to ride in class," he said, lifting his shoulder and shrugging.

Just then, Judge Steele, the constable, and the four-pack of Blood Royals burst through the door. Sofia watched as she saw a hooded figure come out last. A thick dark cloud shrouded his body and face; next to him was the Holy Seer Cardinal Villere.

"Oh, my God," exclaimed Sofia.

"Hop in, blondie," said the mysterious man.

"Excuse me? I have a name; it's Sofia. And you are?" She said as she jumped wildly in the car.

The young man with raven black hair got in, buckled his seatbelt, and, for the first time, smiled wide at her. "Collins, Everette Collins."

"Well, let's get the hell out of here, James Bond! That is the Holy Seer, and he is not one to be messed with!"

Looking in the rearview mirror, Sofia could see the dark hooded figure shimmer, going in and out of existence like a hologram. The Holy Seer waved his hand at Sofia and smiled. "*This can't be good,*" Sofia thought.

Everette started to speed down the parking garage. Sofia and Everette could feel the car getting heavier and heavier. It wasn't until they looked out the window that they saw hundreds of thousands of small little maroon squares the size of one millimeter attaching themselves to the car.

"What the hell are those?" Sofia screamed.

"Our worst nightmare," Everette proclaimed, "Microbots."

"Micro–what?"

"Microbots. They are a sophisticated technology that people use to kill or repair."

"I'm guessing it's not for the latter," Sofia remarked tartly.

Everette's car sped out of the parking garage, almost hitting a bystander. "Be careful, you nitwit!" Sofia carped. "There are actual people on sidewalks, you know!"

Turning the first corner, the man, shrouded in the robe, and the Holy Seer appeared before them, the man still shimmering in and out.

"What in the hell! How did they get here so fast?" Everette asked.

Sofia held her breath and gripped her armrest; they were zooming straight for them, "I don't care, get out of here before they kill us!"

Everette lifted the black covering in the middle of his car and pressed a red button.

"Do I even want to know what that does?" Sofia asked as a rhetorical question.

"No. You don't. Close your eyes because it's about to be a bumpy ride."

Everette slowed to a dead stop right in front of the Holy Seer and the man in the black robe. The Dodge Viper turned invisible and went into stealth mode with no sound. Everette flipped three switches and grinned a cocky grin. "There, the nanobots have been deactivated; they won't be able to find us."

"How did you do that?"

"The finest technology Britain can offer," he smiled.

The sports car started to hover and ascend upwards, going over the two men. The Holy Seer walked towards the spot where the car was, waving his hand in the air to try and feel the vehicle.

Sofia looked down at the man as they crossed over him. The man shrouded in darkness looked up and smiled at her as they did.

Sofia's *fleur-de-lis* began to burn intensely; she started to wither in pain, screaming with all her might. The only thing Sofia could make out from the man was his icy blue eyes. Sofia's eyes closed, and she passed out; her mind seeing only darkness.

#

"Master, they're getting away!"

"No, they're not. The microbots are invisible, but that doesn't mean the tracking system is not," Kieron said coolly.

The Holy Seer smiled. "You are always one step ahead of everyone."

"I need to finish my meeting with the Prime minister; I'll be on a jet back to New York tonight. Tell Tom to get the girl prepared. I have work to do."

The Holy Seer nodded, and Kieron shimmered out of existence, his presence awakened back in Israel. Walking back to the conference room, Kieron brushed his hair aside and smiled at the camera.

"It is my privilege to be working side by side with Prime Minister Yonathan Mizrahi, and my pleasure to introduce to the world a game-changing technology by my company *New Light Technologies*. A technology that can produce a forcefield around any city. A forcefield that can deter any missile or bomb. Israel will never again be threatened or mistaken for weak. For I am with them, and they will be my people, my sheep."

As Prime Minister Mizrai placed the Crown of Thorns on his head, Kieron fell on one knee.

"It is my great honor to introduce the new king of Israel, Kieron Gedron. The last king that led the Jews was King Zedekiah. He was evil in the sight of the Lord. Now, we have a new king to over-right his wrongs. Kieron's DNA has been tested, and he comes from the tribe of Dan. He is worthy of being King of the Jews over the Israelites. The Crown of Thorns placed upon his head represents a new beginning for Israel. Now, we replace the previous deceiver who claimed to be God and override the Crown of Thorns from defilement to glory."

Kieron's scalp started to bleed from the crown placed upon his head. He rose up with every Jew in the conference room, bowing to him.

Kieron smiled at the camera showing his pearly white teeth. "It is time for a new era for the people of Israel and a time of rebellion towards those who wish us harm. Russia and China…" Kieron paused, "I'm coming for you."

CHAPTER 23

September 7th, 2023, 2:46 P.M– Undisclosed part of England

Sofia woke up to her head pounding. She looked outside and saw they were still undetected, flying above the clouds. Nobody was chasing after them, and no one could look up and see them. Sofia was confused now more than ever; who was the man with the Holy Seer? But before going down the rabbit hole, she needed to gather more information on her new friend....

"How long was I out for?" Sofia asked.

"Give or take three hours," said Everette.

"You're MI6, aren't you?"

"What gave it away," he pronounced more as a statement than a question.

"Oh, I don't know: the suit, the name, the car," Sofia suggested playfully with an eyebrow raised.

"Smart lass."

Sofia shrugged and slightly smiled. He was good-looking, but she didn't trust him. Even if he technically saved her life, it was his employee, the British government, she didn't trust. They were the ones testing and torturing Blood Royals. She was in a car with her enemy. She was behind enemy lines. She would have to play smart, especially if they were the ones who were letting Blood Royals run amuck, collapsing towns and cities with their abilities, but why...?"

"Where are you taking me, Everette?"

"Most people call me Collins, you know, the whole Bond thing."

"Well, I'm not like most people."

"No. You're not," he said quietly. The way he said it almost sounded like he admired her. "But then again, you *are* a Blood Royal, so who knows whose side you're really on."

And there it was. He was a bigot against her kind.

"Are you intolerant towards my kind?" Sofia asked. "Or are you just thick-headed?"

"Wow. You don't waste time, do you?" He shook his head, taken aback, "I'm not a racist, Sofia; I'm just weary of you in particular."

"Please do tell."

"Because you can bring back people from the dead, Sofia. Anyone with that power controls reality and controls destiny. Next to the Pope, the President of the United States, Kieron Gedron, and the Rothschilds, I'd say you're in the top five of the most powerful people on the planet. And let me tell you, the *world* isn't ready for that. The *British government* isn't ready for that. Who knows what kind of people you will bring back."

"What like a Hitler or a Stalin? Never in a million years would I do that. You do know I worked for a hospital, right? Healing is my thing."

"Yes, and you took an oath to help anyone in need, poor or rich, good, or evil, it doesn't matter who. Did you not?"

Sofia sat in silence. He was right about the hospital thing.

"That may be true at the hospital, we cannot turn anyone away, evil or not,

but that is not true of my own free volition."

"It's not always the ones who seem evil on the surface, Sofia. Sometimes it's buried within so deep you can't see it until it's already too late."

"I would never do it, Everette."

"You say that, but if it's someone you love and they're evil?" He caught her eye. "Then you might just do it."

"I don't care or love anyone who is a monster," she returned his gaze. "Sorry to disappoint you."

"We'll see."

"How did you know there would be an earthquake inside the courthouse?"

"I didn't. Not exactly. Headquarters noted seismic activity in the area; I was told to check it out after attending your court case. After the ground started shaking, I just put two and two together."

"Why would headquarters have you go check out an earthquake area?"

"Because it wasn't coming from underground. It was coming from above.

"Huh?"

"Blood Royals have been causing earthquakes all over the world. We've been watching them; it's been happening for a few months now. It started when we were doing aerial testing with some jets. We found two people on top of mountains in the Swiss Alps hovering over the mountain, producing shock waves to the mountains. Safe to say we captured them after that. That's why the British government has been rounding up Blood Royals. Those two people could have created an avalanche and killed hundreds of skiers and tourists."

"Why would they do that?"

"We don't know yet."

Sofia was left speechless. Her own people were causing deaths all over the world, and she couldn't understand why. She had to assume the Holy Seer had something to do with it. Or was it the British government and not the Holy Seer? Did they want to shut her up because of the hospital case? Or was there something else sinister going on? She tried to free her kind, so why were they against her? It made absolutely no sense.

"We're here."

"Where are we?"

"Somewhere safe. For now, anyway."

The Dodge Viper landed on the ground near a picturesque cottage. Sofia could only see a forest that looked like the scenery from the movie Snow White; she was expecting to see talking birds or deer any second now.

"It's beautiful out here."

"Should be. This is my getaway spot. There's no one around for sixty miles on either side of us. I can't tell you exactly where. It's against protocol, of course."

"Of course. Either way," Sofia shrugged, "it's lovely."

#

Brother Guiden was sick and tired of constantly being watched by the Italian guards. They had finally let him out of the bunker at least. It was strange to be both protected and accused at the same time. He'd endured a series of depositions. The Italian government was trying to ascertain if he had anything to do with the death of Pope Aloysius. At the same time, they were keeping him secure from any outside threats. With this kind of surveillance, Brother Guiden could barely get a moment alone.

It had been ten days, and he was no closer to discovering the locations of Crown of Thorns, the Stone of Destiny, or David's harp. Zach and Sam had called him about an hour ago with revelations about the Holy Grail. They thanked him for his suggestions of where to look for clues in the Hagia Sophia. One down, three to go. He had had an inkling of what the Holy Grail was, a specific woman who would change the course of destiny. Now, all they had to do was find who it was.

Brother Guiden turned on the TV to watch the world news. He needed to keep up with the events just in case he could use the information to help Zach and Sam. After a few minutes of flipping channels, he landed on a station with the Prime Minister of Israel speaking about Kieron Gedron.

"Smart kid, that one," he spoke with confidence.

Brother Guiden turned around to make a cup of tea. After adding four sugars and stirring, he turned back around to face the TV. Shocked by what he saw, the color in his face drained, and Brother Guiden dropped his cup of tea which shattered to the floor. Seventeen-year-old boy genius Kieron Gedron stood to his knees with the Crown of Thorns on his head, blood coming down his face and dropping to the ground.

The camera followed Kieron outside towards the balcony, where hundreds of thousands of Jews were bowing down before him. He was their new king, their savior, their God. It had finally been revealed who the Antichrist was, seventeen-year-old Kieron Gedron. A shiver ran down Brother Guiden's spine. He must find a way to warn Zach, Sam, and Sofia! He was the Pope, for heaven's sake. If he couldn't protect them…then who could?

CHAPTER 24

September 8th, 2023, 12:28 P.M–New York City

Delaney couldn't tell you what day it was, if it was light or dark out, or how much time had passed since the revealing of the comet on national news. She assumed her missing persons' report might say:

"Delaney Woods, a news reporter who broke worldwide news of the red comet cover-up, has been reported missing by her boss after failing to show up for her news segments."

She couldn't believe the person she had been working with for the past year was behind all this. Delaney shivered thinking about all the women, men, and children she had seen in the underground facility being tortured and experimented on. Delaney could still feel the sensations of needles and prods being poked into her skin; she wondered how long it would take for that feeling to go away. She knew she had been kidnapped for at least two or three weeks, but she just didn't know anymore, and she sure as hell didn't know exactly *what* they were trying to find in her blood or DNA.

She knew Tom had said something about her "glowing red" and having people "falling to their knees" asking for her forgiveness after her blast of red energy went out from her body, but she couldn't remember it; she could hardly remember anything of that encounter. It was as if the whole entire memory was erased from her mind. Probably caused by the trauma of almost being stabbed by that crazy man; that was the only thing she *could* remember, everything else was a blur or a blank.

No matter how many times she was poked, prodded, and tortured, she just couldn't remember the rest of the events that day, and that was bad, considering they were going to keep at it until she could remember. She needed to think of something to get the hell out of this situation; maybe she could play dumb and hit on Tom and try to convince him to let her. She was willing to try *anything* to get out of there.

Delaney could hear footsteps coming towards her. The sound of keys swinging and whistling gave the person away every time.

Tom came in with a brown bag that said Firehouse Subs and sat at the dining room table. "I assume you're hungry," he said, dropping the bag on the table.

Delaney turned up her nose at him to face the white-washed walls. She didn't want to give him the satisfaction of taking food from a kidnapper.

"No, not really."

"You haven't eaten in three days. I know you're hungry."

"Oh, I'm hungry, but I'm not taking food from the likes of you; you're a monster."

"Fair enough."

Tom reached over to grab the bag and opened it up. He took a sandwich out of the paper bag and began to eat it in front of her.

"This would go a lot easier if you just told us when you started noticing your powers."

"I don't have any powers."

Tom cocked his head and gave Delaney a look. "You and I both know that's not true."

"Well, I have no memory of that day, *Tom*," Delaney said sarcastically.

"As I told you a hundred times before, the only thing I remember is that guy coming at me with a knife, and no amount of torture, needles, or probes will give me my memories back magically."

Tom finished half of the sandwich and put it down. "Then it's time to show you what you did."

He took his phone out and typed some words. "Sit. Now."

Rolling her eyes, Delaney got up from the chair with her pen, pad, and paper and sat across from Tom. Tom swiveled his phone around to face her and pressed the play button. The video was of Delaney reporting the news of the red comet. After watching herself for a few minutes, Delaney squinted her eyes and watched herself glow faintly red, and then later on, a blast of red light and energy struck both Tom and the crazed man with a knife. She saw people falling to their knees, praying in all different tongues of the nations. A few had even cried as they held up their hands toward her.

Shaking her head, "I…I…I don't understand," Delaney cried out, "I don't understand how this happened; I've never done anything like this before."

"Which is interesting… considering how every Blood Royal on the Earth started to gain their powers two and a half years ago after Sofia and Zach's connection in the spirit realm."

"Who are they?"

"A thorn in our Lord's side. You probably heard of them when they started the Church of Christianology."

"Oh yes, I remember that news a few years back, they saved the pope, too, didn't they? Well, then I'm rooting for them. I hope they kick your "lord's" ass."

Tom squinted his eyes and then smiled in arrogance. The door opened as if right on cue to a young man with a laptop. He was a young man with the iciest blue eyes she had ever seen.

"That was fast," Tom declared.

"There's no rest for the wicked," the young man stated.

Tom got up, gave one last look at Delaney, and slightly smiled. His eyes told her this was not going to be a pleasant conversation. Tom walked out the door, swinging his keys and whistling down the hall.

"You much excuse his–"

"Personality?"

"Abruptness."

"Yeah, I'll hold my breath."

Kieron looked down at the Firehouse bag and opened it up to reveal the other half of the sandwich had not been eaten.

"Please; eat."

Delaney was about to refuse when she felt a slight tingle and warmth come over her body, wanting the sandwich more than anything she had wanted her entire life. Kieron took the sandwich and placed it in front of her. She snatched the sandwich and scarfed it down in front of the mysterious man.

Kieron turned around his laptop to face Delaney.

"Do you know what this is?"

Delaney inched forward with her body to see her name attached to a piece of paper. It was her family tree printed from Ancestry. She read her DNA report of her ethnicities and nationalities, a few countries she had no idea she had family from, but that's not what perplexed her. It was two names she didn't recognize above her family tree that confounded her. Her parents' names were different from those she had grown up with. Delaney swallowed the last bite of her sandwich and shook her head.

"No, that's not right; my parents' names are wrong."

Shaking his head, "I'm sorry to have to be the one to tell you this, but you are adopted, and these names here are your real parents. We took a sample of your DNA after you drank from a cup of water the first night you were here. I needed to confirm my suspicions before I came to talk to you. You are of the Royal Bloodline of Jesus Christ and Mary Magdalene, an absolute abomination… but nonetheless, here you are. Here you *all* are," he said while tilting his head and giving a grimace look.

Staring with a confused look, Delaney shook her head in protest again, "No, this can't be right. I *know* my family. They would *never* lie to me."

"People lie all the time, Delaney," he said with no emotion. "You must know that, especially if it's to protect the ones they love." He sighed. "Have you ever wondered why you are the only child out of five who doesn't look like their parents? I'm sure the thought has crossed your mind a time or two."

She had thought that a few times before, especially when she was a little girl and in middle school, she was constantly made fun of for her red hair. All her siblings were blonde or had light brown hair, she was the only redhead in the family, and as far as she knew, nobody as far back as four generations before her had red hair.

"What do you want from me? Who are you?" Delaney started to think quickly to get out of this prison, "Listen, kid, if I could just…." Delaney stopped what she was about to say and blurted out her response, "Wait…don't I know you from somewhere?"

Kieron smiled and waited patiently for her to come up with the answer.

"Oh my god, you're that boy genius with the billion-dollar company, Kieron Gedron!"

"I'm more than in on this. I'm behind this."

"And why are you telling me all this? What does this have to do with me?"

"Because I'm going to resurrect you, Delaney, and then make you, my wife. I have many plans for you. Your DNA profile matches Sofia, and I need someone up to par to defeat Sofia.

"Resurrect me? To what? What do you mean up to par? And the hell I'm going to marry you! You're like, what? Seventeen years old? First of all, gross because I'm twenty-two years old, and second of all, you know I can take you down, right? I've been boxing since I was a child. My brothers taught me everything I know."

"I'm counting on it," he spoke with intensity in his eyes; well, not for me, of course, but for the others, that is," Kieron said nonchalantly. "But before I use your powers, I need to do one little thing."

Delaney gave Kieron a confused look. Kieron finally smiled.

"I need to kill you."

A thick black cloud of smoke started to roll off Kieron's body into the room and enveloped the room. The black smoke circled around her throat and started to choke her until she couldn't breathe. Delaney grabbed her neck and tried to shoo away the black smoke from her mouth, but it was useless. It was as if the smoke had matter and weight to it, as if it was a state of solidity.

"Hee...hel...help me," she said hoarsely.

Delaney fell to her knees and opened her mouth, gasping for air, and as she did, the black smoke entered her making her body convulse. Every cell in her body felt like it was on fire. Bursts of black smoke and red rays of light came out of Delaney, her eyes changed from blue to red to black.

Delaney stopped convulsing on the floor, stood up, and sat back on the chair. She placed her hands on the desk, on top of the other. Her eyes, which once gave life, came off as dead and cold. Bits of red and blue speckled her black irises.

"Where do we begin?" Delaney said coldly.

"At the beginning," Kieron imparted as he grabbed her hand and slipped an eighteen-carat diamond on her finger.

CHAPTER 25

September 8th, 2023, 12:48 P.M–The Vatican

Brother Guiden had finally managed to slip one of the guards' phones into his pocket and made his way to the restroom. He knew he had to make the phone call quickly, or else he would get caught.

"Here goes nothing," Brother Guiden said to himself.

Brother Guiden dialed Zach's phone, but there was no answer. He decided he would leave a voicemail encrypted just in case Kieron would intercept the voicemail to erase it. That boy was smarter than hell, and he was not risking this voicemail being intercepted.

"Zach, it's Brother Guiden. I'm alive and well, and boy, am I craving some crawfish back home in New Orleans. How's the research going for your book? I hope all is well with you...if you can email me and let me know how you're getting along, maybe we can find a way to meet up and discuss your findings on the 10

Commandments. There's a new restaurant in town that is getting terrible reviews. People are complaining because it's supposed to be a hot soup, but it keeps coming out ice cold. It's not what people believe it to be. He gaslights the customers into thinking they wanted cold soup the whole time. Anyway...we should skip that restaurant and go somewhere that is heavenly. Email me when you can. Love you, my boy."

#

Back in Istanbul, Zach and Sam were having lunch at a nice Turkish cafe. Zach noticed his phone ringing but did not recognize the number, so he let it go to voicemail. He wanted nothing more than to enjoy this blissful moment with Sam, his wife, the mother of their unborn child, and the woman of his dreams. Sam was eating a meat pastry when Zach heard a beeping sound go off, indicating he had a voicemail. Zach picked up his phone and put his phone on speaker to listen to the voicemail.

Brother Guiden had started leaving him encrypted messages with him as a kid to teach him how to decipher what he was truly saying. It started out as a game and then led to more serious messages that Zach would need to figure out if they couldn't speak on the phone or in person.

"What in the heck was that voicemail about?" Sam asked, puzzled.

"The chef represents a new player in town, someone who people are not expecting to be difficult but, in reality, is a monster. Someone who presents themselves as one way but is the opposite in reality."

"Who is he talking about?"

"I think Brother Guiden found out the identity of the Antichrist," Zach gulped solemnly.

"Then we have no time to waste. What do we do next?"

Zach carefully thought of all the clues he had amassed, from the parchments to the revelation at Hagia Sophia, Sofia's key, and Brother Guiden's voicemail.

#

Back in Istanbul, Jax and Loch asked around for days about the two Americans; they went to museums, mosques, and churches but had no such luck. After twenty-four hours of searching every nook and cranny, they took a break and grabbed lunch at a café. Jax and Loch were seated next to a couple who were paying their bill to leave.

"If we can't get a hold of Sofia or Brother Guiden, then we have to go in a different direction until we can contact them. I will send an email to Brother Guiden letting him know we're both okay and an encrypted email to Sofia. The Divine Mother told me about two people who will help us on our journey. They live in Turkey, so our best bet is finding out where they are and getting in touch with them."

"What are their names again?"

"Yousef and Raziah."

"Excuse me," A young man asked.

Zach and Sam slowly turned their heads toward the two men; they eyed the front entrance, got up, and whizzed past both men.

"Wait! Jax cried, but it was too late; Zach and Sam were already twenty feet

ahead of them, running into the crowd.

"You didn't think this would be easy, did you?" Loch asked, standing up.

"I guess I did!" Jax replied.

Loch shook his head, "You really thought that, huh? I love ya mate, but sometimes you are really naive. Well, come on then, we gotta go after 'em. But let me do the talkin', will ya? Or you'll scare the poor lads."

Agreeing, Loch and Jax took off running into the sea of faces hoping to

catch up with the fleeing couple.

CHAPTER 26

September 8th, 2023, 1:03 P.M -Istanbul

Jax and Loch wove in and out of the crowd of vendors and tourists, hoping to catch up with Zach and Sam and explain the situation. It felt like the American couple was running away from them for some other reason than just them asking a question.

"Well, at least we know what they look like now," Loch said, breathless.

"Loch, we won't catch up to them if you don't run faster! Now come on! You go left, and I'll go right in the market."

Zach pulled out some change and hurriedly bought scarves for himself and Sam. Then they waited in line pretending to buy some meat.

"What are we gonna do, Zack? Do you think the Holy Seer sent those guys after us?"

"I have no clue, and I don't want to find out…come on, let's go inside this shop and hide out for a while."

Zach and Sam entered an unknown shop with no sign and walked down the stairs; heavy smoke engulfed the staircase as they made their way down to the bottom. When they got down, what they saw shocked them. Boys and girls, no more than fifteen years old, were helping older adults strap themselves and shoot them up with drugs. Zach and Sam could see their eyes rolling to the backs of their heads, some with their heads and bodies slumped on couches, and others crushing up pills, talking a million miles a minute. They were in a drug den.

"Oh my god, Zach!"

"Shhh, we can't draw attention to ourselves; just keep your head down low while we try and figure out our next move."

CHAPTER 27

September 10th, 2023, 3:23 P.M–Ireland

Jacan couldn't believe he was spending his fifteenth birthday in this hell hole. It wasn't like he could ask Cara for a favor and get filet mignon steak delivered to him. The Blood Royal kids would know something was up if that happened. Jacan would give anything for a steak and a glass of whiskey. He didn't want to become an alcoholic like his parents, but it seemed he was heading that way.

"Earth to Jacan…you okay?" Alora asked.

Jacan shook himself out of his pity, "Ya, I'm fine."

"No, you're not. Tell me what's wrong?"

Jacan sighed as he picked up the shovel to remove the horse manure from the barn.

"Oh, if you must know…" Jacan said, rolling his eyes. "Today's my birthday. Happy fifteenth birthday to me, right," Jacan said bitterly.

Alora shot Jacan a smile while she fixed her braid. "Well then, we're just gonna need to change the outcome of your predicament."

Alora grabbed Jacan's arm and pulled him outside the barn towards the bunker where the other kids were. They would have to make it quick and get back to their job before any of the guards noticed they were missing from their post.

"Hey, y'all, guess what? Today is Jacan's birthday; he's turning fifteen years old! You're as old as me now," Alora said gleefully.

"Great," Jacan said sarcastically.

"Oh, come off it, Jacan. Everyone likes to celebrate their birthday," Vladimir said in his Russian accent.

"Yes, they do," Alora said in her Southern Texan accent. "And I've got just the way to celebrate. After dinner, show up here, and I'll have everything situated.

Jacan had never had a birthday party with friends before… only the snobs and socialites' mothers who would bring their kids. None of them wanted to come, but they were made to. Jacan didn't have a single friend to his name, but oddly this group of Blood Royals had taken him in as if he were one of their own. "*No, Jacan,*" he thought to himself, "*You have a job to do. Now do it.*"

"Alright, you won me over," Jacan grinned. "What time should I come?"

Jacan had been placed in a room by himself about twenty feet away from the others. He may have acted up once or twice to a certain guard.

"Don't come until the guards have gone to bed, so let's say 10:15 P.M. sharp.

\#

10:15 P.M. couldn't come sooner. Jacan had to take three showers to get the stench of horse shit off his body. Jacan looked at his geo-tracking watch to see it was 10:14 P.M. He got out of his bed and stuffed his pillows underneath the covers, making a body just in case a guard came to check in on him. Jacan opened the curtain and walked towards the other room.

When he opened the tattered brown curtains, Jacan saw all the Elite Blood Royals were there to greet him—even Rune had shown up, which he found interesting since she had shown distaste for him since the beginning.

They had made streamers by tearing up old tattered brown curtains and hanging them alongside ivy, daisies, and forget-me-nots. Sianna had even ripped up her sparkly royal purple shirt to place the jewels and sequins scattered about on a table with gifts next to it.

Alora held a small white cake with Jacan's name written on top with green icing. Jacan almost started to tear up but collected himself not to show his emotions. He began to recite their names, ages, and abilities in his head to keep him on the mission:

Fifteen-year-old Alora from Texas—has prophetic dreams and visions that come to pass. Eleven-year-old Sianna from Wales—has the gift of healing but not bringing people back from the dead. Nine-year-old Mei from Japan—has the power to grow plants, flowers, fruits, and vegetables with one touch of her hand.

Twelve-year-old Albie from England–has the power to become invisible. Sixteen-year-old Vladimir from Russia–has the ability to control the weather and electricity.

Eight-year-old Rowan from Ireland–has the power to conjure fire, and last but not least, sixteen-year-old Rune from Turkey–is a skilled fighter and has the ability to change elements at will, which includes atoms at their basic elements. If Rune wanted, she could create a black hole or even a miniature sun. She was the most powerful Blood Royal in the camp. One thing she couldn't change was the forcefield that was keeping them all there; she had tried about half a dozen times, but it was no use. Rune claimed there was some sort of power that went beyond technology that kept them entrapped. Jacan, of course, knew what that power was–it was Kieron's supernatural power as the Antichrist.

Rune was the most powerful Blood Royal here, with Vlad being right under her. Jacan wondered if one day soon, Alora would have a dream or vision about who he was. He would need to keep an eye on her.

"Well, what do you think?" Alora asked. Jacan thought Alora was very beautiful. She was African American with medium dark skin and had the most beautiful amber eyes he had ever seen. But Jacan didn't need to focus on that; he needed to focus on how to kill one of them in the next battle-to-the-death match. He was also to report to Zara any new abilities they might possess or were hiding.

"Thank you all so much...I've never had a birthday with real friends before...."

"Well, get used to it, mate, cause we're here to stay," Albie said brightly.

Rowan walked over to give Jacan a small dark blue box. Jacan scrunched his eyebrows and opened the small box, a small silver ring with a clear crystal inside.

"What is it?"

"It's a ring, silly duck."

"Well, I know that," Jacan laughed, "but I've noticed that you all have the same ring on, so what's it for?"

Alora was about to speak when Rune cleared her throat. All of the kids looked at Rune; she hadn't been a part of the ring process for Jacan and didn't know the kids had come together to make him a ring.

"I'm sorry, Rune, but I think he should have one. He's one of us."

"No, he's not, but he sure as hell is about to be after this. You all agreed to this?"

One by one, the kids nodded their heads. Rune looked at Vlad, "Even you, Vlad? I thought you didn't like the kid."

"What can I say? He grew on me. He's cool in my books, particularly after he kept standing up to that pissant guard."

Rolling her eyes, Rune walked to Jacan and took the ring from the box. All of the kids held their breath except for Vlad.

"Listen, kid; this is not a game. Do you understand me? When they put you in the arena, it's life and death. They want to see what you're made of. Thankfully we've never had to use the rings on each other, but there will come a time when we will..."

and when that happens, we must be ready to beat them at their own game. This ring is only used for special circumstances. Life and death circumstances. Got it?"

"I do."

"Good. I still don't trust you; there's something about you I can't put my finger on…but if the others trust you, I will at least *attempt* to give you a shot."

"Attempt?"

"It's the best I can do."

"Fair enough," Jacan said.

"Just remember, the moment I think you are against us, I will end you."

"Understood."

"Good."

"Now, let me tell you about the ring."

CHAPTER 28

September 10th, 2023, 9:40 P.M – England

Sofia didn't know if she wanted to laugh or cry. Getting to know Everette these past three days was something for which she wasn't prepared. She wasn't ready to like him, *actually* like him. He could be aloof, cold, and a smart ass, but other times, when he would let his guard down, he would take off his mask and show her the real side of him, a soft, welcoming, comforting, and loving side.

Half the time, she wanted to kill him in his sleep; the other half, she wanted nothing more than to have his toned arms holding her. Other times she felt like she wanted to slap him. Although she never would slap a human being, there were times he tested her patience. Sofia didn't want to feel these feelings with him, the back-and-forth tug-of-war feelings inside her. She had dated a few men briefly but had never had a real boyfriend. She was always so busy with school and working at the hospital that most men she had dated had fizzled out to be friends. They could never keep her attention long enough, to be honest. Some great men had tried to court her, but each had something missing to attain her affection. She never could figure out what that missing puzzle piece was; maybe one day she would.

"What's that thing you say again?" Everette placed a cup of steaming tea on the coffee table in front of her, "the quote you always say?"

"Thank you," Sofia accepted the tea. "Which one?" she laughed. "I have many."

"The Spanish one."

"Que Sera Sera, whatever will be will be."

"That's right." Everette placed his tea down and took a seat next to her on the couch. "What's the specific meaning behind it to you, Blondie."

Sofia shot him a look. Everette didn't squirm. He held her gaze.

"We've gone over this a hundred times, Everette."

"And will go over it a hundred more times; I'll keep calling you Blondie if you keep calling me Everette. It's Collins."

Sofia shoved Everette toward the other end of the couch. "It's Sofia."

Everette looked deeply into Sofia's eyes and smiled. "You got an arm on you," he teased.

Everette moved back over to Sofia. "You know I admire you, right?"

"Is that so?"

"I like that you can fully be yourself; you've shown that to me these past few days."

"I don't see any point in hiding who you are." Sofia added milk to her tea.

"But you did, to the whole world. You didn't even tell your own people you were one of them."

Sofia sighed. "That's because I didn't want to be the face of the cause. That's Zach's thing, or it should be his face, not mine."

"Why do you say that?"

"Because he was the one who saved me. It was Brother Guiden and Zach who put it all together. I only contributed a couple of times. He was born to be in the limelight. I wasn't. That's not me."

Everette inched closer to Sofia, "And who are you, Miss Boudreaux?"

"I'm just a girl who wants to do the right thing, someone who stands up for the underdog. That's why I didn't tell my people." Sofia stirred her tea thoughtfully. "I don't want to be revered or worshiped as a god: that's not me or who I am. I want Blood Royals to find the divinity within themselves. We all come from God. We are all children of God." She blew on the tea and took a sip.

"Maybe with you lot—Blood Royals, everyone else who is not a Blood Royal, well, we don't have that right. Non-Blood Royals aren't children of God."

Sofia thought long and hard before responding. "We may be the literal bloodline of Jesus and Mary, but we still have a choice to accept the gift of salvation; free will is given to all."

"Tell that to the angels. I think they would beg to differ." Everette lifted his cup to his lips.

"Who said anything about angels? I'm talking about human beings…why would you bring them up?"

"No reason. I find it interesting that God gives free will to humans and not angels."

Sofia was about to rebuttal his response when Everette's phone rang; he jumped to his feet and went into the other room, talking in hushed tones. Everette returned to the room; all the color in his face had drained.

"What is it?"

Everette said nothing, his expression dour.

"Everette, tell me."

Everette took out his phone and showed her the news segment. She was on National News for the UK and wanted for the crimes of conspiracy, evading arrest, and kidnapping. She was number one on the most wanted list of criminals in the United Kingdom. The government had pinned all the disappearing Blood Royal children to her, Zack, and the Christianology Church.

"They can't be serious, Everette! We would *never* do anything so monstrous as that. I literally said in court that the British government kidnapped Blood Royals, and now they're trying to pin it on me." Sofia rubbed her hands on the knees of her jeans. Her eyes pleaded with Everette, "Do you see it now? What your own government is trying to do? What did they tell you to do with me? Are you supposed to kill me? Is that why I'm here? Are you gathering information about me and Zach to report to your superiors and then kill me dead in my tracks?"

"No, I don't report to them." Everette shook his head. "I report to another agency, one that protects Blood Royals."

"Then why do I feel like you hate my kind?" She asked. "The way you talk to me about Blood Royals…it seems like you're a bigot."

"It's complicated." He took a step forward.

"Then uncomplicate it!"

"Sofia…you wouldn't understand…." Everette began but was interrupted by a knock at the door.

"Nobody knows where I live," Everette said, "not even my superiors, quick! Hide in the cloak closet!" He pointed to a door in the hall.

Sofia ran into the closet and hid behind a bunch of cloaks. She held her breath as Everette put a gun in the back of his pants and answered the door.

"Hello, Everette."

Sofia knew that voice; she knew it *all too well*. The Holy Seer had found them.

"It's so nice to meet you in person. And Sofia, I know you're in here. The nanobot technology tracked you both here. We've been watching you for days now."

"Who's we?" Everette asked.

Kieron stepped out of the shadows with Delaney and smiled. Kieron's eyes settled on the cloak closet; he smiled slightly.

"Hello, Sofia."

CHAPTER 29

September 10th, 11:42 P.M – Sea of Galilee

Jesus closed his eyes and listened to the waves crash in the Galilee Sea. Today was his birthday, and he spent it alone, without his Mary or daughter, Sarah. Jesus kept a low profile as his Father in Heaven instructed. He was to wait until the sign of the spirit of Elijah came back to the Earth before he could reveal himself. Both Elijah and Moses must be presented before they can defeat the Antichrist. Jesus stayed away from social media, cell phones, and the news, anything that could distract or deter him. All Jesus knew was that he was waiting for his Mary; to hold her in his arms once more and forever be one again. He was home, but he wouldn't be for long. He needed to pray to receive divine revelation.

"Heavenly Father, if it is your will, please show me where to go next. My people are hurting. I have heard from my travels the woe that has come upon Israel. Russia and China must be stopped, and it seems as if people think Kieron Gedron and his technology is the answer. I know this is not the way. I know the Antichrist will use technology to deceive the people. Show me how I can help Father and what I can do to make way for Elijah. Please, Holy Spirit, divine Mother, what must I do? I can only do what you send me to do. Let your words flow through my mouth. What must I speak to make them come to pass?"

Jesus sat on the beach as he listened to his Father's words and the words of the Mother, the Holy Spirit. It was a revelation like no other. A revelation of who was the new incarnated Eve, her mission, and what he must do to help her overcome the Antichrist. Jesus was the new Adam, he redeemed mankind's sins of the world, and this mysterious woman is the new Eve. She must also redeem women's sins as well as her sins. It had to be both of them. Both Adam and Eve had to make amends, or God would not allow half of the population to enter the kingdom of Heaven. Jesus understood that even the elect would be deceived in the end times; he needed to do his part, but not before it was his time.

"Let your will be done, Father, on Earth as it is in Heaven. Let your will be done, Mother, on Earth as it is in Heaven."

Jesus slowly got up and looked up into the night sky. He smiled as he saw the Star of Bethlehem, the same star the three wise men had used to navigate their way to find him as a baby. Now, he would use the star to find Eve to get back to his wife and child in heaven.

CHAPTER 30

September 11th, 2023, 8:30 A.M – The Vatican

Brother Guiden was finally in the clear. The Italian government had thoroughly investigated and cleared him of all accusations set against him for the murder of Pope Aloysius. He could, once and for all, put the tragedy behind him and focus on helping Zach and Sam with clues for the Stone of Destiny and David's harp. Zach had conveyed in his email that the Holy Grail was not only a chalice of great power but that it would also be an individual woman.

Now all he had to do was go to the underground library where only he and a few select priests were allowed to view a few hidden books that had been locked up for centuries away from the public eye. He had waited his whole life to get his hands on any secret teachings left out of the Bible. He also hoped to find diary or journal entries from priests, popes, or anyone else that could lead them to the magical items requested.

#

After hours of flipping through books, parchments, and journal entries, Brother Guiden had finally found something of substance. He couldn't believe the Roman Catholic Church's audacity in who they deemed worthy or not worthy to know secret information. It was wrong on so many levels, and he wanted to be the one to change that. Brother Guiden found a journal entry from someone called 'The Black Pope.' The black Pope is the Superior General of the Society of Jesus, also known as the Jesuits. If the Jesuits had anything to do with hiding the Stone of Destiny, locating the item would be much harder. There would be multiple people keeping an eye on and protecting the sacred object.

Brother Guiden's head was starting to pound. He had been having more dreams about Zach and Sam, and he didn't like what he saw…He had to figure out any information the journal entry gave for the Stone of Destiny, or he would lose both forever. Brother Guiden took some Ibuprofen and downed a Coca-Cola to help with his migraine, and reread the journal entry:

'The Jesuit order has finally found the Stone of Destiny. After countless searches for over 700 years, we have located the sacred object. The Stone of Destiny has immense and great power. I have seen it with my own eyes. If a person who is not worthy sits on the stone, they are annihilated. When a righteous person sits on the stone, the stone cries out, naming the man the next king of the kingdom. An immense surge of power emerges from the stone, rising to the heavens to declare him sovereign king of the nations. The stone then empowers the king with capabilities unknown to the common man…he has the power to create and destroy life,

the ability to speak something into existence or take away something in existence.

This is why we do not see creatures like the giants of old and unicorns; they were spoken out of existence. We must always keep the Stone of Destiny in the hands of the Black Pope and the Jesuits. It must never leave our sight. I have taken it upon myself to hide the sacred object so that when one who is worthy of becoming sovereign over all life, it shall be revealed to him. The Stone of Destiny's whereabouts will only be handed down from the current Black Pope to the next Black Pope. Let it be known the riddle of the Stone of Destiny that only a Black Pope will know.'

"From the darkness we mise,
From the ashes, we rise,
Fire and smoke will be their disguise,
They are the ones who will burn this world free,
They are the one who is the true light of the three.
The Stone of Destiny is hidden out of sight,
Only True Darkness and Light can unearth it with might,
There are only four left in the world who can be the one,
Choose wisely, my friends; it cannot be undone,
The Stone of Destiny hides where one cannot see,
Don't use your eyes; they will only deceive thee."

Brother Guiden had a lot of work cut out for him to figure out this riddle. He would need to find out who the Black Pope was and find a way to converse with him. He was the Pope, after all.

CHAPTER 31

September 11th, 2023, 12:48 P.M - Istanbul, Turkey

Lennox couldn't think about walking another step. She plopped her butt on the ground and closed her eyes; taking in the sea breeze, she inhaled deeply. It was a cloudy gray day in Ireland. Where they were exactly, she didn't know, but she knew they were getting close to the touristy area of the Cliffs of Moher. They had started to see more cars on the road. A few people had offered to give them a ride, but Raziah politely refused. She said when the time was right, the Divine Feminine would show them where to go next. If only that sign could be now because her feet were killing her.

"Is there any way to speed up the process of getting a sign?" Lennox asked. "We've been walking for four days straight. I don't think I can take much more of this."

Raziah sat next to Lennox and looked off in the distance. They could see the Moher Tower with a few people taking pictures just up ahead. It was a Monday, so there weren't too many tourists out and about. Yousef walked over to the edge of the Moher Cliffs, looked out to the ocean, raised his hands to the sky, and started to worship.

"Why does he keep doing that every hour?" asked Lennox.

"He's trying to get God's attention."

"I'm pretty sure God sees everything, so why isn't He/She, whatever, you know what I mean, responding?"

"We don't tell God what to do, Lennox." Raziah explained gently. "We are on God's time; He's not on ours. When the time is right, God will supply our needs. And, yes, I know what you mean," Raziah smiled.

Lennox was starting to feel achy, so she excused herself to go to an area without tourists in sight. She looked down at her phone; she had a missed text message from Jax:

'Hey Len, I know it's been a few days since we saw you. I'm thinking of you and hope you're doing okay. Loch and I miss you. Can't wait to get back to digging and back to normal. Hang in there. We're praying for your dad.'
-Jax

Lennox began to think about Jax's smile and how he would brush his brown hair off of his face. He always seemed to be fixing it when she was around him, which was strange to her, considering he wasn't a primadonna or anything.

Lennox removed her backpack and took out a clipboard and a dollar bill. She made sure no one was looking and dumped a large amount of the brown powder on the clipboard. Taking the dollar bill, she rolled it up, made two thick lines of the substance, and snorted it. Opening her bag, she rummaged through the bottom and felt something unfamiliar. She put her hand on the item and lifted it from her bag. It was a pack of needles.

"How in the hell did these get in here...?" Lennox said out loud to herself. Lennox thought back to every encounter she had had since the drug den. She thought of the man who tried to offer to shoot up for her when she declined.

"He must have put a pack of needles in my bag when I nodded off," She thought. "Get me to think about shooting up, and then I do it, which then, in turn, makes me a drug user on a whole other level. Clever man, that one."

Lennox realized she had been talking to herself out loud, but she didn't care. How she didn't notice the pack of needles in her bag this whole time was also a mystery. It was as if they were invisible to her this entire time and only became visible when she became weak. And she was weak. She was tired of walking for four days straight. She was tired of having feelings for Jax that were unreciprocated and tired of feeling depressed about losing her father. She was just tired of it all.

"Lennox." A voice whispered very lowly.

Lennox turned around but didn't see anyone around her.

"Lennox," the voice said again.

Lennox started to breathe heavily. She closed her eyes. She didn't want to hear the voice. She had been hearing the voices of supernatural entities since she was a child. Some were benevolent; most were not. Lennox didn't want to admit it to herself, but she was what the Bible called a "Seer." She could see demons and angels, hear them, or sense their presence when they were invisible. That was one reason Lennox started using pills when she was nineteen. She just couldn't take it any longer, feeling like an outcast, feeling so different from others. Her parents told her she had a gift. She told them it was a curse. Her father expressly called her special. That's why the thought of losing him hurt so much. Even though her dad was an alcoholic, he still understood spiritual things.

"Lennox," the voice said a third time in a growl.

"What! What do you want from me!?"

"You know what you must do."

Lennox looked down at the pack of needles. She kept having visions of her putting a needle in her arm while crying. It was always the same vision at the same place. This was not the place she saw herself shooting up. Today was not the day she was going to die, not if she had any say in it.

"No. Now leave me alone!"

Lennox ran, threw the pack of needles over the Cliffs, and watched them fall into the choppy deep blue sea. The vision could no longer come true if she didn't have the needles on her.

"Lennox!" Raziah called, "Yousef heard from the Divine Feminine! We know where we're going next!"

Lennox put the clipboard, dollar bill, and drugs back in her backpack and headed toward Raziah and Yousef. Little did she know that one needle fell out of the pack and was lying at the bottom of her bag.

CHAPTER 32

September 11th, 2023, 3:47 P.M – Ireland

Jacan stood his ground as the other Blood Royal kids moved out of the way when Rune and the Elite Blood Royal kids came walking through. Jacan hoped to God his name would be called. He needed to show Kieron that he could do this. So far, there had been four battles, with sixteen Blood Royal children who had died. If he were lucky, Zara would put him in the arena next.

"You ready if your name is called?" Alora asked in her southern drawl.

"I'm counting on it."

Rune eyed Jacan. "Why would you be counting on it?"

"To show those assholes who's boss."

"You realize you would have to kill a kid in the process, right?" Rune looked him up and down. "Maybe even all three. Four kids go in; only one comes out."

Jacan thought carefully about the words coming out of his mouth. He must play this smartly. That was a dumb move to say his comment out loud. "Unless there's another way..." he suggested.

"There is no other way. You have to kill to get out," Rune said, bothered.

"The ring amplifies your powers, correct?"

"Yes," Rune said abruptly.

"Then I gather you could amplify other Blood Royals' powers as well."

Rune was stunned. She had never thought of amplifying other Blood Royals' powers before. She arched her eyebrow as she regarded Jacan.

"Now listen here, maggots, when your name is called, come up to the front and get a bag from Zara," announced the guard. "If you run away, you die. If you do not come to the front when your name is called, you die. Understood?"

All the kids nodded yes in unison. All were holding their breaths as the first name was called.

"Breya Anderson. Thirteen years old from Connecticut. Breya has the power to control the wind and rain."

"So, I was saying," Jacan whispered, "you could technically amplify other Blood Royals' powers. You could even switch or take someone else's powers as your own."

"Wow, that's insane," Alora stated with unbelief.

"It's just physics, really. With Rune's powers endowed in the black opal gemstone, it only makes logical sense that her powers

to manipulate matter at the quantum level means you could theo-
retically manipulate the ring to transfer those powers to yourself."

"You're a freaking genius, kid," Vlad said as he playfully
punched him in the shoulder.

Jacan smiled and shrugged. "I like physics. It just makes
sense to me."

"Mei Quan. Nine years old from Japan. Has the power to
grow plants, flowers, fruits, and vegetables at will."

Everyone that was a part of the Elite Blood Royals gasped.
Out of all of the Blood Royal kids and teenagers in the compound,
Mei was the least powerful of them. She was only stuck in the
Elite section as she was the only Blood Royal who could grow
food out of thin air.

"Why would they stick Mei, our only food source, in
the arena?" Albie cried. "She's one of the youngest here; that's
not fair!"

Rune grabbed her hand, looked Mei in the eyes, and whispered, "Do exactly what Jacan said. Focus all your energy and will
on the ring, take others' powers into yourself, and use it against
them. It's your only fighting chance."

Rune kissed her head and gave her a hug.

"Mei Quan to the front, now!" screamed the guard.

Mei held her head high as she moved past the Blood Royal
children to the front. Some pointed and laughed at her, while
others bowed their heads as she passed them. Mei Quan was
the third youngest kid at the compound, with only Braydon and

Rowan being one year younger than her. Most kids were at least eleven years and up.

The guard picked his canine tooth as Mei took front and center stage next to Breya Anderson.

"Jeffery Matthews. Fourteen years old from Georgia. Has the power of night vision, camouflage, and x-ray vision."

Jacan eyed Zara as she looked down at her clipboard. She looked up and caught Jacan's eyes. He was telling her with his eyes he wanted to go in. She let out a slight curve of a smile and then composed herself. She crossed out a name and wrote another name on the board. She handed the clipboard to the guard.

The guard read the last name on the board.

"Frank Cummings. Seventeen years old from England. Has the power of invisibility."

"Frank has the same power as Albie!" Sianna yelled out.

Frank started making his way to the front when he saw Jeffery's eyes turn from green to red. Just thinking that Jeffery only had night vision, Frank soon realized he also had the power of laser fire in his eyes. Without thinking, Frank started to move slowly backward and then took off running toward the invisible fence.

"Stop! Don't go past the fence!" Rune took off running after Frank. He just arrived last night. Jacan had been there a week, and he hadn't been called into the arena yet. Rune would need to have a word with Zara. "Frank, stop! Don't go past that pole, or you'll get electrocuted!"

But it was too late. Frank whizzed past the pole and was instantly turned into a black pile of dust.

Zara walked over and stood next to Rune. Her face was solemn, not saying a word. Rune started to shake in anger. Zara put her hand on her shoulder and eyed her, nodding no. Zara walked over back to the front of the stage. All eyes were on her.

"Which one of you guards was the one who brought in the boy last night?" The man who had picked his teeth and called out the children's names spoke up.

"I was the one who brought him in," he said with a grin.

"And did you not tell him about the fence?"

"Must've slipped my mind."

"I see."

In the blink of an eye, Zara took a blade from behind her back and slit the man's throat in one clean move. The guard fell to his knees with his hands covering his neck, blood seeping between his fingers and hands, staining the green grass crimson red.

"If any other guard decides to accidentally forget to mention the electromagnetic fence to any other Blood Royal that comes through here, this will be your fate. They are here to battle each other; they are here to be tested. They are NOT here to be burnt into a pile of ashes. Do I make myself clear?"

Every single guard nodded. "Good."

"Now then." Zara grabbed her clipboard and looked at the name she crossed off her board. It was Rune's. Zara looked to Rune, who was still by the fence looking at Frank's ashes. A single tear rolled off her cheek and landed on her collarbone. Zara looked back over at Jacan. He was watching Rune as she walked over to the group. Rune stood next to Jacan without saying a word or looking at him. Her eyes were laser-focused on Zara. Zara looked back over the crowd and then back to Jacan. He was mouthing 'me' to her silently.

"Jacan Eisen," she announced. "Fifteen years old from New York City. Has the power of superhuman strength."

Rune tensed her hands and made them into a ball of fists. She shot a look of anger towards Jacan.

"Don't worry," he whispered, "I have a plan."

All eyes were on Jacan and Rune. She couldn't risk saying anything else to him, so she nodded yes and stepped back as Jacan made his way to the front where the others were.

"The battle begins at 10:00 P.M. tonight." Zara announced. "Say your goodbyes now because only one of you is coming back."

CHAPTER 33

September 11th, 3:13 P.M. – Everette's Cottage

Sofia and Everette awoke to the smell of burning sulfur wafting in their noses. When they opened their eyes, they could see that they were both bound by chains and tied to wooden chestnut chairs sitting two feet apart from each other. Delaney was off in the corner on her phone, but Kieron and the Holy Seer were nowhere in sight. Seeing that they were awake, Delaney quickly said goodbye to her mother and gave Sofia a wide grin.

"So, you're my competition, huh? Not much to look at if you ask me."

Sofia blinked her eyes a few times to collect herself. The stench of burning sulfur was really getting to her, not only by giving her a headache but the unholy reason for the smell of sulfur in the cottage.

"Competition for what?"

Delaney sat down on the third wooden chestnut chair and crossed her legs. Putting both hands clasped on one knee, she responded delicately but sternly.

"World domination."

Sofia raised an eyebrow. "I haven't the slightest clue what you're talking about."

"Sure you don't."

"Ladies, ladies, let's not jump the gun here. Excuse me, young maiden, but what is your name?" Everette asked with a sweet smile.

"Delaney."

"Delaney, a beautiful name for a beautiful girl."

Delaney blushed and smiled. "I don't think my fiancé would like it if he saw you hitting on me."

"Tell him to come and see me if he doesn't like it."

"With pleasure," Kieron announced as he entered the room.

"I don't find what you are doing tasteful, Everette. It's deplorable. People will do or say anything to get out of their situation," Kieron promulgated.

"And just what *is* our situation?" Sofia asked plainly.

"There she is." Kieron moved slightly closer to Sofia, putting his hand on his jaw. He looked her over from the top of her head to the bottom of her feet. She was a pretty little thing, he must confess. More than pretty, if he were honest with himself, she was stunning. Her eyes glowed with hate, but her aura was the most beautiful silver, white, and navy blue he had ever seen in a human being. Her light made him ache for her, not just sexually but for the immense power she held inside her.

"The beautiful and almighty Sofia Boudreaux. You have no idea how long I've been waiting to meet you. I have been waiting thousands of years to set my eyes upon you. And I must say, you do not disappoint."

Delaney shot Sofia a hateful look full of jealousy.

"Now, now my sweet, you are my prize and the one who will sit with me while I take my throne. She is a means to an end. This I promise you."

"Excuse me?" Sofia exclaimed with alarm. "You're only a teenager, a rich and intelligent teenager, but a teenager nonetheless. You have no power over me."

Kieron cleared his throat and looked down at her chains.

"What are these things?" She rattled the chains. "I can get out of these in a blink of an eye."

"Not if they're laced with black magic, you can't," Kieron smiled as he tilted his head at her.

Sofia closed her eyes and whispered a phrase in Latin inaudible to Kieron. When she opened her eyes, she could see she was still in the cottage, chained up in front of Kieron. Sofia's blood began to boil in anger. "What did you mean when you said you have been waiting for me for thousands of years? You're what, sixteen, seventeen?"

"I'm seventeen years old in human terms, but in spiritual terms, I'm immortal."

"How can that be?" Sofia questioned.

"I'm endowed with the spirit of Lucifer. I AM Lucifer incarnate, to put it into technical terms."

Sofia's mouth dropped so low you could have picked it up off the floor. Everette stayed quiet while he contemplated his next move.

"So, you're the Antichrist."

"Yes," Kieron said with a slight smile.

Sofia needed to tread lightly. "Why does it smell like sulfur in here?"

Kieron raised his eyebrow at Sofia, "Oh, you noticed that?"

"How could I not? Japan could smell it from here."

Kieron let out a belly laugh, a laugh he didn't think in his seventeen years he had ever done. "It does take some time to… get used to," Kieron said in a mischievous tone.

"Are you planning on killing us with sulfur? Is that it?"

"No, my delicate little flower, your death will not be until later. What you are smelling is the sulfur coming from hell."

"Like, literal hell? Like heaven and hell?" Sofia asked in shock.

Kieron walked towards Sofia. "Yes. Like THE literal hell."

Kieron brushed a strand of hair out of Sofia's face. He bent down and looked into her hazel eyes deeply and kissed her lightly on the lips. She pulled back, but he only kissed her harder, biting her lip in the process. It felt like a thousand razor blades making tiny cuts all over her lips.

"Ouch!" Sofia exclaimed, jerking away.

"Hey, leave her alone!" Everette demanded from his chair, pulling against his chains.

Kieron ignored him and looked intently into Sofia's eyes. "It's only a matter of time before the red horse of Revelation is loosened. Once that happens, my demons will cause havoc on the Earth, and I will be Lord over all of Heaven, Earth, and Hell."

"Get off of me, you perv!" Sofia demanded. She tasted blood.

Delaney's eyes grew wide with jealousy. The look on her face told Sofia that she would have tried to kill her right then and there if she could have. Kieron smiled and backed away from Sofia and rejoined Delaney at her side.

"Don't you EVER do that again," Sofia said in disgust. "Why are you telling me this stuff?"

"So you can tell Zach my plans."

"Why? Can't you tell him yourself?" Keiron looked away briefly. Sofia smiled, slowly realizing an opening, "You can't find him, can you?"

"I know exactly where he is," Kieron asserted, "but it would be better if it came from you."

"Why is that?"

"If Zach and Sam want to live, he must bring me the Holy Grail and David's harp. He must also find the location of the Stone of Destiny and tell me its coordinates. Here is my card for you to call me when he does."

Kieron inched closer to Sofia's face and whispered in her ear, "I know about the baby. If all three want to live, tell him to find those two items and bring them to me in Ireland. I will give more specific directions when he has those items."

Kieron slipped his card into Sofia's bra while copping a feel before slowly backing away smiling.

"Kieron! They weren't supposed to know that, you know," Delaney said.

Kieron gave Delaney a look from hell and returned to face Sofia. "And that's exactly why I'm saying it now, Delaney, this is our bargaining chip," Kieron spat out.

Sofia's eyes were wide with terror, "How do you know about the baby?"

"I have my ways," Kieron said as he looked at Everette.

Everette looked at Kieron, then over at Sofia, and shook his head no.

Sofia looked over at Everette. "How did you know?"

"I don't know, I didn't know!" He insisted.

"But you did, Everette. Gadreel sees all." Kieron explained. "So, when Sofia saw the pregnancy stick on the ground, so did Gadreel." Kieron gave Everette a look of pity. "Shame, just when I thought I would move you up in the ranks, Everette. Well, you won't be, but Gadreel will be."

"Who is Gadreel? My name is Everette Collins!"

Kieron smiled, "Your head says no, but your heart says yes."

"What is he talking about, Everette?" Sofia asked.

"I don't know what the hell he's talking about!"

"Yes, you do. Your body is occupied by a fallen angel named Gadreel," Kieron explained. "Both you and he occupy the same body. I have many fallen watchers occupying human bodies. You are both at war with each other for this body. It's only a matter of time before he completely takes over. Fight it all you want, but Gadreel will win over your mind."

"Is that why you were asking me if there was redemption for angels earlier" Sofia asked.

"No, I–"

"Don't lie to me, Everette! This whole time you've known, you have had a fallen angel inside you, and you never thought to tell me? You're basically working for the Antichrist."

"But I'm not. It's Gadreel letting Kieron know all these things, not me."

"That's not entirely true," Kieron said as he cocked his head with a slight grin. "A fallen angel must have permission from the host to enter. A host must be on the wayward path of destruction and make a wish or pray for power. Then the fallen angel may enter. You called Gadeel to yourself without even realizing Everette. What did you wish for? Let me guess. To be the most powerful and famous MI6 agent in the agency?"

Everette was speechless, "How could you have known that?"

"I'm Lucifer incarnate, you pathetic piece of dog shit; I know everything, and I can read you like a book. Do you really think I, Satan, Lucifer the Morning Star, don't know the desires of every human being when I encounter them? You must be dumber than a sack of rocks." Kieron sighed, hitting his forehead with his palm. "The atrocity of the human race astounds me."

Before Everette could say another word, Sofia chimed in, "Why would I do this if you're just going to kill me anyway? Why would I need to be murdered and not Zach? We're both Blood Royals from the line of Jesus and Mary. Not that I want my brother murdered, but what you're saying makes no sense."

"Because, my dear, you and Delaney are two picks from the Divine Feminine to redeem mankind."

"Oh, not this again."

"You don't know, do you?"

"Know what?"

Kieron gave Sofia the most sinister look she had ever seen on someone's face. "The Holy Grail is both a chalice and a woman. She will be a sinful woman, not sinless like her counterpart Jesus."

"There is no way in hell that is true, Kieron," Sofia firmly expressed.

Kieron went out of the room into the kitchen and returned with a glass with parchments inside. "I received these parchments from an Archaeologist in Istanbul, where, by the way, Zach and Sam reside at this very moment. These parchments reveal truths about the Divine Feminine and her redemption of Eve and all females of the human race."

"I thought Jesus Christ of Nazareth took care of that," Sofia said defiantly.

"Why do you think Jesus says you must be born again and that if you are saved, you will be like the angels in heaven, neither marrying nor given in marriage? There are only male angels, no female angels. Jesus only redeemed half of humankind, the masculine. The Holy Roman Church removed scriptures from the Bible as well as replaced scriptures to make it seem like Jesus redeemed all of mankind. They did it by way of controlling the masses and especially to have control over the feminine. It says the Holy Grail will be able to bring men to repentance, which Delaney can do, and she will also bring back man from the dead, which you can do. It is logical to assume you both make up half of the whole."

"How do I know you're not lying?"

"Why on earth would I lie about this?"

"To get me to do what you want."

"I may be evil to my core, but there is no point in lying if I want to possess the items I need to sit on the throne."

Kieron walked over to Sofia and spoke in a language she had never heard on Earth. The shackles fell to the floor in a thud. Sofia slowly got up and walked over to Everette.

"Now, his." She pointed to Everette's chains.

"I don't think so."

"If you want me to find Zach and tell him, undo his shackles, or there's no deal."

Kieron thought carefully and began to smile. "I will do this if you kiss me of your own volition. Otherwise, I will throw him into the portal of hell where his soul can never be redeemed. He will live in eternity for hell. The choice is yours."

Sofia was mad as hell at Everette; more than angry, she was furious. She would rather gouge her eyes out than kiss Kieron, the Antichrist incarnate in an seventeen years old body. Sofia looked over at Everette. His head was hung low where she couldn't see his eyes. She saw tears streaming down his face. He was hiding his face from her because he was crying. In her right mind, Sofia could never condemn someone to hell for all eternity, no matter how mad she was at him for lying to her.

"Don't do it, Sofia. I don't deserve redemption," Everette said bitterly. "I'm not worth you kissing that monster."

Sofia closed her eyes and gulped hard. She hoped to God that Everette would be free of Gadreel's hold one day. Until then, she knew in her heart of hearts she needed to do the right thing. Sofia slowly walked over to Kieron and faced him head-on. Sofia glanced over at Delaney; instead of looking for a face of disgust or envy, she saw pure joy written across her face. "*What in the world*," Sofia thought, "*she really is batshit crazy.*"

Sofia inched closer to Kieron and looked him dead in the eyes. His ice-blue eyes began to change to a burnt orange color. Sofia inched closer, and his eyes changed from burnt orange to fiery engine red. Sofia closed her eyes and leaned in to kiss Kieron. His lips were smooth like rose petals. Sofia's heart said to back away, but her head and the blood coursing through her veins told her to stay. She leaned in to kiss him harder. His lips began to burn like fire on hers. No matter how hard she wanted to stop kissing him, she couldn't. The more she tried to stop, the more she wanted him to take her to bed. Kieron picked up Sofia and held her in his arms. He would be putting the Antichrist's seed into Sofia. Delaney was incapable of becoming pregnant, but Sofia was not. Kieron began to walk out of the living room, heading towards the bedroom.

"Sofia! No!" Everette was aghast; he strained against his chains but was unable to break free.

Sofia could not hear Everette's screams. She couldn't hear anything except Kieron's voice in her head saying beautiful and lovely things to her.

Delaney hated that Sofia was about to have consummation with Kieron, but it needed to be done. He needed an heir to help rule hell while he ruled Earth. After the baby was born, he would sacrifice Sofia to Satan and take his throne. Kieron smiled as he opened the bedroom door and tossed Sofia onto the bed. This would only work if she willingly gave herself to him. She needed to be the one to kiss him first for his spell to work. Now that she conceded, the dark magic spell could take place, and he could rule Heaven, Earth, and Hell for all eternity.

CHAPTER 34

September 11th, 2023, 5:31 P.M – Istanbul, Turkey

Zach was beginning to get worried that Sofia's phone had been off for three days. Every time he called; it went straight to voicemail.

"Zach, it won't do you any good to worry. We need to get a plan in order. If we can get the item from Sofia to open the crypt at the Hagia Sophia, then we need to focus on David's harp or the Stone of Destiny."

"Based on what Brother Guiden just texted, I think the Stone of Destiny will be in Ireland, so let's go for the harder object to find, David's harp."

Sam sipped her cappuccino, rubbed her belly, and smiled. "If it's a boy, I like Alexander; if it's a girl, I like Alexandria. They both mean 'defender of mankind' and coming into this world, they will need a strong name to face whatever evil comes their way."

Zach lovingly looked at Sam, "I absolutely love the names and love you. I couldn't imagine my life without you." He reached for her hand.

"Well, I am the ball to your chain," Sam teased, giving his hand a squeeze. "Let's go back to the hotel and research where David's harp was last seen."

Sam gathered up her purse while Zach went inside to pay the bill. She started rummaging through her purse for a piece of gum when she saw two pairs of feet standing before her. She looked up to see that it was the same two men who were chasing them three days ago. One had purple hair and tattoos all over, the other looked like a young, bespeckled Hugh Grant. Sam was about to scream when the man with purple hair put a finger to his lips and smiled warmly. "All we want to do is talk, scout's honor."

Sam eyed them suspiciously but proceeded to let them sit down at the two empty chairs in front of her.

"My name is Jax Kingsley," the tall one with glasses said, "and this is my comrade Arran Lachlan."

"Loch, just Loch," the tattooed fellow insisted.

"Why not Lach?" Sam said, letting out a small laugh.

"I'm Scottish lassie. It's a nickname given to me by my mates. Loch stands for the Loch Ness monster."

Sam squinched her face, not knowing how to take that answer, but she already felt a rapport with his joking nature.

"Don't worry, lassie, I don't bite…. Much." He flashed a wicked grin.

Sam raised an eyebrow, and Loch continued. "I'm always disappearing into an adventure, just like how Nessie is never caught, so am I."

Sam sighed a sigh of relief and grinned at Loch, "Well, that's an interesting nickname for a mysterious man."

"Oh, he's not mysterious. He's an open book, believe me," Jax laughed.

Zach came out briskly holding two dinner mints when he saw Jax and Loch sitting across from his wife. Zach could see they had no weapons and were all laughing at a joke. Curious, he sat down next to Sam and stayed quiet. He wanted to let them do the talking.

"Hello lad, my name's Loch, and this here is Jax," Loch held out his hand for a shake. "We were just telling your hilarious wife the reason we've been looking for you."

"Which is…?" Zack asked hesitantly.

"To tell you what was said on the parchments we found."

"How did you know we were looking for parchments?

"A couple told us where to find you, Raziah and Yousef. They claim the Divine Feminine told them where to find you and why you needed this information."

Zach sat stunned in disbelief. "When the Divine Feminine took me into a portal into another dimension, she told me that Raziah and Yousef were two people I would encounter who would help me on my journey!" Zach looked around, "Where are they?"

"They're with our friend Lennox. Apparently, the Divine Feminine took them on a side quest to Ireland."

Zach's eyes widened, "To find the Stone of Destiny!?"

Loch shook his head no, "To find their daughter who was kidnapped."

"Is she a Blood Royal?"

"We think so."

Sam chimed in, "There are kids who are Blood Royals who are being kidnapped every day. I think they're being taken to be experimented on."

"Why wouldn't they just kidnap adults? Why kidnap kids?" Jax asked.

"I haven't a clue. Zach, what do you think?"

Zach pondered on this question for a minute before responding. "Maybe as a child, they're closer to the source of God. Maybe it's because they're more innocent. Maybe it's because the kidnappers are wicked people. My guess is all of the above."

"So, where do we go from here?" Loch asked.

Zach was about to respond when he felt his *fleur-de-lis* mark burn, but it wasn't the normal burning sensation he felt…This felt different. The sensation felt like he was being encapsulated with fire and ice. The stench of burning sulfur engulfed his nostrils. Zach fell to the floor, withering in pain.

"Oh, my God, Zach! What's wrong!" Sam screamed.

Zach couldn't describe what he was feeling; all he could mouth was one word. "Sofia…."

#

Walking along the Cliffs of Moher, Lennox was trying to keep it together. She kept hearing a voice that was calling her name. Granted, it wasn't the scary demonic voice she had heard earlier; it was a soft feminine voice, even pleasant, but she just couldn't respond to it. She was too scared to ask what the voice wanted. Most of the time, what the voices were asking her to do was evil.

Lennox noticed Raziah and Yousef stop dead in their tracks.

"Do you hear that?" Raziah asked Yousef.

Yousef nodded solemnly. Raziah centered herself and went inside her mind's eye to the source of the screaming. She could see Zach withering in pain, holding his chest. Raziah fell to the grass holding her own *fleur-de-lis* birthmark.

"I…have…to go," Raziah said breathlessly.

"What are you seeing?"

Raziah caught her breath, getting up very slowly. Zach is feeling something tremendous, something awful. I must go to him and find out. You guys go on ahead, and I'll catch up. This cannot wait."

Yousef kissed Raziah on the lips softly and nodded. "Go, my love. You know where we are heading."

In the blink of an eye, Raziah was gone. Yousef looked at Lennox. She was covering her ears and crying.

"Lennox, what's wrong!"

Sobbing uncontrollably, "I keep hearing voices telling me to do bad things to myself and to you and Raziah. There is a shadow figure standing just off to the side of you." Lennox pointed at the figure. "I keep denying it, but I can't deny it anymore. I can see and hear angels and demons, Yousef. The shadow figure has been following us this whole time while we've been in Ireland."

"I understand what you're feeling. I can't see them, but I can sense them. I've known this whole time something has been following us. The shadow demon wants you to kill yourself. It's the drugs, Lennox. Doing drugs opens the door to the spiritual side. The more you do drugs, the more open you are to receiving demonic influences."

Lennox stopped her sobbing and became very still. She seemed unsure if she should say what was being said to her. "There is one voice I keep hearing that's unlike the others. It's soft and feminine, like a warm summer breeze on a hot day."

Yousef lifted both of his eyebrows and smiled. "That's the Divine Feminine Lennox! That's the voice telling me where we should go on our journey. Call unto her."

Lennox waited until the voice called unto her again. "Lennox," the voice asked.

"Yes, here I am," Lennox responded.

"You must expunge Gadreel. Only you can do this. When the time is right, you will know."

"Gadreel?" Lennox asked, "Who or what is Gadreel?"

But she did not hear the voice again.

#

Onlookers watching Zach writhe in pain gasped as Raziah popped onto the floor, coming out of thin air. People started to scream and scatter, leaving only Zach, Sam, Jax, Loch, and Raziah outside the cafe. Sam could hear sirens getting closer as she held Zach's hand.

"Who are you?" Sam asked with tears streaming down her face.

Raziah looked over at Sam and lowered her blouse. Sam could see the *fleur-de-lis* birthmark pulsating the same as Zach's.

Sam's eyes widened, "Please, help him!"

Raziah put her hands on Zach's chest and closed her eyes. She could see in her mind's eye a woman with dirty blonde hair lying on a bed with a young man undressing his shirt. Raziah went deeper into the vision. She looked around to see she was in a small cottage in the country. She saw a man chained up on a chair, yelling the name Sofia.

"Oh, my God, it's Sofia!" Raziah gasped, pulling her back to where Zach and Sam were.

"Listen, I don't have much time to explain who I am; all you need to know is that I'm on your side."

Sam nodded understanding. Raziah closed her eyes and focused on the cottage. She could see the young man about to take off his pants when she popped into the room and landed next to Sofia. Kieron's eyes became wide with anger and disgust. Kieron jumped on the bed toward Raziah, but it was useless; she had already touched Sofia's arm and expelled her from the room back to Turkey, where Zach and the others were waiting.

Kieron screamed in agony and threw a lamp against the wall.

"I will find you, and I will kill you," Kieron said, directed at the unnamed woman he had just encountered.

Kieron buttoned up his pants and put his shirt back on. He opened the door to see Delaney smacking Everette to shut up.

"Gadreel. It's time," Kieron smiled.

Kieron linked arms with Delaney and headed out the door, where a helicopter was waiting.

"Where are we going?" asked Delaney. "What about Sofia? We need her."

"I'll deal with it. Right now, we have a date with the President," Kieron said with a wicked smile.

CHAPTER 35

September 11th, 2023, 9:20 P.M. - Compound in Ireland

There was an eerie feeling throughout the compound that Rune couldn't explain. She tried to shake off the strange energy that made everyone feel more unsettled than usual. Rune smiled as she watched Vlad pick up Rowan and put him on top of his shoulders.

"You're getting soft, Vlad," Rune said.

Vlad shrugged his shoulders and looked up at Rowan. "Maybe I'm just starting to become more human."

Rune turned to Jacan to go over the plan once more. "Remember, if you get hungry, use Mei's powers to grow food. You never know how long you're going to be in the arena for, especially if what you're trying to do is have one up on Zara; she's not going to be happy about that."

"Has no one ever thought *not* to kill someone?"

"No. No one has tried to attempt that before. I'm sure we would have tried if any of us were put in the arena together."

Vlad gave Jacan a handshake. "You got this. Don't cave in." Vlad walked out the door with Rowan, Albie and Sienna followed behind them.

"Use the ring on Jeff, if necessary, but be discreet about it," Rune advised. "We don't want our only weapon against them taken up."

Just then, Alora started to scream as she woke up from a nap. Rune and Mei rushed over to Alora and began to hold her. Jacan watched as Rune put her hand on her forehand to wipe off the beads of sweat dripping down her face.

"What did you see?"

Jacan held his breath, anticipating the worst.

"I saw a lamb with a dragon's horns surrounded by thick clouds of smoke and fire. There was destruction and chaos all around, but the lamb started to shine and glow brightly. Cities had fallen to destruction, but people were bowing down to worship the lamb with dragon's horns even though the lamb was the one causing the destruction. Then I saw two stars fall from the heavens. One was red, and the other was blue. They were intertwined and were trying to separate but could not. Then I saw a cross piercing both stars so they could separate. The red star grew in power and stature while the blue star grew dim. Then I saw eight stars shine brightly, but one star was not shining its own light; it was giving off a false light; it was corrupted. A different kind of light, not like the other seven stars. Then I saw a red dragon sweep one-third of the stars from the sky, and they all fell to Earth. The red dragon became a comet and circled the Earth, trying to find a way to land. Then I saw a battle take place where millions upon millions of people died. People were screaming about the comet coming. They were screaming from the locus coming out of the Earth. They were screaming from missiles being pointed in every direction. Every which way you looked, it was total chaos and destruction," Alora cried.

"Shhh, there, there. Everything is going to be alright." Rune comforted Alora, rubbing her back. "What you see can always be changed; remember that. Your visions are not set in stone. Remember those two visions you had about me? Remember how I was in a battle, and I didn't die?"

Alora nodded.

"You saw me go up against a star, but I overpowered the star; I overcame the star and lived. I think God wants us to pray about your visions and develop strategies, so they don't come to pass. That's all. Now come on, sweetie, we need to get Mei and Jacan to the arena, or else Zara will kill them both, and we don't want that. Now why don't you get yourself cleaned up with Mei and let the grown-ups talk, okay?"

Alora wiped away her tears and nodded. Mei took Alora's hand as they left the room for the bathroom.

"That was…intense."

Rune bit her lip, not responding.

"Why are you worried? You just said that her visions don't always come to pass."

"I lied."

"What? Why?" Jacan asked, alarmed.

"Because I don't want her worrying."

"But you said you overcame a Blood Royal when you were supposed to die."

"You really think I would die against another Blood Royal if I'm the most powerful one here? No. Her vision of me against the star talks about a future event that has yet to happen." Rune crossed her arms and turned away. "There has been only once where her vision has not come to pass."

"Rune?"

She turned back around. "Vlad was supposed to die in a battle but survived by a miracle." Rune didn't explain what happened but did tell him about another vision. "Before you came, Alora had the same vision of the eight stars since the beginning. At first, it was just three of us: Me, Alora, and Albie. One by one, our group became bigger with each Elite Blood Royal that was added. If you haven't noticed, we have eight Elite Blood Royals nearby. One of these stars represents us. One of us is a false star, a false light."

Rune eyed Jacan as Mei and Alora walked back into the room.

"Ready?" Rune asked.

Mei nodded.

"Let's go before Zara chains us in the torture room." Rune put her arm around Mei and gave her a good-natured squeeze.

CHAPTER 36

September 11th, 2023, 10:00 P.M

The compound was stirring with hushed whispers and chatter as the four Blood Royals entered the arena one by one. The biggest television screen Jacan had ever seen was in front of him as he entered the arena. Jacan looked up to see every single Blood Royal kid in the stands. It was more than he thought. If Jacan had to guess, there were 500 Blood Royal children between the ages of eight and eighteen.

"This place must have other compounds," Jacan said aloud. "If not, I would have seen everyone here by now.".

Zara walked out to the middle of the arena next to the four Blood Royals lined up for battle. She began to speak to the crowd of Blood Royals. Zara's long midnight black hair was tied in a long simple ponytail. Her dark amber eyes were piercing Jacan's soul.

"Each of you is descended from the bloodline of Jesus Christ and Mary Magdalene. Each and every one of you carries a special power. Some say it's a gift, while others say it's an abomination. It's not up to me to decide that, but rather my Lord, our Lord. He is our shining light, our Savior, our one true God. He calls each and every one of you an abomination in his sight. Prove him wrong and use your power for evil instead of good. Then you will have favor with him."

Jacan leaned over to whisper into Zara's ear. "I know your secret, Zara. Don't make me use it against you."

Zara's eyes squinched, wondering what he meant, but she continued her speech.

"Before us are four contenders: Jeff, Mei, Breya, and Jacan. Each one of them is strong and capable in their own way. Let fate decide who lives and who dies." She turned her gaze to the four Blood Royals, "Each one of you go to your specific corner and wait for the bell to ring."

Zara looked at Jacan, whose eyes were settled on Rune in the crowd. Jacan smiled at Rune and then looked over at Zara and smiled. Zara's eyes widened as she started walking out of the arena to a platform with a golden chair and a silver chair. Sitting in the golden chair was a man dressed in a white robe. It was the Holy Seer, Cardinal Villere. Zara sat down in the silver chair with a grave face.

"What was that about?" The Holy Seer asked.

"Nothing of importance. He was just asking about when he would get to meet Kieron."

"And you responded with?"

"Soon."

The Holy Seer nodded. The bell rang. All four Blood Royals were on opposite sides of the arena's corners.

"Have you had any luck finding the Black Pope?" Zara asked.

"Not yet," the Holy Seer responded. "He doesn't want to be found, apparently."

"I see."

Jeff looked up and saw the Holy Seer talking with Zara. He smiled, knowing he was someone of importance. Jeff ran towards the trees and camouflaged himself to the trees. Breya started to move toward Mei, who was standing still. She put her hands together to form a rain cloud and pushed the cloud toward Mei. Mei couldn't move. She was paralyzed with fear.

"Mei! Run!" Jacan yelled.

As if something sparked inside her, Mei ran toward one of the trees and touched it. A branch started to grow and travel towards Breya.

The arena, which was lit with flood lights, began to dim.

"Of course, they would dim the lights; Jeff has night vision and X-Ray vision," Jacan said out loud to himself.

Just then, Jacan was knocked over by a camouflaged Jeff. Jacan hit his head on a rock; blood poured from the side of his head onto the ground.

Jeff walked over to a knocked-out Jacan, whose eyes were closed. He looked up at Mei and Breya. Breya's rain cloud was now producing wind of mammoth strength. Mei held on for dear life to the tree trunk as the rain cloud began shooting lightning at the tree. The lights dimmed even more so that only a soft orange glow was in the arena. Jacan awoke and saw Mei get hit by a lightning strike.

"Mei!"

Not realizing his mistake, Jeff removed his backpack and opened his bag to get a knife out. Jacan grabbed Jeff's ankle and, in one sweep motion, made Jeff's body fall to the floor, his elbow catching the ground, knocking out the knife in his hand. Jacan grabbed the knife and stared at it. Kieron's name was engraved on the knife. Jacan opened his backpack and saw the same knife in his bag. Zara must have put the same knife in each bag. Jacan watched as Breya walked over to Mei's lifeless body. A smile crept on her face as she began to form another lighting strike to hit Mei's heart. Jacan closed his eyes and focused on the black opal ring he was wearing. He began to circle the ring with his thumb, putting all his energy and intention into the ring and ran toward the trees.

"What is he doing?" The Holy Seer asked. "The boy is right there for the taking!"

Zara squinted and saw Jacan begin to blend in with the trees. Breya didn't notice Jacan running toward her as he became camouflaged with the trees. "Looks like Kieron's microchip has added new gifts to Jacan. The gift of camouflage just like Jeff," Zara said tartly.

"Ahh. The more, the merrier," the Holy Seer said as a matter of fact.

Jacan ran full blast into Breya, knocking the wind out of her and causing her to fall and roll onto the ground. Jacan investigated the crowd to find Rune with her mouth agape and tears streaming down her face. Jacan looked over at the other Elite Blood Royals with tears in their eyes, all of them except Vlad, whose face was solemn. Jacan threw Jeff's knife toward the front, landing just before the platform where Zara and the Holy Seer sat.

"I thought this battle was for us to use our powers against each other. So why are there knives in our backpacks?" Jacan yelled.

The Holy Seer smiled at Jacan. "To make it more interesting!" the Holy Seer yelled back.

"I didn't know you put knives in the backpacks, Cardinal Villere." Zara hissed. "That wasn't a part of the plan. You know how Kieron wants this done."

"There was an incident in England. Kieron wants the battle amped up because of it." The Holy Seer replied. "That's all you need to know."

Jacan looked at Zara, whose eyes told him she didn't know about the knives. It was the man dressed in the white robe who had done it.

"And who are you to make that decision?" Jacan demanded. "Who the hell are you?" He screamed.

The Holy Seer rose from his chair, "I am the Holy Seer, right-hand man to Kieron, our Lord. And if I were you," the Holy Seer smiled, "I would be paying attention to the battle at hand."

Jacan cocked his head to the side to see Jeff running toward him with Jacan's knife. Jeff smiled as he let out laser beams from his eyes at Jacan. Jacan screamed in pain as the laser light sliced through his shoulder. Jacan fell to the ground holding his shoulder. He saw Breya stirring, holding her head as she sat up. Her anger was stirring deep inside her bones; she got up and put her hands together to produce another rain cloud with rain, wind, and electricity. She shot it at Jacan, who blew over to the left, just missing Jeff's downward knife hit to his heart. Jacan got up and started zigzagging away from the raincloud that was headed right toward him, a lightning strike hit Jeff in the process. Jeff screamed in pain and fell to the ground, his eyes wide with terror as he slowly dropped the knife. Breya screamed and hit Jeff with another lighting strike in the head, causing him to fall backward and land on his back. Jeff's face was burnt to a crisp, with no recognizable features on his face.

"Now, this is getting interesting," the Holy Seer laughed.

Jacan kept zigzagging, averting each lighting strike that Breya sent his way; when he finally reached her, he ran into her for a second time, pushing her toward the tree that Mei had clung onto. He looked out onto the crowd and focused his energy on finding Sianna. Once he did, he rubbed the black opal ring and channeled her power. Jacan walked over to Breya, whose eyes were wide with anger.

"I will kill you," she said.

"Not before I do, love." Jacan walked closer to Breya, put his hands on her neck, and squeezed hard, superhuman strength kicked in as Jacan heard the crack of her neck pop. Breya's eyes bulged as she slumped to the ground. Jacan walked over to Mei, whose body was still lifeless.

"Come on, Sianna, don't fail me now."

"Finish her! The Holy Seer yelled.

Jacan put his whole body on Mei's and rubbed the ring, putting all his energy and intention into healing Mei.

"God, if you're real, please use Sienna's gift of healing. I know she can only heal and not bring back people from the dead, but if you're real, show me."

Jacan's hands started to produce a soft yellow light. His eyes widened in disbelief as he watched Mei's eyes open with fear.

"Jacan," Mei cried. "My body hurts."

"I know, Mei, I know. Everything is going to be okay. Jacan picked up Mei's body and held her in his arms. He walked over to the platform where Zara and the Holy Seer were sitting.

"Zara, do not fail me as your twin sister Cara did. Finish this."

Zara stood up and faced Jacan. "What are you doing, Jacan? Finish her."

"No."

"If you do not finish her, I will finish you."

"I'd like to see you try. We both live, or you die. You both die if we do not live," Jacan said as a matter of fact to the Holy Seer and Zara.

"I will make a deal with you," Zara amplified.

Knowing that Jacan knew the truth about her and Rune, she needed to think quickly on her feet.

"And what deal is that sweetheart?"

"I will let you both live, but you will endure the machine. Deal?

"Deal," Jacan agreed.

The Holy Seer eyed Zara. "I hope you know what you're doing. If Kieron gets a hold of this information—"

"I'm in charge here, Holy Seer. Not you."

"This is true. But you are letting him make a fool out of you. He must be punished, so the others do not get any ideas."

Zara nodded. "And one more thing Jacan."

"Now what?" he said with beady eyes.

"If you do not endure the machine, you will die," Zara smiled.

"Let it be known to all other Blood Royals that this behavior is unacceptable. If any of you defies me like Jacan or decides not to participate in the battles, you will die by my hands. Jacan will undergo the machine. He will be tested beyond imagination; if he survives it, he may never be the same."

CHAPTER 37

September 11th, 2023, 5:38 P.M. - Istanbul, Turkey

Zach fluttered his eyes open to see Sofia lying next to him. He didn't know if Sofia was still mad at him for the trial and everything else he had done wrong, but he was ready to make it up to her.

"Sofia," Zach whispered.

Sofia awoke and started to sob. Her shirt was missing, but she still wore her bra. Embarrassed, Sofia turned away from Zach and covered herself with her hands. Sam ran over, took off her plaid shirt tied around her waist, and put it on Sofia. Sam hurriedly buttoned up the buttons so that Sofia could stand up. As she did, Zach stood up alongside her and gave her a bear hug.

"Sofia, I'm so sorry for everything! I was so foolish to talk to you like I did back at your flat. Please forgive me. I should have been there for you at the trial," Sofia allowed him to hug her and gave him a squeeze back.

"I should have called you and offered my services to help in any way I could," Zach continued, speaking into her ear. "I was awful to you and said some pretty mean things. You aren't a prima-donna; you aren't selfish; you are the second most wonderful woman I have ever known."

"He's talking about me," Sam laughed.

"Oh, okay, we were wondering," Loch laughed.

"Can you ever forgive me?" Zach backed away and looked Sofia in the eyes.

Sofia stayed quiet for a moment, collecting her thoughts. "I forgive you; of course, I forgive you…." She sighed. "Why didn't you tell me that you and Sam were pregnant?"

"I just found out four days ago. Sam kept it a secret until she passed the three months mark. She wanted to make sure everything was okay before telling us. Her family has a history of losing children before the first trimester."

"It's true. I couldn't tell a soul until I knew for sure," Sam smiled. Sofia walked over to Sam and gave her a hug. She put her hand on her stomach and smiled. Sofia closed her eyes and tuned into the baby's heartbeat.

"Do you want to know the sex of the child?"

"You can tell?"

"I can."

Sam thought for a moment and shook her head no. "You can tell Zach, but I want it to be a surprise," she gleamed.

"Zach? Do you want to know?"

Zach laughed, "I've always been one for knowing secrets, so yes, come over here and whisper it in my ear."

Sofia walked over to Zach and whispered in his ear the sex of the child.

Zach smiled as he thought about the lineage of Jesus and Mary. It only made sense to him what the sex of the child would be.

"Hey gang, we need to go; the police are here!"

Two police cars stopped forty feet in front of them and were yelling out to them in accented English.

"Stay right there!" Four policemen yelled.

The six of them took off running out of the café.

"Over here!" Zach yelled at the others. Loch and the others followed Zach as he took them to an undisclosed building. They went inside the door and walked down to the basement. It was the drug den that Zach and Sam stumbled on a few days back.

"What is this place?" Jax asked.

"It's where people come to get high," replied Raziah.

Jax watched in horror as a girl of about twelve years old pushed a needle through an old man's arm, his eyes rolling into the back of his head with a smile on his face.

Raziah knew in her heart of hearts this was where Lennox had been getting her drugs. Every way she looked, she saw men, women, and teenagers either getting high or about to get high. She could see bruises on every arm; no arm was safe against the needle.

"This is absolutely sickening," Jax remarked. "I don't understand how someone could do this to themselves."

The twelve-year-old girl made her rounds to shoot up three more people before finally settling in on a chair at a table. She took out some brown powder and laid it across the table. She picked up a straw and started to snort the substance. Jax walked over to her and sat down next to her.

"What's your name?"

"Why? Are you a cop? Have you come to arrest me?"

"No, I'm not a cop; I'm an archeologist."

"I always wanted to be an Archeologist. I've always been fascinated with the pyramids."

"It's not too late, you know. You can stop all of this and still become one. You have your whole life ahead of you."

"That's true," she replied, "but I can still do drugs and become an archeologist. I met an American girl here who's an archeologist who does drugs, and she seems like she has it all together."

Jax turned white as a ghost. "This American archeologist, do you know her name?"

The girl smiled wide, "Lennox," the girl replied, "and she's really pretty, too."

Jax thought he was going to be sick. It all made sense to him now. Why she was constantly late, why she was always ill with a stomachache, why her eyes were pinpoint even at nighttime. The red flags were there, but he just didn't want to see them. Lennox was a heroin user and had been for at least six months, from what he could remember.

"My name is Lilyanna."

"Lilyanna, what a beautiful name. I'll tell you what, Lilyanna, if you quit drugs right here and now, I'll put you on the list for my dig site. You can start learning what it is to be an archeologist. I will teach you everything I know; we can start with the weekends. Here's my card so you can call me anytime to set it up. Just know I will be drug-testing you each time we meet; that's the deal. If you want to be an archeologist, your mind must be clear. You could damage the item you're digging up, and you wouldn't want that, would you?

Lilyanna shook her head, "No, I wouldn't."

"Good, because those lost items are too precious to get messed up."

Lilyanna nodded, agreeing with Jax.

"Now take my card and go home to your parents. I'm sure you have school in the morning?"

"Yes," Lilyanna sighed.

"Go get a good night's rest and call me next week to schedule a time for you to come in."

The girl looked down at the card.

"If not this week, then a week or two after that," Jax continued. "I'm on a secret mission with this lot," he thumbed at Loch and the group, "so I may be out of commission for a few weeks, but I promise to have you on once I'm done with this, okay?"

Lilyanna looked up from the card and nodded, understanding. She took a small bag out of her pocket with brown powder and placed it on the table. She walked out with Jax's card in hand, smiling.

Loch walked over to Jax whose eyes welled with tears. Loch placed his arm around Jax's shoulder, "Let it out all, mate, let it all out." Jax's shoulders shook as he cried. He buried his face in Loch's burly chest.

Zach, Sofia, and Sam, not knowing what was going on, looked over to Raziah, who mouthed, "I'll tell you later." The three all nodded in unison.

"Come on, gang, let's get out of here! We have a lot to talk about," Zach announced. "But first, let's all get a good night's rest. We'll reconvene tomorrow at our hotel at 1:00 P.M."

CHAPTER 38

September 12th, 2023, 12:00 P.M - The White House

Kieron watched as the President of the United States finished his brisket and moved his plate to the side. President Frank Hill was a fat man but an intelligent man; he had to give him that. He was outspoken and had won the people's hearts with his wit and charm.

"So, young man, what brings you into my office today?"

"We both know why I'm here, President Hill."

"The comet." The president took a long swallow of iced tea.

"That is one of the reasons, yes."

"I must say, I was not expecting Israel to place Jesus's Crown of Thorns on top of your head. Sacrilege it is."

"If you say so."

"And you don't think it is?"

"He was an imposter. Anyone who dies and only shows himself to fifty people can't be trusted. If I were to die and come back to life, I would broadcast it for the whole world to see."

"They didn't have cameras back then, sonny-boy."

"Touché. But if he were truly God, he would have flown worldwide to let the people know exactly who he was. There are too many discrepancies if you ask me."

"Now that we can agree on." He took another sip of tea. "How can I help you today, King Gedron."

"I like the sound of that."

"I bet you do," Frank retorted.

Kieron raised an eyebrow with a smirk at Frank.

"What's wrong, Frank? Is being President not satisfactory for you? That's okay because I'll take over your position here shortly."

"You pompous little shit," the president laughed. "You won't be able to even apply for the presidency for another eighteen years."

"Not if I have a say in it," Kieron leaned across the table. "Rules are meant to be changed, President Hill. You would be wise to understand that."

"You may have fooled everyone, Kieron, but you don't fool me," as the president leaned across the table and pointed at Kieron's chest, "I know what you really are."

"And what's that?"

"A con artist with a lot of money," the president leaned back and grinned.

"I'm no con artist, but yes, I have a lot of money."

Kieron looked at his watch and smiled. He would only need to put up with this arrogant man for ten more seconds.

"By all means, Mr. Gedron, if you have other places to be, please be my guest and leave," the president gestured to the door of the Oval Office.

"About the comet."

"We are handling the situation; now, if you please, I have important business matters to attend to."

"Tell your wife I say, hello."

"My wife is dead, Mr. Gedron."

"And now, so are you."

In the blink of an eye, President Hill was shot dead in the head. Kieron stood still as he heard bullets coming through the window. He lifted his arm, so he was shot in the shoulder and in his right hand. Kieron dropped to the floor and closed his eyes. He had undercover Russian spies shooting up the white house. They would take out the Vice President and half of the cabinet. All Kieron had to do was play dead until someone came to get him. This would cause the United States to go into a panic with, once again, with him coming to the rescue. His plan was falling perfectly into place.

CHAPTER 39

September 12th, 2023, 1:00 P.M - Istanbul, Turkey

Sam was placing a salad bowl on the counter when she heard a knock at the door. She opened the door to see Raziah, Loch, and Jax holding a brown bag.

"We brought chicken," Loch grinned.

"Great! I've got salad and steamed potatoes with garlic and cheese."

"Magnificent," Loch said with a smile.

Sofia was texting Everette, but it was useless; she hadn't heard a peep from him since the incident. His phone kept going straight to voicemail.

Sam turned to Sofia, "I'm sure he's okay…he's a…umm… fallen angel after all."

"Sam!"

"What! It's true!"

Sofia glared at Sam.

"I mean, like, he's a fallen angel, so I'm sure the fallen angel inside of him, Gadreel, will not let him die any time soon. That's all I meant…"

Sofia rolled her eyes.

"Fallen angels? Now I've heard it all," Loch remarked.

"Okay, just so everyone is up to date, Everette is an MI6 agent. He saved my life. He just happens to also have the spirit of a fallen angel inside of him named Gadreel. He may or may not have made a wish to be the top MI6 agent which may have opened a door for a fallen angel spirit to come inside of him. He didn't do it on purpose, nor did he expect it to happen." Sofia looked around the room, meeting each person's eyes. "We've all made wishes before. It doesn't mean we meant to sign a deal with the devil. So, let's just cut him some slack, okay?"

Everyone nodded in unison.

"Good. Now can we eat and get to the matter at hand."

"Here, here because I'm starving!" Sam said. "I'm eating for two now, you guys."

Everyone in the room laughed. Loch handed Sam a plate, "Dig in, lassie; the world is your oyster."

"I thought you'd never ask," Sam winked. Sam piled her plate with chicken, salad, potatoes, and bread. She sat down and made another plate, putting the same amount of food on the second plate. Everyone stared wide-eyed at her.

"I eat a lot for a girl," Sam grinned, "but now I have an excuse for the second plate right off the bat."

Everyone chuckled and let Sam finish her second round before the others made their plates. After an hour of everyone chit-chatting and stuffing their faces, Zach broke the silence. "Okay, everyone, we have a lot to go over. Should I begin with sharing what I know?"

Everyone murmured and nodded.

"Sam and I made a discovery at the Hagia Sophia," Zach began. "After Sam made a wish at the wishing stone, we were taken to a column with a riddle written on it:

'As above, so below,
The connected ones will start the show,
If it is the harp that you seek,
Sound and vibration will start at the teeth
But first, blood and sweat must be unleashed.'

After I made a wish, I put my blood into the wishing stone and spoke a prayer with the sound of my voice. We were led to a woman who told us the key to getting inside the crypt lay with Sofia."

"I don't have any key like that," Sofia remarked.

"What do you have on you?"

"Nothing. I don't have anything that could—wait."

Sofia took off her cross necklace and handed it to Zach. "Agnes bought this cross necklace for me at a bookstore. She said the owner told her a man had sold it to him. A man who had special powers of healing. And that man was Jesus Christ."

"How in the heck did that happen?" asked Sam.

"Pure luck, I guess," Sofia laughed.

"Not luck, divine intervention," Zach said confidently. "The cross is the key to getting into the crypt and getting the last fragments of the Divine Feminine. The gospel should be able to tell us where David's harp is as well as the Speaking Stone of Destiny. The old blind woman who told us about the key said only two Blood Royals could open up the crypt with the key. My guess is it has to be me and Sofia. We're both Blood Royals and are related. The closer the genealogy, the better our chance of opening the crypt." Zach grinned. "Who wants to go next?"

"You haven't had a chance to meet Lennox yet," Jax jumped in, "but she's the one who found the lost parchments at the dig site. She sold the parchments…but we know what the parchments say. They read as follows:

'Shrouded in darkness, she will come,
Only made known by the Son of God,
Blood, light, sound, and water will have their part,
But not before life imitating art,
She will bring back the dead and bring them to their knees,
Only by repentance and the rule of threes,
What is to come has come before,
Make sure you don't open the wrong door.'

"What the heck does that mean?" asked Sam.

"My words, exactly, when I heard that!" exclaimed Jax.

"Something about the phrase 'life imitating art' stands out." Raziah said, picking up the narrative. "I'm just not sure what it could refer to yet. But this is what we do know. The incarnation of Eve will be shrouded in darkness. This represents her being hidden until her time comes from her meeting with the Messiah. When that time comes, the four aspects of water, blood, light, and sound will have their part in her revelation." She gestured with an open palm toward Sofia, "We know that Sofia can heal and bring back the dead, but she cannot bring people to repentance by the sound of her voice. Only by repentance of the first Eve can she undo all of this. A single woman will have Eve's spirit living inside her as well as wisdom Sophia— the Divine Feminine."

"Zach," Sofia said, suddenly anxious. "When I was with Kieron, he told me he was the Antichrist incarnate," she rubbed her hands over her arms as if cold. "He told me to tell you his plan and what he wants from you or else...."

"Or else what, Sofia?"

"Or else..." Sofia looked down, avoiding his gaze, "he would murder your unborn child."

"How does Kieron even know about that?" Zach slammed his fist on the table. "Not even Brother Guiden knows!"

"Oh, my God!" Sam exclaimed, placing a hand on her stomach.

"When I saw the pregnancy stick land on the courthouse floor, Everette saw me look at it," Sofia explained. "Gadreel lives inside Everette, so he must have relayed the information to him utilizing telepathy."

"I have to tell you, Sof," Zach said, running his hands through his hair. "I like this guy less and less each time you speak his name."

"I already told you it's not his fault. He didn't know he had a fallen angel spirit living inside of him!" Sofia leaned forward and touched Zach's arm. "If we can just get him to do more good than evil, Gadreel has to leave his body…. I think."

Zach tilted his head at Sofia, wondering if she really believed what she was saying.

"All I know is that Kieron told me to tell you to give you his card and to find David's harp, the Holy Grail Chalice, and the coordinates to the Stone of Destiny," Sofia continued. "He also said that he would kill me eventually. Sacrifice me since Delaney and I are both parts of the Holy Grail."

"Wait, what? Kill you?" Zach asked, stunned.

Sofia nodded.

Zach took her hand and shook his head. "Who is Delaney?"

"Delaney is Kieron's bride-to-be," Sofia explained. "She has the power to bring people to repentance just by her presence."

"Zach," Jax interjected, "Loch and I watched a video of this girl with red hair…."

"Show me the video."

Jax showed everyone the video of Delaney airing her segment on the red comet. Delaney was in a state of confusion when she saw a man with a dagger run at her. Her body emitted a powerful red energy that blasted him and another man. Hundreds of people fall to the ground asking and begging for forgiveness.

"I'm speechless," Zach replied. "How can there be two incarnations of Eve? It doesn't make any sense." He turned to Sofia, "you both each have a gift that would define the incarnation of Eve. Would the Divine Feminine really do that?"

Sofia shrugged. The group sat in silence, pondering this question. If anyone knew anything, it would be Brother Guiden.

"I'm going to call Brother Guiden and see if he has any revelation or insight into this," Zach announced.

\#

After Zach got off the phone with Brother Guiden, he was even more dumbstruck. "Okay, everyone, this is what Brother Guiden told me…. he found a journal entry of an order called "The Black Pope." The Black Pope is the one who holds the secret and whereabouts of the Stone of Destiny."

He looked around at the group and divided them with his hands, "I think we should split up into two groups. Half of us go to the Hagia Sophia to get the Chalice and find David's harp; the other half will go on the search for the Stone of Destiny."

"I think it's better if we all stick together," Jax pointed out. "It's safer that way."

"With my gift of teleportation, I agree with Zach." Raziah said. "All he would need to do is call me and tell me the coordinates of their whereabouts, and I can take us to him. We need to make the most of our time. I need to get back to my husband and Lennox in Ireland. We are searching for our daughter, a Blood Royal who has been kidnapped. We've already lost two children…" Raziah started to tear up, "and I *will* not lose another."

"How many children do you have left?" asked Sam.

"Two."

"May I ask how the others passed away?"

"My son's name was Ahmet; we lost him to a heroin overdose. My daughter, Cara…" Raziah paused, unsure if she was ready to share this information. She looked directly at Sam, "…was killed in the crossfire of your battle against the Holy Seer."

"Cara was your daughter?" Zach asked, baffled.

"Yes, she is a twin to Zara. My other daughter Rune is sixteen years old and, we believe, has been kidnapped by the Holy Seer to an undisclosed area in Ireland. That's where the Divine Feminine took us when we teleported out of Istanbul. We didn't ask to go there; we just arrived there. I could feel her presence when I was there. I know she's there."

"The Speaking Stone of Destiny has been in Ireland, Scotland, and England. If the Divine Feminine took you to Ireland to find your daughter, then the Stone of Destiny must be there, too!" Zach exclaimed.

"What did the journal entry say about the Black pope and the Stone of Destiny?" Raziah questioned.

"The journal entry said this:

'From the darkness we mise,
From the ashes, we rise,
Fire and smoke will be their disguise,
They are the ones who will burn this world free,
They are the one who is the true light of the three.
The Stone of Destiny is hidden out of sight,
Only True Darkness and Light can unearth it with might,

There are only four left in the world who can be the one,
Choose wisely, my friends; it cannot be undone,
The Stone of Destiny hides where one cannot see,
Don't use your eyes; they will only deceive thee.'

"Brother Guiden deciphered the journal entry. He said only four people would be worthy to use the Stone of Destiny and not be killed by it. These four people have risen from the ashes and are the light of the three. The three being the Father, the Son, and the Holy Ghost, or Lucifer, Satan, and the Antichrist. The Stone of Destiny is hidden where we cannot see with our earthly eyes but with our spiritual eyes."

"How can we find something we can't see?" asked Loch.

"I think it's going to be like the Indiana Jones movie. The platform was there the whole time, but he had to take a leap of faith and step out. It was always there, but you had to believe to see it," Zach replied and paused thoughtfully. "Okay, so here's the plan. We'll all go to the Hagia Sophia after dark. Raziah will teleport us all inside. Then we will use Sofia's cross to open the crypt to find the last remaining parchments and find the location of Davis's harp and the Stone of Destiny. Then we will split up and reconvene and go from there."

CHAPTER 40

September 12th, 2023, 3:00 P.M. - Compound in Ireland

Jacan was walking to his room when he heard his name being called by Zara on the P.A. system, "Jacan Eisen, please report to Zara in one hour in front of the cemetery. And don't be late."

As Jacan headed inside the room, he saw Rune talking to Vlad in a heated but hushed tone. Vlad kept his cool, but Rune stormed out of the room.

"What was that about?" Jacan asked.

"Nothing much," Vlad shrugged, "just Rune being Rune."

"Well, if she stormed off like that, it can't be nothing."

"She thinks you are the false star who will betray us."

"Are you kidding me? Still? After what I did in the arena yesterday? I proved my loyalty to her and to all of you. I risked my life for Mei's. I stood up to Zara and the man in the white robe."

"He's called the Holy Seer. He's the right-hand man of the man who's running this place."

"And who's running this place, do you think?" Jacan asked, wondering if Vlad knew.

"Some say it's a billionaire; some say it's the government."

"But what do you think?"

"I think it's someone with immense wealth and power. How else can you hide five hundred people without being noticed by other people? To do that, that person needs to have technology beyond what we know or can even comprehend. They must have the government, CIA, or MI6 at their disposal because they have one guard for every five kids here. And half of these guards aren't like that dumb ass one that got himself killed. They're armed and dangerous. They're intelligent and know what they're doing."

"How did you figure that out?"

"I overheard two of the guards talking about it while I was shoveling cow manure one day. One talked about how he was an MI6 agent; the other said he was a CIA agent."

"That's pretty dumb for them to talk about it out loud like that."

"I'm sure whoever hired them had them all meet and disclose information beforehand. That way, they can use it against one another if something goes wrong."

"So, tell me about this machine," Jacan spoke more urgently. "What is it, and what does it do?"

"So far, only one person has survived it," Vlad said. "It's a machine that tests your wits, strength, and DNA."

"Who survived it?"

"I did," Vlad smiled.

Jacan nodded. "Congrats, man."

"Thank you," Vlad said. "When I was in the arena, I won by default, or what Rune calls a miracle. Zara didn't like that, so she put me in the machine. The machine is hooked up to your brain and produces a hologram video game. It will test your wits, strength, and your DNA. If you fail any one of those tests, you die. The trick is to know it's not real," Vlad paused to make sure Jacan was paying attention. "You must remember it's not real," he repeated adamantly. "The second thing to remember is to use all your knowledge and wits to beat the second round. When it comes to the DNA, you're on your own."

"What is the test?"

"How much of a Blood Royal you are. If you're over fifty percent, you pass."

"Piece of cake," Jacan responded.

But it wasn't going to be a piece of cake. Jacan, as far as he knew, wasn't even one percent Blood Royal; Zara knew that. She was either out to kill him or had some master plan to save him.

#

At exactly 3:00 P.M., Jacan appeared in front of the cemetery where Zara was waiting.

"Are you going to kill me?"

"You will pass the test as long as you pass the other two tests. I have to make an example out of you. You cannot defy me like that again, Jacan. Do you understand me? Or else you battle me in the arena, and I am a trained Punarjanam. You are no match for my skills, even with your super strength."

"How am I going to pass the DNA test?"

"I'm going to put drops of blood from another Blood Royal in the test tube."

"Why did we meet at a cemetery?"

"To show you your mortality. You are not a god or a Blood Royal; once your mission is completed, your body will return to what it was. Kieron controls the microchip unless he decides to keep the chip in you. He can also keep the microchip in you and turn off your powers. Everything is decided by him. Now let's go and get this over with."

After walking for what seemed a millennium, Jacan arrived at a building he had never seen with other Blood Royal children outside. It was the same unfamiliar kids he had seen at the arena.

"Why are we separated? Why are these kids here and the other half there?"

"These are less potent Blood Royals. We have them here for other reasons."

"Which are?"

"You ask a lot of questions."

"I'm an inquisitive kid."

"I can see that."

"So what do they do here?"

"Mostly labor with some arena battles."

As Jacan and Zara walked inside the stonewashed building, they took a left down a corridor and made their way to the back. Jacan could hear kids screaming the further they got to the back of the building.

"Why are their kids screaming in every other room?" Jacan asked timidly.

They're undergoing testing with a prototype of the machine. It's less intense but still effective."

Jacan gulped as Zara opened the door to find the Hoy Seer waiting for them.

"We haven't been properly introduced. I'm the Holy Seer, right-hand man to Kieron, the Antichrist himself. And you are causing a stir within the compound. I'm hearing kids speak of a rebellion after your little impromptu yesterday. This cannot happen. So, your testing will be broadcast for the whole compound to see. This is what happens when you defy me."

"Holy Seer, you know he's not a Blood Royal, right? Kieron has him as an undercover agent acting as a Blood Royal." Zara said flatly.

"I know this, Zara, which is why he must still undergo the machine. He defied you, me, but most importantly, he defied Kieron; he must be punished."

"What will Kieron think?"

"Kieron gave his blessing, of course," the Holy Seer smiled.

The Holy Seer leaned into Jacan's ear, "Kieron says the next time you defy him, you will die a slow and painful death by his hand. Just pass the first two tests, and we will go from there," the Holy Seer spat.

"But the DNA test...."

"I said pass the first two tests, and we'll go from there. Do not ask again."

The Holy Seer placed his hand on Jacan's shoulder and forced him to sit down in a metal chair while Zara hooked up a mechanism to his head. The Holy Seer glared his teeth, "Let the games begin."

CHAPTER 41

September 12th, 2023, 2:03 P.M. - The Vatican

Brother Guiden hung up the phone with Zach and paced the room, pondering the latest paradox of two Eves. Was it possible? If so, what was the purpose? He thought back through the imagery the Divine Feminine presented to Zach when she first appeared to him. He combed through the riddles, looking for clues. He perused online pictures of the paintings hanging in the Hagia Sophia. He cross-referenced previous research. It was like feeling for a light switch in a dark room, he could feel the answer nearby, but couldn't quite find the switch. When he pictured Sofia in his mind's eye, the feeling grew stronger. He knew she was a part of the enigma, but what part did she play in the overall divine plan?

Brother Guiden made himself a cup of tea and asked the guard stationed outside his quarters to accompany him up the circular staircase to the Vatican Roof. He knew they wouldn't allow him to go up there alone, but he didn't mind a quiet guard joining him. He needed to pace and to get a new perspective. He hoped the literal new perspective of looking out over the orange rooftops of Vatican City would help him. Taking such a physical action had helped him solve problems before.

As usual, the first glimpse of St. Peter's Square, the Vatican Gardens, and sparkling rooftops took his breath away. He still wasn't used to his position here or the opulence of Vatican City. He missed his regular walking route in New Orleans where he thought the best, beneath the live oaks and concentrating not to trip on the roots lifting up a sidewalk, this kind walking - where he had to focus on his feet often helped him work out a question. Nature found its way through the human made concrete; the imperfections also had a purpose.

He paced the smooth roof of the Vatican alternating from looking at his feet to the roofs, to the dome of St. Peters, and the statues of the apostles and eventually started to follow a train of thought about dualities. It certainly wasn't the first time the divine plan had included "both/and" in a duality; the incarnation of Jesus being a founding principle of Christianity - Christ was both divine and human, so perhaps two Eve's served some kind of similar purpose: sinner and redeemer; and often God had used flawed people, Peter for example, with his temper and his questions, to do powerful spiritual work in the human realm. There was also Mary, who said yes to bringing Jesus into the world when she was scared and not yet married.

Brother Guiden paused to look at the green dome of St. Peter's Basilica. He pictured the statue of Peter as the first Pope inside the Basilica. The statue depicts Peter holding the keys of heaven aloft in one hand, while his other arm is bound in a sling. The dichotomy depicts both strength and weakness: the weight of the keys is too heavy to be borne by human strength alone; the first pope must rely on the divine. The Holy Spirit guides the hand that holds the keys, while the sling reminds the viewer of human weakness.

Brother Guiden felt more certain there were two Eve's for a reason, and any sins Sofia might have made certainly did not prohibit her from being the agent who could heal this rift and redeem all womankind. But she would need to tap into the holy spirit to know what actions to take in order to allow the Eve incarnate out. A flutter caught the corner of his eye, and he looked up to see a flock of white birds rise up and dart around the dome of St. Peter's. He knew intuitively it was a sign from the Holy Spirit. He'd figured out the riddle, at least the spiritual purpose of it. He wasn't quite sure how it would manifest physically, but he knew without a doubt that their dear Sofia was a key player, and she would have to make the right choices. He pulled out his phone to call Zach, but his ring only led to voicemail. He texted an encrypted message. He said a prayer that the group was still safe and that the Holy Spirit was guiding their steps.

CHAPTER 42

September 12th, 2023, 3:57 P.M. - Ireland

Jacan held his breath as Zara flipped the switch to start the machine. His eyes went blurry as he was transported through the darkness. Jacan woke up to his father hitting him.

"You piece of shit, get up and face me like a man!"

"But dad—"

"But dad, no! Why aren't you getting straight A's anymore? What the hell is your problem? Are you dumb? Is that it?" he slurred.

"And why are you skipping school," his mother replied. "What will the others think of us?"

Jacan could see that his father was drunk again.

"Maybe I wouldn't skip school if my father wasn't a drunk and always hitting me."

Jacan's father ran over and knocked him across the face so hard that he fell straight to the floor. Jacan could see blood spilling from the floor from his mouth. His father had split his lip.

"Children are to be seen and not heard."

"I'm not a child; I'm a teenager."

Jacan noticed that the photograph sitting on the dining room table was different. He then looked at the wallpaper; instead of being laced with ivy, it was laced with roses. Jacan realized some details about his home were different.

"Dad, when's my birthday."

"June 12th. Why? Do you think you're getting a huge party this year? Because you're not."

Jacan's father hadn't remembered his birthday for the past four years.

"This isn't real; you aren't real."

"What kind of nonsense are you talking about, boy. I'll give you something real to think about."

As Jacan's father began to punch him in the face, Jacan closed his eyes and smiled, "This isn't real."

Before Jacan's father could touch him, the scene dissolved in front of him. Jacan was now in front of Zara, smiling from ear to ear.

"Hello, Jacan. You failed the machine. Are you ready to go into hand-in-hand combat with me?"

"As ready as I'll ever be."

Zara began to slink towards Jacan, holding a dagger. Zara zipped past Jacan slicing his left arm. Zara did a one-eighty spin and slashed Jacan across his stomach. Jacan fell to the floor; blood was gushing out of him so fast he started to get light-headed.

"Had enough?"

"Not. Even. Close."

Jacan got up, spat blood from his mouth, and headbutted Zara, knocking the wind out of her. The dagger flew out of her hand, landing on the grass next to a headstone in the cemetery. Jacan got on top of Zara and punched her in the face, giving her a black eye. He got up, walked over to the dagger, and picked it up; sauntering back to Zara, he got down on one knee and shoved the dagger through her heart.

"I win," Jacan smiled.

Jacan came to and could see the Holy Seer and Zara's mouth agape, their eyes glued to the television as an AI's voice spoke the percentage.

"Blood Royal percentage is 50.5%.

"That can't be possible. He was supposed to die!" The Holy Seer screamed.

It was then Jacan realized Zara had never put another Blood Royal's blood in the test tube. He was half Blood Royal from Jesus and Mary Magdalene all along.

"Get him out of here and lock him up. I need to speak with Kieron!"

CHAPTER 43

September 12th, 2023, 3:04 P.M. - The White House,
Washington D.C.

The look on the paramedics' faces was priceless to Kieron. "We don't understand how you're not bleeding," the young paramedic said, feeling his Kieron's arms for any injury.

"Yeah, we saw you on TV getting Jesus's Crown of Thorns placed upon your head, and you bled then." A heavyset paramedic joined in. "Why aren't you bleeding now?"

"Technology."

"What does that mean?"

"It means I can't die. With the new technology I will introduce very soon, you all can have the same fate as me. To live forever."

"Until I see a bullet go through your head or heart, then I'll believe it," said the heavyset paramedic.

"You'll see. You will all see very, very soon."

The paramedics looked at each other and rolled their eyes.

"The bullet went straight through your shoulder and exited out of your body into the wall over there. You're clear to go, Mr. Gedron; there's nothing else we can do since there are no bullets inside you or wounds. Just a scar...."

Kieron smiled and thanked the paramedics for their time.

"Mr. Gedron, a moment, please."

Kieron shook the paramedics' hands and walked over to see a middle-aged woman in her early fifties with mousy brown hair and glasses. She had six bodyguards beside her who looked like they could kill a man with their pinkies.

"We must get you to the underground bunker where the others are waiting. We must keep you safe while we figure out our next move against Russia. The United States of America would like to officially offer you a position on the cabinet."

"And which position would that be?"

"Warfare. Let's get underground so we can talk more. We don't know if they will be implementing a second attack."

#

Once in the bunker, Kieron sat down in a black leather chair while the others hushed their voices.

"It has come to our attention that you were shot twice but received no medical attention. Is this true?" The woman with mousy brown hair asked.

"It is."

"And how is this possible, Mr. Gedron?"

"Please, call me Kieron."

"How is this possible, Kieron?"

"By AI technology and microchips."

Kieron watched what was left of the group of the cabinet talk in hushed tones and whispers, their faces changing from disparity to sanguine.

The Secretary of the Treasury stepped forward and addressed Kieron, "The government of the United States would like to offer you a contract as the Secretary of Defense," he began. "Today, we lost many great men and women, including the President, Vice President, Speaker of the House, Attorney General, President Pro Tempore of the Senate, and Secretary of Defense." He glanced behind him, and the others nodded for him to continue. "We know you are young and inexperienced, so we will have an ex-Attorney General and an ex-Secretary of Defense guide you as you make the transition. The United States will offer you thirty billion dollars to access your technology with *New Light Technologies*. Is this something you can do?"

Before Kieron could answer, a guard interrupted, "Madame Secretary of State, you are the next in line as acting President of the United States of America. We just received word that Russia and China have bombed five major cities of the United States: Chicago, New York City, Los Angeles, Boston, and us here in Washington, D.C. What are your orders?"

Kieron watched as the Secretary of State bit her lip. She was the same woman with mousy brown hair that came to get him. She didn't have a clue what to do.

"If I may, Madam President," Kieron interjected, "The United States of America needs to show strength now more than ever. The first question I would be asking is how were they able to bomb us without our notice? If their aircraft entered our land, why weren't we notified? Seems to me, there is a Russian or Chinese spy within the cabinet or the Defense. I would do background checks on everyone in the cabinet as well as high-ranking officers of the Defense. Once you find who the rat is, I would put a bullet through his head on national television to show Russia and China we are united more than ever."

Kieron looked about the group to see if he had their attention; he read their eyes to see who was in agreement with him. "I would then announce to the world that the President and King of Israel stands with the United States. We cannot let this act of warfare go unpunished; with my technology of cloaking invisibility, microchips, nanotechnology, and AI technology, we will surely win the war against Russia and China. And believe me, when I say, ladies and gentlemen, that we have entered into World War III against the communists."

"Madam President, if I may, are you really going to listen to a seventeen-year-old kid?" one of the cabinet members protested. "Are you really going to give a seventeen-year-old kid the position of Secretary of Defense? He has no experience with warfare any more than I do. The people of the United States will not allow it; I will not allow it. The Secretary of Defense position description states that a person must be retired from service for at least seven years. This is not going to fly with Congress. I don't care how intelligent he is, how much money he has, or what technology he has; he cannot be Secretary of Defense."

"Fine. Then as acting President, I will create a new job for him," the Madame Secretary said. "He will be Head of Technology & Warfare, a position next to the new Secretary of Defense, and there's nothing you can do about that, John."

"Madam President, we're getting word that they were Russian and Chinese spies as well as Blood Royals," the guard touched his earpiece. "Earthquakes are occurring around the areas of the bombings, and we already know of a few Blood Royals who have that kind of power."

"As Head of Technology and Warfare," Kieron asserted, "it's my duty to implement a plan to stop Blood Royals from causing total chaos against our people. I want a decree put out to round up all Blood Royals. I want them tested to see what their powers are. We need to categorize them on a level from one being the least dangerous to ten being the most dangerous. We will have categories in both intelligence, strength, and abilities."

"What will we do with them?" the Madame President asked.

"I will find a solution to extract their powers and put them in a serum for us to use against the Russians and Chinese."

"Kieron, I'm sure they have Chinese and Russian Blood Royals; it's not just Americans."

"I never said there wasn't! But if they have Chinese and Russian Blood Royals working for them, then we need to put a plan to stop them from annihilating us. With Russia and China joining forces against us, it's only a matter of time before they get others to join them against us. We must act, and we have to act now."

Kieron could see all nodding in agreement with him but one, the man who refused him the cabinet position of Secretary of Defense.

"Is there a problem, John?"

"Just you, you're my problem. I'm not taking orders from a seventeen-year-old kid who doesn't even have the right to vote. This is absolute nonsense! Look at all of you, a bunch of wimps and dumbasses."

"I'd like to be President one day," Kieron smiled. "However, waiting until you're thirty-five years old, *that* is an issue for me. I would like to change the rule to eighteen years old."

"Now I really think you're delusional," John said, huffing.

"John."

"Yes, Madam President?"

"You're fired. Get your things and leave this bunker. You're on your own. I'm tired of your smart-ass comments and your negativity."

"But, Madam President!"

"But no, John! Guards, get him the hell out of my sight."

John ran at Kieron and was eight inches away from knocking his lights out when Kieron put up his hand and created a forcefield around him and President June Crawford. John ran into the forcefield knocking his head into it. John kept punching the invisible glass making his knuckles bloody, but no matter how hard he tried, he couldn't penetrate it.

"You'll regret this! You'll see! You'll all see!" John yelled from outside the forcefield. "He's going to be the demise of America. You just wait and see!"

CHAPTER 44

September 12th, 2023, 9:00 P.M. - Hagia Sophia Mosque

As soon as the sun rolled away and the stars came out, Zach, Sam, Sofia, Jax, and Loch touched a part of Raziah's body to teleport inside the Hagia Sophia. They ensured the coast was clear of guards and rushed to the wishing column. Zach took off the cross necklace and inspected the wishing column.

"Does anyone see a cross imprint on here?"

Everyone looked on all four sides but to no avail.

"Zach! Remember the column where the riddle was located?" Sam asked glcefully, "I remember seeing a small cross on the other side!"

As they rushed to the column, they could see the indentation of a cross in the exact spot. Zach placed the cross inside the indentation, waiting for something to happen, but nothing did.

"I don't understand why nothing is happening," Sam said, defeated. "The blind woman said the cross is the key to opening the crypt."

"I think we need to find a cross where there is an opening of a possible crypt," Zach pondered. "Everyone search the floors for a cross or a wall that could open up. Look for any paintings of women in threes," he directed. "That should be our clue. The lost parchments said she is in threes like the Father, the Son, and the Holy Ghost…." Zach thought for a second. "Or look for something that could be life-imitating art like a sculpture."

As everyone searched the floors and the walls, Sofia stood looking at a painting on the East side of the wing. It was a painting of Eve taking a bite of a fig. She was covered in ivy leaves with Adam beside her and the snake wrapped around the tree. There was something about this painting that was calling out to Sofia. Something she couldn't explain but nonetheless beckoned her to it. Sofia walked closer to the painting. She could see the snake's tail was wrapped around Eve's foot. Sofia looked down at her birthmark in the shape of an "S" by her ankle.

"It can't be," Sofia whispered to herself.

Zach noticed that Sofia wasn't looking for a cross but stood looking back and forth from the painting to her left ankle.

"What is it, Sofia? Did you find something?"

"Zach, I've had this birthmark in the shape of an "S" since I was born," Sofia pulled up her pant leg to show Zach the birthmark. "You said to find a painting of life imitating art, and I think I found it," she pointed to the painting. "This painting shows Eve's fall from grace by eating the fruit God told her not to eat. If the

Divine Feminine is shrouded in darkness and has both light and darkness in her, this would be why. She was good and full of light until she sinned and fell, taking Adam and all of humanity with her. Look at the snake's tail wrapped around her left ankle, then look at my birthmark."

Zach peered closer at the painting, then bent to look again at Sofia's ankle. "They're almost exactly the same!" he exclaimed.

"I think it's a sign, Zach. I think I'm finally starting to believe you…. I think Delaney and I both have part of the fallen nature of Eve inside of us. I wonder if she also has the same birthmark on her left ankle? Could Eve really be put into two separate bodies? Why would God do that? It just doesn't make any sense to me. I really hope it's just me and not the both of us, so I can put a stop to all of this."

"Don't worry, Sofia, whatever happens, we'll figure it out. We always do," Zach put his hand on Sofia's shoulder to comfort her.

"I can't mess this up. The whole female half of the population is riding on my shoulders," Sofia said, crying.

Zach could see that Sofia had completely lost her bearings. It was too much pressure for one woman to handle. Sam walked over and put her arm around Sofia's other shoulder.

"I overheard you and Zach talking," Sam said. "You are the most wonderful woman I have ever met, Sofia. You're kind and generous. You always put others before yourself. If God did split Eve's soul into two bodies, we would find it out, I'm sure, by the next parchments. No matter the results, you are worthy of love as a human being." She gave Sofia's shoulder a squeeze. "If the Divine Feminine didn't believe in you, she wouldn't have incarnated you to live again. Now what do you say we continue with the mission of finding the cross?"

Sofia wiped away tears from her cheeks and smiled at Sam. "Let's do it, sister." They embraced in a hug. As Sofia looked over Sam's shoulder, she saw a cross at the wall on the right of the Eve painting.

"Found a cross on the north side of the wing," said Loch.

"I found one over here on the west side of the wing," yelled Jax.

"If we put the crosses all together, they point to the Eve painting," Zach deciphered, "they make the shape of a diamond."

"I bet it refers to that scripture!" said Sam.

"What scripture?" asked Loch.

"She is more precious than rubies; nothing you desire can compare to her. Long life is in her right hand; in her left hand are riches and honor. Her ways are pleasant ways, and all her paths are peaceful. She is a tree of life to those who take hold of her; those who hold her fast will be blessed. Proverbs 3:15-18," Raziah said with a smile on her face.

"Do you know what that means, Sofia?" Raziah asked.

"No, I don't. What does it mean?"

"It means that you are the tree of life and the way of salvation for all womankind. It is you who fell, and you who will save. God holds you in high esteem, and you are worth more to him than rubies or gold. Know that; feel it deep inside your bones. By blood, we have been made; by blood, we have been saved, and by blood, we will be saved again—by your blood."

Sofia knew what she had to do. Raziah handed her a small dagger. Sofia pricked her finger and put her blood where the indention was for the cross. She smeared her blood and then put the cross inside; as she did, a wall with the Eve painting began to move with stairs leading underground.

"Come on, gang! Let's go!"

Everette watched as the group descended the winding spiral staircase into the darkness.

"Follow them," Everette said out loud to himself.

"No, Gadreel, I will not do your bidding!"

"Follow them, or I will kill you."

"You can't kill me, you need me, and I'm telling you right here and now, I'm not following them."

Zach led the way down the spiral staircase when he stepped on the next stair, which triggered a timer causing the step to crumble and fall into a pit. Almost losing his bearings, Zach tumbled back and Jax grabbed hold of him under his arms, so he didn't fall into the black watery abyss of the pit.

"Whoa! Nobody move!" Jax yelled.

Each person stayed on their step and didn't move a muscle. The steps where the others stood started to shake, causing the first step to crumble, with the others following suit.

"Think, Zach, think!"

Zach had to hurry, or they would all fall into the dark pit. He noticed a second set of stairs across a gulf. A cross was on the wall next to the third step before him. He jumped and landed on the step without it crumbling. As he did, the original steps stopped crumbling behind him just two stairs from where Jax stood across the gulf.

"Raziah! Teleport over here to this step with the others. As long as we're standing on a step with a cross on the wall, we'll be fine!" He yelled.

Zach noticed every third step had a cross and hopped down to the next stair.

"Make sure you guys jump every third step! And whatever you do, DON'T touch any of the other steps!"

One by one, Raziah teleported each person over the gulf and put two people per step to avoid overloading the steps or making it difficult for them to squeeze by. As each person jumped, they landed on a stair with a cross on it; they were almost to the bottom when Sam accidentally landed on a second step causing the steps from behind them to crumble.

"Sam!" Zach yelled.

Sam was the last one in the group; she lost her footing and grasped the railing. She hung on the side of the staircase with her feet dangling toward the pit.

"Zach!" Sam cried.

"I got her, Zach! Stay put!" Raziah yelled out.

As Raziah teleported to Sam her body landed so hard on the step that the rest of the staircase came falling down. The others had either already made it down, or were close enough to the ground, that their falls were minimal.

"God, please give me superhuman strength to save this girl!" Raziah cried out as she clung to the single remaining step.

Raziah picked up Sam with all her might and threw her down to the ledge where Zach was waiting. Zach, Loch, and Jax caught Sam with their bodies watching in horror as Raziah, from the force of her throw, fell into the gulf. Raziah did not cry as she fell or even scream. The only thing Raziah repeatedly said was, "Save my daughter, Rune," which echoed up to the group as Raziah fell to her death in the black abyss.

CHAPTER 45

September 12th, 2023, 10:03 P.M. - Hagia Sophia Mosque

Sam cried profusely as she put her head on Zach's shoulder.

"Zach," Sam cried even louder," it's all my fault! You told us to be careful, and I wasn't! Now Raziah is dead because of me!"

Sam couldn't control her tears as she repeatedly saw in her mind's eye the rest of the stairs fall into the abyss.

After a moment, Loch said, "I don't mean to be crass, but how in the hell are we going to get out of here?"

Everyone gave Loch the side-eye.

"What? We're all going to die in here if we don't figure this out. I knew we should have split up into two groups."

"Now is not the time for woulda's, coulda's, shoulda's, Loch. Have some decency; Raziah just saved Sam's life. What if it was you instead of Sam? Would you be saying this now?" Sofia barked.

Loch hung his head and shook his purple head no.

"I didn't think so. Let's move forward. I, for one, will not have her death be in vain. We will find her daughter and save her."

"This can't be the only booby traps there are, there has to be more." Zach said cautiously. "Everyone be on the lookout for anything out of the ordinary or strange."

The group strolled as they came to a fork in the walkway. The right-hand side had a single cross, while the left did not.

"Stay to the right, gang; the left is booby trapped."

At each fork was a lantern; Zach smiled as he took a lighter from his jean pocket. He always carried one around for this one reason. He learned it from the movies; sometimes, just sometimes, films saved people's lives; whether the writers knew it or not, they were saving theirs tonight.

"Come on, guys, let's go."

Loch, Sofia, Jax, and Sam followed suit after Zach; all sticking close to him as he navigated the way underground. Another fork would pop up every few minutes, and Zach would always pick the side with the cross on it. After what seemed like he had done it five times, the last fork in the road had a cross on both sides of each side of the wall.

"What do we do now?" Sam asked.

Zach studied both walls but couldn't find a difference in the crosses. "There's nothing here to differentiate which tunnel to take. They both look exactly the same."

Loch came up to the front and pointed his index finger up above. "My time for redemption is here; look up, mate."

"Oh, right," Zach laughed.

Zach read the contents in Hebrew in English for all of them to understand.

'The Holy Grail that you seek is not one that is always meek,
In order to know which road to take, give your life,
but no soul can take,
Only one who has a chamber may drink from thee; only one
with a chamber is the one who can set you free.'

"What does it mean?" asked Jax. "It's all so alluding."

"We have to pick a side and put the cross in," Zach said. "Chamber, chamber, what could that mean?" Zach asked the group.

Sam's motherly intuition began to kick in as she pointed to her belly, "A chamber, guys, you know, like a womb. It's where darkness resides, creating the light, a human being. We create a child in us, and sometimes a woman can become a mama bear to protect her children. That's what it's talking about, where it says, 'not always meek.' We will give our life for our child, even if that means we die ourselves, but no man can take our soul; it is only God's to take."

Zach walked over and kissed Sam on the lips. "You are amazing, you know that? You are beyond brilliant and beautiful. I still can't believe I get to call you my wife," Zach said with a wide grin.

"I know, I know, I'm a genius. Applause later; we gotta keep moving."

Zach handed Sofia the cross. Use your intuition and pick a side. It should be you, not me, who does this. You are Eve; you are Wisdom, Sophia. I know you will make the right choice. Sofia closed her eyes, stood in the middle of the fork-way, and touched each cross. She closed her eyes and began to pray.

"God, I know you are real. Jesus, I know you hold the keys to life and death. Holy Spirit, if you can connect me, Mary Magdalene, and help me choose the right path, I will be forever in your debt; *we* will be forever in your debt."

Sofia's right hand grew hot as she saw a vision of Mary Magdalene etching the cross symbols on the wall. In the vision, Mary Magdalene smiled at Sofia and pointed to the right wall. Sofia smiled back as the vision began to fade. Sofia put the cross inside the cross etching on the right wall. A stone moved in the wall and fell to the ground. Inside the opening, they could see the Holy Grail, the chalice. It was a plain wooden cup made by the hands of Jesus Christ himself. The cup read, "Yeshua the Christ & Mary Magdalene the Beloved Disciple."

Sofia took the cup gently from inside the wall and looked at it. The water turned into wine, and she drank from the cup. A warm sensation went throughout her body; she began to give off a soft, warm red glow. Sofia felt more alive than she had in her entire life. She felt rejuvenated, she felt clean, she felt pure, she felt whole. The wine represented Jesus' sinless blood, and she drank from it gladly.

"You guys, the water turned into wine, and now I feel like I can take on the whole world. I feel like I've been given a new body, a new mind. I feel whole, a feeling I have never felt in my entire life."

"Just wait until you meet Jesus for real. Then, you will really feel whole," Zach gleamed.

They took the right path and walked down it for a few minutes before stopping at a crypt with a white-washed stone wall. Along the wall were multiple imprints where the cross would fit. Each cross had a Hebrew letter on it.

"How are we supposed to know where to put the cross?" Jax asked.

Zach was completely stumped. "I have absolutely no idea... for once, I'm completely stumped. If we make a wrong move, it could be our last night on Earth."

CHAPTER 46

September 12th, 10:23 P.M. - Hagia Sophia

Sofia thought about the painting with Adam and Eve with the snake wrapped around the tree and Eve's ankle. It suddenly dawned on her like a ton of bricks.

"Zach!" Sofia grabbed his arm. "The password is Eden. The painting of Eve is what led us down here. The first original sin takes place in the Garden of Eden. It's where everything started, and the story of Eve's redemption unfolds. I can feel it deep within my bones. Zach, I know without a shadow of a doubt the password is Eden.

"Sofia, you're a freaking genius!" He hugged her.

Sofia smiled as she shrugged her shoulders.

Zach spelled 'Eden' in Hebrew, putting the cross in each Hebrew letter. After Zach had finished spelling out Eden, the ground began to shake as the wall opened to reveal a large stone with parchments on top of it. Zach walked slowly but stopped just in front of it. He could see these were ancient parchments, so he must be careful. The pages were written In Hebrew and read: '*The Gospel of the Divine Feminine, written by Mary Magdalene.*'

Zach walked closer to the parchments and read the first page which was a table of contents for the gospel. Zach quickly read over the contents to find the parchment they sought.

"There's a chapter here called Genesis Revealed, a chapter on the Holy Grail, a chapter on the Ark of the Covenant, and a chapter on David's harp!" Zach exclaimed. "There are eleven chapters in here, and I can't wait to go over them all, but we need to focus on the Holy Grail and David's harp right now. The chapter for the Holy Grail reads:

'The Holy Grail that you seek is not one that is always meek,
Covered in darkness, but her light you seek,
She must be the one to give her life, don't think once, but twice you see.

She is the one who gave life to us all; she is the one who started the fall,
If it is the divine that you seek,
Look within and give her your weak.

Fall to your knees, repent! Repent!
Just make sure it was blood that was spent,
For all to be saved, this must you do; don't let your sin keep it from you.

You must remember and beseech thee,
Call upon the name of the Divine Feminine and come back
to me,
Then you will have peace, and I will sanctify thee.'

"That's all there is for the Holy Grail; we will figure that out later. Now let's read about David's harp," Zach said.

'David's harp is hidden in light,
The sun, the moon, the stars, which light?
David's harp repels evil spirits,
Be deliberate, don't be incoherent.

Hear what I'm saying and follow your heart,
Only one who is true can give a fresh start,
She must put down her vices and believe in thee,
Then she will find forgiveness and be set free.

There are many women who can use the harp,
Not just one, but many who fit the part,
Follow the sign of the wandering star,
Then you will find rest and not have to spar.

Which light is true, you must deduct,
Know your scripture, induct and unlock,
Choose wisely, my friend, or you may not live,
The Divine Feminine will not give you a second chance.

By blood, you have been made, and by blood, you will be saved,
Look within and be amazed,
Use the harp for good, not evil, or else,
Destruction will come upon your house.'

"Everyone be on the lookout for a pictograph or an etching of a star in this crypt," Zach directed.

Everyone began to look for a star etched in the walls, Soon, Sam called out,

"I found a group of stars over here on the left side of the wall!"

"I found a group of stars over here on the right," said Jax.

"And I found a group of stars by the door," said Loch.

Sofia walked over to the north side of the wall, where she also found a group of stars etched. "I found them as well over here on the north side."

Zach started with Sam, then worked his way to Jax and Loch, and ended with Sofia. Sofia's star cluster was different from the others. Each had a cluster of seven stars, but Sofia's had an eight-star off the side. It was the wandering star.

"Sofia, Raziah was always saying that quote, by blood, you have been made, and by blood, you have been saved," said Jax. "Use her dagger to cut yourself and put your blood in the wandering star etching."

Sofia took the dagger out of her purse and pricked her finger again. Blood started to ooze out, and she placed her finger in the etching. Three apparitions began to form in front of Sofia, a sun, a moon, and a star. A feminine voice began to speak, "Pick the right symbol, and the harp is yours."

Sofia began to look over each symbol as she pondered the riddle. David's harp represented goodness and light. She knew from scripture that angels were called stars in the Bible, the sun represented Jesus Christ, and the moon represented Mary and the church. She discarded the symbol of the star, which left only the sun and the moon. In scripture, it said David was a man after God's own heart. That would represent the sun in masculine form. But it seemed to Sofia that God was doing a new thing. To pass on the harp from the masculine to the feminine. The church represents mankind, but the moon represents the women and their monthly cycles.

"I pick the symbol of the moon," Sofia said.

"You have chosen wisely," said the feminine voice. "All who have sought the harp before have picked the star and failed. They think because the riddle says, 'wandering star' that it must be the symbol, but they do not know their scripture as you do."

"Thank you," Sofia beamed. "May I ask…How are we supposed to get out of here? All of the stairs have fallen, and there is a deep pit."

"By flying, of course."

Sofia had forgotten all about her new gift of flying. She had done it a couple of times, and it was exhilarating. But she only thought she could carry Sam. "I don't have the upper body strength to carry the men," she nodded.

"You drank the wine, did you not?"

"I did, yes."

"You have drunk the blood of Christ, my beloved Son whom I cherish. Ask anything, and I will give it to thee."

"I wish for superhuman strength."

"Your wish is granted, my child."

David's harp magically appeared out of thin air. It was smaller than Sofia had expected.

"David's harp is bigger than this," said the Divine Feminine, "I shrunk the size, so you wouldn't have to lug it around everywhere you go. It's quite big," the Divine Feminine laughed.

"Well, I'm glad you did," Sofia laughed, "thank you for doing that."

"It's my pleasure; now go forth and finish what you started."

"Wait! What about the Stone of Destiny?" Zach pleaded, "It wasn't listed in the fragments, and we have no idea where it could be."

"You must go to Ireland. Follow the path of the rising sun. Jesus will be waiting for you there. Only he can unlock the full potential of what is inside Sofia."

"But where in Ireland?"

"What are some famous landmarks in Ireland that could hide the Stone of Destiny?" the voice questioned.

Zach thought long and hard about where a natural landmark could be to hide the Stone of Destiny. He thought back to the journal entry that Brother Guiden told him about.

'From the darkness we mise,
From the ashes, we rise,
Fire and smoke will be their disguise,
They are the ones who will burn this world free,
They are the one who is the true light of the three.
The Stone of Destiny is hidden out of sight,
Only True Darkness and Light can unearth it with might,
There are only four left in the world who can be the one,
Choose wisely, my friends; it cannot be undone,
The Stone of Destiny hides where one cannot see,
Don't use your eyes; they will only deceive thee.'

"The journal entry that the Black Pope wrote states that it is hidden out of sight and must be unearthed. We cannot use our earthly eyes but must use our spiritual eyes instead. So, what I think you're saying is it's hidden in plain sight but can't be seen with natural eyes."

"That is correct," said the Divine Feminine.

"What natural wonder could be made of stone that could hide the Stone of Destiny in Ireland?" Asked the Divine Feminine.

"Giant's Causeway," Loch said, grinning.

Everyone turned to face Loch, stunned.

"I may be a brute sometimes, but I know my history of the UK. Giant's Causeway would be the perfect place to hide the Stone of Destiny. It's hidden somewhere in plain sight, yet it's never been found."

"You are correct, Loch," the Divine Feminine spoke.

CHAPTER 47

September 12th, 2023, 8:33 P.M - Ireland

Lennox looked up at the stars. She began to name the constellations to Yousef.

"There's Orion," she pointed, "And that's Andromeda over there. And my favorite constellation is the seven sisters, the Pleiades."

Lennox felt her phone vibrate in her backpack. She had forgotten to check her phone all day; she was having such a great time with Yousef, learning about him and Raziah and their adventures, that she completely lost track of time. She had six missed calls from her mother. Lennox's eyes became blurry as tears started to well up as she read a text message.

'Lennox, your father passed away this morning at 10:00 A.M. He loved you dearly and was so proud of you. Know that. We will be having a funeral for him in a week. We hope you can make it.

Love,
Mom'

Lennox fell to the grass and began to cry. Yousef, who had continued on walking, ran back to Lennox and held her tightly, brushing her hair out of her face as she let out her anguish and pain.

"He's, he's, he's dead, Yousef, my father is dead," she cried. "I will never forgive myself for not being there for him."

"Lennox, you cannot blame yourself for not being there. Your father knows you love him. It says in the Bible that every man must die sometime. It was your father's time to go."

"But it wasn't! He still had another year or two to live. I don't understand why his time was cut short."

"We don't always understand the ways of God, but we trust him anyway. It is not up to us who lives and who dies."

"How does God pick? Who lives to be just a few years old, and who lives to be ninety years old? How does he pick?"

"No one knows the answer but God. We just don't know. Why does an innocent kid with cancer die at five years old, but the mass murderer lives to be eighty years old? To me, that is unfair. It should be the righteous who live long and not the wicked ones. Maybe God gives them more time to repent from their sins? We just don't know. God's thoughts are higher than our thoughts, and God's ways are higher than our ways. When we start thinking that we could do better than God, remember Jesus. He gave his life so that we may live. He lived a perfect and sinless life so we may be in heaven one day with our God. No matter how you look at it, who lives a long life and who doesn't, for God to give his only Son to us so that we can be redeemed and live forever, well, that shuts me up real quick. I will put my trust in God because I know God is good and fair. He will always do the right thing. God cannot lie, God cannot steal, God cannot sin. So however he decides to take someone, that is how he wants it. Trust in God, trust that he is good, that she is good."

Lennox wiped the tears off her face and stood up. "I just need to be alone for a while, if that's okay."

Yousef nodded as he watched Lennox walk away.

Lennox took out her phone and dug for her bag of drugs. Her hand landed on something long and skinny. Lennox took out the item; it was a singular needle. All she needed was a spoon, and she could complete the task. She was tired of living, tired of the pain, tired of the rejection. Tomorrow she would have a date with the needle.

"Lennox, are you ready?"

"I guess…"

"I've just had a vision from the Divine Feminine; we're almost at the compound. Get ready to fight and use the gifts that God gave you. You're gonna need it."

CHAPTER 48

September 12th, 2023, 11:38 P.M - Hagia Sophia

Sofia easily picked up Loch as she carried him flying over the pit.

"Wow, lassie, you really are strong now. Can your gift rub off on me?" Loch laughed.

"I don't think it works like that," Sofia laughed.

"It was worth a shot," he joked.

After Sofia had flown everyone back inside the Hagia Sophia, they realized they wouldn't be able to get out without Raziah.

"Uh, guys… how are we going to get out of here?" Sam asked. "We don't have Raziah to teleport us out."

"I think I may be of service."

Stepping out of the shadows was Everette. He had stubble on his chin and looked like he had been hit by a bus.

"Everette!" Sofia exclaimed, "you look like hell."

"I know."

"What took you so long?"

"Kieron is not a forgiving person."

Sofia noticed that Everette had a black eye and burned cigarette marks on his left arm. "He did this to you because of me?"

"He did this to me because he can. He's the Antichrist. I have no power over him."

Sofia's cheeks began to burn with anger. She hated Kieron for almost raping her, and she hated him for hurting Everette. "If it's the last thing I do, I will make him pay for this, for all of this."

"I'd like to see you try," Gadreel said in a deep voice out of Everette's mouth.

"Gadreel is getting stronger," Everett said, sounding defeated. "We have to move quickly before he completely takes over my mind. I don't know how much longer I have."

"Let's all get our things, hop on the Concorde jet, and head to Ireland."

As they climbed into the jet, Zach's phone clicked into service, and he noticed Brother Guiden had sent an encrypted text when they were underground. He read and deciphered it in his head. He looked up at Sofia who was chatting with Everette. Brother Guiden had just confirmed everything he'd thought about Sofia. His sister was the one to lead them to the Stone of Destiny. Zach said a quick prayer to the Holy Spirit to guide Sofia's mind and choices. She was the one who held all the keys now.

Zach walked over to his sister and whispered into her ear, "Brother Guiden just confirmed what we've discovered. He says when the time comes, if you don't know what to do, ask the holy spirit and Divine Feminine to guide you. You're not alone."

Sofia looked up at him and smiled. "I know," she replied.

CHAPTER 49

September 13th, 2023, 7:17 A.M. - Concorde Jet

Sam was dreading calling Yousef to tell him the news. She still felt responsible for Raziah's death and didn't know how she would tell him. They had been aboard the Concorde jet for five hours and still had two more to go before landing in Londonderry. They would need to rent a car and spend another hour on the road before getting to Giant's Causeway.

"Zach, I don't think I can do it…" Sam said weepily.

Zach put his arm around Sam and kissed her on the forehead.

"Sam, Yousef is an understanding man, from what I've been told by Jax and Loch. This isn't your fault; it could have been anyone one of us who triggered those steps."

"But it wasn't any of you. It was me." Sam buried her face in her hands and began to cry.

Loch walked over to an empty seat, sat down, and faced Sam.

"Sam, I owe you an apology. I'm not good at apologizing, as I'm usually right, but in this case, I was dead wrong to act the way I did. I shouldn't have spoken like that. I'm sorry. Raziah knew what she was doing; she gave her life for yours, but that doesn't mean what happened was your fault. I'm a brute man myself, and I'm not agile; I can tell you that right now."

Sam wiped away her tears and laughed a little.

"I've seen you while you eat with a fork. It scares me," Sam laughed.

"I'd rather use my hands, to be honest, but that would make for a messy meal," he winked.

The whole cabin laughed at Loch's remark and settled back down. Zach dialed Yousef's number and handed the phone to Sam. We're all behind you, Sam. Everything's going to be okay," Zach said lovingly.

"Hello?"

"Yousef, it's Sam Dorsey."

"Hi Sam, how are you? How's the treasure hunting going?"

"Well, we found what we were looking for. We have David's harp, Jesus' chalice, and the Gospel of the Divine Feminine."

"That's wonderful news!" exclaimed Yousef. "All you kids need is the Stone of Destiny and the Crown of Thorns to complete your mission."

"Kieron has the Crown of Thorns, but we know where the Stone of Destiny is. It's hidden at the Giant's Causeway in Ireland."

"Wow. I would have never guessed it would be there."

"Us either. If it wasn't for the Divine Feminine giving us a clue and Loch figuring it out, we would have been out of luck."

"Tell Jax he needs to call Lennox…she's having a hard time right now. She just lost her father to cancer, and I'm afraid she's going down a dark hole fast."

"Noted, I will tell him…."

"What's wrong, Sam… I can tell there is something wrong by the sound of your voice…."

"It's about Raziah…she didn't make it. She gave her life to save mine. Yousef, if I could take it back, I would. It's all my fault. If I wasn't so clumsy, she would be alive today." Sam began to cry as Yousef comforted her.

"Sam," he choked up, "don't you dare blame yourself…"

Sam and Yousef both listened to each other cry for a moment over the phone until Yousef recovered enough to speak. "Sam, I would have done the exact same thing for you. Raziah is the love of my life, and I will miss her more than you will ever know…. Raziah fought the good fight; now it's her turn to rest in peace with God."

"I know she was deeply faith-filled," Sam said, catching her breath.

"Deep in my heart, I know she would make the same decision if faced with it again. She knows you're an expectant mother-to-be, and she has lived a joyous life of being a mother of four kids. She saved your life so you can experience what it is like to be a mother. I know that's why she saved your life."

"Thank you for your kind words, Yousef." Sam said, wiping away her tears. "You have no idea how much it means to me."

"There is one thing you can do for me, Sam."

"Name it. I will do anything."

"If I give you the quadrants to my location, can you drop by here first before going to the Giant's Causeway? Lennox and I could use all the help we need to bust those kids out. I know they will have some sort of advanced technology that's hiding the compound. I don't know how we're going to get in."

I think I know someone who will," Sam said, smiling at Everette. "We will, of course, all come to help your cause. What they're doing isn't right, kidnapping Blood Royals like that. Have you seen the news? Russia and China have bombed five major cities. They're saying Blood Royals are behind it, and they're rounding up Blood Royals as we speak all over the United States. The rest of the UN followed suit after the United States put out the order. It's only a matter of time before every Blood Royal is under Kieron's thumb," Sam said weakly.

"Not if I have any say," Yousef said with defiance.

Sam hung up the phone and told the gang what Yousef had asked. Zach went to the pilot and told him to change quadrants to the Cliffs of Moher.

CHAPTER 50

September 13th, 2023, 5:15 A.M. - The White House,
Washington D.C.

Kieron had yet to hear an update about Zach and the precious items he was hunting. He decided to track down the Concorde jet and see what the group was up to. They were no longer in Istanbul but in Ireland.

"Naughty, naughty boy."

Kieron tried calling Everette, but it went straight to voicemail. Kieron began to concentrate and project himself into the Concorde jet. He could see Sam trying to play David's harp. He saw her laugh as she kept messing up on the strings.

"I can see you found my items, Zach Dorsey," Kieron's voice said, echoing throughout the jet.

"And we're not giving them to you," Zach said.

"Ya, you can't make us," Sam said, chiming in.

"No, sadly, I cannot. But I know what will."

Kieron's body became see-through as he became a hologram on board the jet. Zach walked up and punched Kieron in the nose, but his fist went straight through the hologram.

"And what's that?" Zach said defiantly.

"I thought you were smart," Kieron said.

"And I thought you weren't a coward," Zach said.

"If you don't hand over the relics, I will enable a bloodbath between the Blood Royal children."

"You wouldn't."

"You must know me better than that by now, Zach. You know what I'm capable of. You have twelve hours before my jet lands in Ireland. Better yet, make it four hours. I will just teleport myself after I meet with the president and the cabinet. You're keeping up with the news, are you not?" Kieron asked, smiling.

Zach bit the inside of his cheek, "We are."

"Then you know it's only a matter of time before your church of Christianology will shut down, and the people will come against you. People are terrified of Blood Royals and what they can do. It will be a modern-day witch hunt, and I have already started implementing policies and procedures toward Blood Royals. I will give you the quadrants of the compound. You will give the Holy Seer the relics, or you will watch the Blood Royal children murder each other one by one. Now, if you'll excuse me, I have a date with the President."

Kieron vanished from the jet, leaving everyone stunned in their seats.

"What are we going to do, Zach?" Sofia questioned.

"We'll call Brother Guiden and go over everything in the Gospel of the Divine Feminine with him. We'll review every parchment we've found and piece it together on how to beat Kieron."

"I have a plan to get past the invisible barrier," Everette said. "But you're not going to like it, Sofia."

"Tell me, then I'll decide."

"I will let Gadreel take over my mind but not completely, just enough to where he is in more control than I am. This will enact Kieron to tell the Holy Seer to trust me while I give him the relics. Then you guys can run in while the pilot flies the jet inside the compound."

"Can you signal to your headquarters at the site so we can have backup to get the Blood Royal children out?"

"I could, yes, with my watch, but…"

"But what," asked Zach.

"My government has been testing Blood Royal adults. They have started segregation from Blood Royals to Non-Blood Royals. If they came, they wouldn't be helping us. They would just round them up and test them, or worse."

"Do you trust anyone who could help us?" Sofia asked.

"How do we know you won't pull a fast one on us?" Loch asked.

Everette turned to face Loch and the others. "I deserve that; I do. But I want to help. After what Kieron tried to do to Sofia… everything changed."

"What changed?" Sofia asked.

"Knowing that I have feelings for you. I couldn't stand not being able to protect you. Let me protect you now."

Sofia blushed and smiled. "We'll talk about that later," she said sheepishly. "Back to my question, do you know anyone who could help us that has any planes, jets, ammo, anything?"

"I know a few people who are team Blood Royals who are MI6. If I can use someone's charger to charge my phone, I can make some calls."

"Great. Let's call Brother Guiden and see if he can help send some people our way too and go over the gospel and the parchments. We need to be ready for anything."

CHAPTER 51

September 13th, 2023, 9:15 A.M. - Ireland

Lennox took out some brown powder and set it on a piece of paper. She took out a straw and snorted it up. Knowing that one line wouldn't get her through, she poured more powder and snorted two more lines. She got up from her spot and walked for a few minutes before standing next to Yousef.

"They'll be here any minute. Are you ready?"

"As ready as I'll ever be."

Lennox took out her phone to text her mother that she loved her and didn't know if she would be able to attend her father's funeral. She didn't know if she would make it out alive, and she didn't want her mother to be disappointed if she didn't show up. She texted that she would try to make it out but had a deadline to meet with the dig site. If she didn't make any progress, she would be fired. Lennox hated lying to her mother, but she didn't know what else to do.

Lennox looked up as she saw the Concorde jet approaching them. She watched as they exited the jet and walked over to her and Yousef.

Jax ran over to give Lennox a hug. He squeezed her tight and lingered longer than just a friend would have. He stepped away to look into her eyes. He could see they were bloodshot and red from her crying. He also noticed that they were pinpoint.

"Lennox, can we talk by ourselves for a few minutes?"

"Ya, sure."

Jax looked to the others to ensure it was okay and that they had enough time to still do what they needed. Zach nodded yes and smiled.

Jax took Lennox's hand and walked out of earshot of the others.

"Lennox, I am so sorry to hear about your father. I can't even imagine what you're going through right now."

"I don't feel anything at the moment. I just feel numb, like it's not real."

"And you may feel that way for a while, and that's totally okay. Just know that you have people who love you and are here for you."

"In what ways?"

"In all ways," Jax said with all his strength.

Jax looked deep inside Lennox's green eyes and kissed her gently on the lips. Lennox was caught off guard. Hungry for him, she kissed him back deeply. She pulled back after kissing him and looked lovingly into his eyes.

"I've had feelings for you for a long time," Lennox said.

"So have I," Jax responded, returning her loving gaze.

"You did?"

"I did, but I thought you just saw me as a friend, like a brother."

"And here I thought you saw me as a friend, a sister," Lennox laughed.

They both laughed as they held each other's hands.

"There is something else I wanted to talk to you about." He squeezed her hands. "I know you're using."

Lennox withdrew her hands from his and looked at the ground. "It wasn't Raziah's place to tell you."

"She didn't tell me. A little girl at the drug den did."

Lennox looked at Jax in question.

"It's a long story, believe me, and I'll tell you all about it once we're finished here, but right now, I just need you to know that I'm here for you, and I love you. I've loved you since the moment I laid eyes on you, Lennox. You're smart, kind, funny. I know that the drugs have changed you. Your humor and the light inside your eyes disappeared when you started using drugs. It's completely changed who you are, and I don't think you realize how much it has. I will help you get clean. I will do everything in my power to help you, but I need you to want it."

Lennox wasn't ready to give up the drugs, but all she ever wanted was to be with Jax. "I'll try for you."

"Not for me," Jax shook his head and pointed to Lennox, "for you."

"I will try."

"That's all I ask."

Loch walked over and stood off to the side of Jax and Lennox. "We're ready."

"Let's go," said Jax.

Yousef and Lennox got the down-low on the plan that the others and Brother Guiden devised.

"We all ready?" asked Zach.

Everyone nodded in agreement.

"Good, let's go."

CHAPTER 52

September 13th, 2023, 9:33 A.M. - Compound, Ireland

Zach walked up, holding the harp, while Everette held the chalice. They stopped just in front of two poles, where they could hear a light buzzing. The Holy Seer smiled and called out to Zach. "Just a little further."

"I know what's in front of me, Holy Seer; even if I can't see you, I can hear the buzzing. Take down the protection wall, or else you're not getting the relics or the location of the Stone of Destiny."

The Holy Seer seethed, pondered his choices, then commanded a guard to switch off the protective shield around the compound. Once he did, Zach and the others could see miles of buildings.

"Where is your sister?" The Holy Seer asked.

"She flew to the site where the Stone of Destiny is located. For safekeeping, of course."

"Naturally," said the Holy Seer.

"Gadreel, come here."

"Yes, master," Everette complied as Gadreel.

The Holy Seer smiled as Everette walked over and stood next to the Holy Seer to give him the chalice.

"Now you, Zach. Hand over the harp."

Zach didn't move a muscle. "Not until you let the Blood Royal children go."

"Oh. Well, I'm afraid you better hurry," a knowing smile crawled across the Holy Seer's face.

"Why's that?"

"Because the bloodbath has started," he spread his arms wide. As he did so, Zach could hear the screams of fighting children in the distance.

Zach's eyes grew wide with anger as he tossed the harp to Lennox.

"Lennox, now!"

Lennox caught the harp and began to play the instrument; as she did, she remembered what the voice had told her:

"You must expunge Gadreel. Only you can do this. When the time is right, you will know."

Lennox had just so happened to take harp lessons when she was a child and all throughout middle school and high school. After the others had revealed the riddle of the harp, it was Jax who put it together that the riddle was talking about Lennox. Lennox was the wandering star, she was not a Blood Royal, but she could see the spirits of both angels and demons. Lennox realized right away that there was something off with Everette. She could sense a presence inside of him. Lennox went over the parchment that Zach had told her about the harp:

'David's harp is hidden in light,
The sun, the moon, the stars, which light?
David's harp repels evil spirits,
Be deliberate, don't be incoherent.

Hear what I'm saying and follow your heart,
Only one who is true can give a fresh start,
She must put down her vices and believe in thee,
Then she will find forgiveness and be set free.

There are many women who can use the harp,
Not just one, but many who fit the part,
Follow the sign of the wandering star,
Then you will find rest and not have to spar.

Which light is true, you must deduct,
Know your scripture, induct and unlock,
Choose wisely, my friend, or you may not live,
The Divine Feminine will not give you a second chance.'

As Lennox played the harp beautifully, Yousef, Sam, Zach, and Loch ran past the Holy Seer toward the screaming of the Blood Royal children. What Zach, Sam, and Loch didn't realize was that Lennox was incoherent, and the prophecy stated she must be coherent to play the harp.

Everette fell to his knees and began to convulse in pain as the fallen angel Gadreel left his body and entered Lennox. Lennox screamed in pain and fell to the ground. The Holy Seer smiled, ran over to pick up the harp, and followed closely behind Zach, Sam, and Loch. Jax ran over to Lennox and held her tightly.

Everette came to and looked over at Lennox. "What happened? What went wrong?" asked Everette.

"She must have used drugs before we got here. The riddle stated that she must be coherent and not incoherent," Jax said quietly. "Now she has to pay the price of the Gadreel living inside her."

"Gadreel has hardly any control of her since he just entered her body," Everette said. "He can only stay if she makes a wish or prayer for a power of some sort."

"Lennox, you hear that?" asked Jax.

"Yes," she nodded, "I will not make any deal with Gadreel."

"Okay, let's find the others, get the kids out of here, and get the relics back," Jax said.

Jax, Everette, and Lennox followed the sounds of the screaming to an arena. They saw multiple kids' bodies on the floor with their eyes wide open.

"Rune! Look out behind you," Jacan screamed.

Rune looked behind her as she saw a boy hurling a fireball at her body. She ducked as the fireball hit a tree. Rowan conjured his fireball and launched it at the kid catching his arm on fire.

"Sianna!" Rune yelled, "Go around and start healing everyone you see that isn't dead."

"Rune!"

Rune looked over to see her father, Yousef, running toward her, "Father!" she yelled.

As Rune ran toward her father, a lightning bolt electrocuted her body. Her body slumped to the floor as Vlad strutted toward her.

"It's been me all along, Rune. I'm the wandering star," Vlad told her. "You were so caught up thinking it was Jacan that you paid no attention to what I was doing."

Rune thought back to all the times Vlad had gone missing for hours and how he managed to win the arena battle when he shouldn't have.

The ground began to shake as a Blood Royal child began to form an earthquake.

"Stop!" Everette yelled, "Don't do it!"

But it was too late; a blonde-haired girl had put her hands to the ground making it begin to open and cause a deep rift.

"Everyone, get away from the middle!" Everette yelled out.

Vlad stayed put. "Kieron wanted me to give you this," he said as he struck another lightning bolt into Rune's body.

The earthquake had created such a large gap that Yousef couldn't jump over to save Rune. He paced helplessly back and forth.

Vlad's eyes widened as he felt a sharp pain in his back. He fell to the ground as he saw a pair of black boots saunter toward him. Vlad pulled the dagger from his back. "Hello, Zara."

"Hello, Vlad."

"Kieron isn't going to be happy to hear this."

"He's not going to find out from you."

#

Zach kicked a guard down and took his gun; he fired it into the air. Some kids stopped fighting and looked over at him.

"Blood Royals! Stop fighting each other!" Zach exclaimed. "You no longer have to fight against one another. We've come to set you free! Follow me if you want to live!"

Vlad dodged Zara and ran over to Zach. He shot a lightning bolt at Zach, causing him to fly back and hit a tree. Vlad then used his ring to channel Rune's power and blast a surge of energy inside Zach's body. Zach's body began to convulse as he felt his insides crawling out from him. Vlad walked over to Zach and smiled. A small black hole began to form as Vlad directed Zach's blood inside the black hole and replaced his blood with Non-Royal Blood.

"You have just been hit with an energy that destroys the basic building blocks of cells. You're no longer a Blood Royal, Zach Dorsey. Zach watched in horror as Sam ran up to hit Vlad on the back of the head. Vlad whipped around to push Sam onto the ground. Sam got up dizzy but ran at Vlad, who blasted her across the way. She fell, hitting her head on a large stone. Vlad slowly approached her and pointed his ring at her belly, "Goodbye, little one."

Vlad shot a surge of energy at Sam's belly; Sam screamed in pain as her eyes fluttered into darkness.

#

"Rune! Rune! Can you hear me?" Zara crouched next to her sister and put Rune's head in her lap.

Rune nodded her head slowly but couldn't speak. She remembered the ring on her finger and tapped into Sianna's healing power to heal herself. She could feel the warmth radiating in her body as her cells repaired.

The ground began to shake as they heard helicopters and jets fly past them. They heard the sound of a bomb going off in the distance.

"We gotta move, and now!" Zara said to Rune.

CHAPTER 53

September 13th, 2023, 10:15 A.M. Compound, Ireland

Loch, Jax, and Lennox were gathering all the kids out of the compound and running toward the Cliffs of Moher. Almost every kid was out of the compound running, walking, or limping toward the sea, where Everette's friend had an Airbus A3380-800 waiting for them. The plane could hold over 500 hundred people.

"Alright, lads and lassies, it's time to board the plane!" Loch directed.

One by one, each Blood Royal went onto the plane and buckled their seatbelt.

"How many did you count?" Loch asked Jax.

"252 kids."

"Okay, we'll wait a little longer, but if we see any fighter jets, we're out of here. We must get these kids to safety; that's our main priority."

Jax nodded. Lennox went inside the plane to calm the children down while Loch and Jax waited outside for more kids to come with Zach, Sam, and Yousef.

#

Zach mustered what strength he had left in him and limped to Sam's lifeless body.

"Sam," he whispered. Zach placed his hands on Sam's body to heal her, but no matter how hard he tried, Sam wouldn't move.

Rune quickly got up off her feet and faced Vlad head-on.

"Vlad, it's you and me. All the other Blood Royals' children have left or are dead. Leave him alone and face me like a man."

"With pleasure."

Vlad channeled Rune's power of quantum power and directed it to her, the surge of energy missing her by an inch.

"Sam," Zach whispered, "please don't leave me."

Zach prayed to the Divine Feminine, but his prayers weren't answered. He was left all alone with his dead wife and child. Zach whispered into Sam's ear the name of their unborn dead child into Sam's ear, "I love you, Sam, I love you, Alexandria."

"I can allow her to live," a dark familiar voice said, walking up behind Zach.

Zach looked up to see Delaney and Kieron walking toward him.

"What do you want in return?" he asked Kieron.

"The location of the Stone of Destiny."

Zach couldn't bear the thought of losing both Sam and Alexandria.

"Heal her first."

"Not until you tell me where the Stone of Destiny is," Kieron said.

Zach knew he couldn't pull a fast one on Kieron, not in this state. He could only think of saving Sam.

"Fine, the Stone of Destiny is somewhere at the Giant's Causeway…Now heal her!" He cried angrily.

"I am a man of my word," Kieron replied.

Kieron placed his hands on Sam, closed his eyes, and began speaking in a language that Zach had never heard. It seemed angelic to him, and he thought it must be the language of the heavenly angels.

Sam's eyes began to flutter open as she coughed and held her stomach.

"Zach! The baby!"

"Shhh, everything will be okay, Sam;" Zach held her hands, "you're alive."

Sam turned to Kieron, "But at what cost?"

Kieron smiled, "At the cost of your child. She dies while you live."

Zach lunged at Kieron, but it was too late. He vanished into thin air, teleporting Delaney and himself to the Giant's Causeway with the chalice and harp in hand and the Crown of Thorns on top of his head.

Zach heard sirens and more bombs go off as buildings began to collapse all around them.

Zach saw a Blood Royal child healing a small red-haired boy.

"Hey, kid! We gotta go, come on!"

Sianna looked up, picked up Rowan, and ran over to Zach.

"Where are all the others?" she asked.

"On a plane, you need to get on; come on!"

Sianna piggybacked Rowan and followed Zach and his group toward the two planes: the Airbus A3380-800 to save the Blood Royal Children, and the Concorde jet to whisk Zach's cohort to the Giant's Causeway.

"Rune," Zach commanded. "I think you should come with us."

Zara embraced Rune. "Go with them and use your powers for what they were made for...for good. I will help the injured children."

The two sisters parted, Zara climbing into the Airbus A and Rune following Zach into the Concorde jet.

CHAPTER 54

September 13th, 2023, 10:46 A.M. - Giant's Causeway

Sofia thought back to the two parchments that talked about the Holy Grail:

'Shrouded in darkness, she will come,
Only made known by the Son of God,
Blood, light, sound, and water will have their part,
But not before life imitating art,

She will bring back the dead and bring them to their knees,
Only by repentance and the rule of threes,
What is to come has come before,
Make sure you don't open the wrong door.'

She thought about the second entry:

'The Holy Grail that you seek,
Is not one that is always meek,
Cast down from the ineffable light,
Drink from the cup; don't put up a fight.

For the two to become one,
Remembrance and repentance must be done,
By blood, you have been redeemed; holy blood, you have
been saved,
It is now your turn to go into the grave.

The Father of Light died for your sins,
The Mother of Life wishes to live again,
For all of this to come to be true,
Look inside yourselves; what will you do?

The act of the transgressor is "The Soul,"
Those who seek will find redemption by not denying
the whole,
The "Self-Perfected Mind" has come forth to live once more,
The Holy Grail must be transformed to be restored.

How this is done, is by gathering the four,
The Holy Grail, the stone, the harp, and the thorns,
Put them all together with the Son of Man,
Then the two will become one and be united again.'

But before she could figure out what to do as the Holy Grail, she needed to find the Stone of Destiny. She took a piece of paper that she had written the journal entry for the Stone of Destiny.

She could hear Brother Guiden's voice in her head and feel his love for her as she read it out loud.

> 'From the darkness we mise,
> From the ashes, we rise,
> Fire and smoke will be their disguise,
> They are the ones who will burn this world free,
> They are the one who is the true light of the three.
> The Stone of Destiny is hidden out of sight,
> Only True Darkness and Light can unearth it with might,
> There are only four left in the world who can be the one,
> Choose wisely, my friends; it cannot be undone,
> The Stone of Destiny hides where one cannot see,
> Don't use your eyes; they will only deceive thee.'

Sofia knew she represented darkness, and that Jesus represented the light. She knew the true light of the three was the Father, the Son, and the Holy Ghost.

"How can I use my spiritual eyes to find the Stone of Destiny?" She pondered.

"Only true light and darkness can unearth it," she said aloud, "which means it's hidden in the stones or underground."

Just then, she felt a wave of peace envelop her. She looked up to see an olive-skinned man with long hair and a beard walk up to her. His blue eyes sparkled with love and grace.

"Jesus, Christ!" She exclaimed.

"In the flesh."

"Oh, sorry!"

"It's quite alright; I knew what you meant," he laughed heartily.

"Jesus, we both must find the Stone of Destiny! The riddle says that both light and darkness can unearth the stone."

"Then unearth it, we shall," Jesus smiled and took Sofia's hand. He began to pray: "Heavenly Father, Heavenly Mother, please open Sofia's spiritual eyes so she may see past the facade."

As Jesus continued to pray for Sofia, Sofia noticed a stone in the Giant's Causeway change shape into a flat rock.

"Oh my goodness, look!"

Sofia pointed to the stone that was now flat where it had been upright. She ran over to the stone and fell at its feet. She could see words written in Gaelic that she could now read.

'Only by blood, sound, light, and water can one use the stone. Choose wisely.'

Just as Sofia was about to speak, Kieron and Delaney popped into their sight. They landed on their feet with a thud. Kieron smiled at Jesus.

"It's been too long, old friend."

Jesus smiled back at Kieron, "Indeed it has, old friend."

Kieron walked over to Jesus and whispered in his ear, "Tell the Father and Mother I said hello."

Jesus knew what was coming but did not flinch. Kieron took Vlad's ring and began to channel Rune's power and blast Jesus with a surge of quantum energy. Jesus fell backward and landed on his back. Sofia could hear bones cracking as Kieron shot another wave of energy at Jesus. Jesus lay crumpled on the ground and cried out in pain.

"Sofia," he whispered.

Kieron walked over to the Stone of Destiny and stood on it. The Crown of Thorns placed upon his head had pierced his scalp so that blood ran down his face and landed on the Stone of Destiny. He took the chalice and drank from the cup of the Holy Grail.

CHAPTER 55

September 13th, 2023, 11:22 A.M. - Concorde Jet

On board the Concorde jet Zach knew they wouldn't make it to the Giant's Causeway without some divine interference.

"Divine Mother, if you can hear me now, please grant my prayer and help us get to the Giant's Causeway in time to save Sofia. And please grant Sam and me back our baby Alexandria. I don't care about being a Blood Royal; I only care about saving Sofia and restoring our child to life."

"You have chosen self-sacrificial love," the Divine Mother spoke in a echo.

Zach bowed his head. In an instant, the Concorde jet was in front of the Giant's Causeway. He didn't have time to ask if the baby was also restored to life. He had to lead the group to action. On his cue, Sam, Yousef, Lennox, Loch, Jax, Rune, and Everette hopped out of the jet and followed Zach as he ran toward Sofia, who was battling Delaney for the harp.

"Let go of the harp, Delaney!"

"Over my dead body, whore!"

Both women played tug of war with the harp, with neither gaining full access. Sofia channeled the divine feminine energy and forced her way into Delaney's mind. She could see the girl Delaney used to be in her mind's eye. She saw Delaney running around, being chased by her brothers on a farm. She saw her in her cap and gown on graduation day, beaming ear to ear. She saw Delaney giving money to multiple homeless people and helping out at soup kitchens. She saw Delaney being drafted as the youngest head News Anchor on CNN. Sofia pushed her mind deeper into Delaney's mind.

She saw a picture of a little girl shaking, cradling herself back and forth while Kieron watched. Kieron placed his hand on the little girl's shoulder as she cried. He smiled as he stroked the little girl's hair. The little girl morphed into the body of an adult Delaney. Kieron's hand glided down her arm as he bent over to whisper a spell in her ear. Delaney was just a scared little girl being manipulated and controlled by Kieron.

"Delaney, I know what it's like to have your life taken away from you. To work for something your whole life only to have it snatched away in a single moment. Can't you see that Kieron is manipulating you? He put a spell on you to make you become who you are now. Someone cold and calculated. But I saw what you were before. You were kind, caring, and free."

Sofia let go of the harp and stared deeply into Delaney's eyes.

"Please, if there is any part of that little girl left in you, give me the harp. You do not want the death of billions on your hands."

Delaney squinted her eyes in shock as she held the harp. She couldn't believe Sofia had just let the harp go.

"Delaney, throw me the harp!" Kieron yelled out from a distance.

Delaney looked at Kieron and then back at Sofia. Anger started to rise out of her, her body began to emit red light, and a surge of red energy blasted from her body, going outwards, producing a shockwave, knocking everyone down on the ground, even Kieron.

"DELANEY!" Kieron growled as he crawled to his feet, "Give me the harp, or I will end you."

Zach rolled over and saw that Sofia had blood coming from her side; a sharp rock had pierced her from Delaney's blast.

"Sofia!" Zach screamed. Sofia's eyes fluttered. She slowly began to get up off the ground but fell back down. Zach looked back at Kieron, who was not paying any more attention to him or Sofia, only Delaney. He knew he wouldn't get a chance like this again. Zach ran over to Rune and looked down at her black opal ring.

"Rune, I need you to conjure up a black hole!"

Rune closed her eyes as she concentrated on a pinpoint of dark matter and pushed out the energy outside her to create a black hole. Kieron saw the black hole come at him and ducked. Kieron channeled Rune's power, creating his own black hole, and threw it at the group, barely missing Zach. Kieron ran toward the Stone of Destiny but was knocked over by Delaney.

"You stole my life, Kieron. You stole the essence of who I used to be. I understand I will never be that person again. Now it's your turn to be my bitch."

Delaney quickly took the Crown of Thorns off Kieron's head and placed it on top of her head. She grabbed the Holy Grail on the grass and ran toward the Stone of Destiny. Delaney reached the Stone of Destiny and stepped on top of the stone, holding the harp with the Crown of Thorns on top of her head. The thorns pricked her head, and blood rushed down her scalp and landed on the stone. All she needed now was to drink from the chalice, and the incantation would be complete. Delaney watched as Sofia came walking towards her holding the chalice. Their eyes glued to one another, without either backing down from the stone.

"Give me the chalice, Sofia. It's over. I am meant to be the Queen of Heaven. I am meant to rule the people."

"No one person is meant to rule Delaney, that is the spell that Kieron placed on you talking."

"Maybe. But I see more clearly now than I ever have before. I always knew I was meant for great things."

"And you are, but not like this. Do you even know what it means to be the incarnated Eve? What that really means? What you have to do?"

"I care nothing for riddles or prophecies. I am the goddess incarnate."

"Then your wish is my command, your highness."

Zach watched in horror as Sofia handed Delaney the chalice.

"Sofia! What are you doing?"

Sofia looked over at Zach and gave him a "trust me" look.

Delaney snatched the chalice from Sofia's hand and turned to Kieron, who was now on his feet. "No!" Kieron yelled.

Delaney drank from the chalice, closed her eyes, and smiled, but her smile quickly turned into a grimace as she fell to the floor, withering in pain. Delaney's body began to seize up and turned gray, solidifying in ash like the bodies of Pompeii.

Sofia knew what she had to do and called out on high to the Father and the Mother. "Holy God, I repent of my sins as the incarnated Eve. I now believe full-heartedly that I am Eve, wisdom Sophia and I repent of all my sins and the sins of all the females of the world."

Sofia picked the Crown of Thorns from Delaney's mummified ashen body and placed it on top of her head. She grabbed the chalice that fell to the floor and gulped the wine. She began to play the harp as her blood from the Crown of Thorns landed on the Stone of Destiny.

"No!" cried Kieron, who was now running towards Sofia.

Even though Sofia had never played the harp in her life, her fingers knew what chords to strike. She played a song that seemed heavenly, as if the song she was playing was the song of heaven itself. The ground began to shake as an earthquake split the Giant's Causeway into two. Sofia began to rise as her whole body filled with light.

"Into your hands, God, I commence my soul and repent of all sins by way of Eve and all the women in the world, past, present, and future…. It is finished."

Delaney began to rise into the air as her body began to fill with light. Sofia now understood what she had done; it had all returned to her remembrance. She was the reincarnation of Eve, and to keep herself from remembering what she had done, she had split her soul into two forms. One of light as Sofia and one of darkness as Delaney.

Delaney's power to cause people to repent of their sins left her and entered Sofia's body. A surge of red light blasted into Sofia as she rose even higher in the sky. Sofia's body exploded into pieces of red and white light that came down, sprinkling on the body of Jesus. Jesus opened his eyes and smiled. Kieron ran to Delaney, grabbed her ashen hand, and faced Zach, "This isn't over, not by a long shot."

Kieron teleported out of Ireland with Delaney's ashen body to New York City.

CHAPTER 56

March 24, 2024, 3:24 P.M - Tulane Medical Center

Six months had passed. Sam and Zach had lost the baby, but they were healing. Even as they grieved, they cherished every day they had together, knowing their lives were a gift. Brother Guiden had counseled them through the darkest days. They knew that loss was a part of life and choosing to do God's will didn't shelter them from the pain of living. They knew they were blessed with being able to help Sofia fulfill her destiny and redeem all women.

They held hands as they walked to the Parkway Tavern to get po-boys. Zach was talking to Brother Guiden on the phone about some new ideas for the Church or Christianology. He hung up the phone and turned to Sam, "Brother Guiden sends his love."

Sam smiled. "Any news about Sofia?"

"Not yet."

"Do you think we'll ever see her again?" Asked Sam.

"I don't know…" Zach said, squeezing her hand, "but I hope so. I really miss Sofia."

"I do, too," Sam said. "She's become like a sister to me as well."

"I know," Zach said.

They rounded the corner, and the Parkway Tavern came into sight.

"Thank goodness, I'm starving for a roast beef po-boy!" Sam said.

"That's my girl!" Zach threw his arm around her shoulder and pulled her close.

"And Zach…"

"Yes?"

She looked up into his eyes. "I'm ready to try again."

Zach smiled and felt like he might cry at the same time, "me, too," he said. He pulled her close and they kissed.

#

Meanwhile, in New York City, Kieron Gedron was heading out to Washington, D.C., where he was to meet the President of the United States.

"Is everything in order?" Kieron asked the Holy Seer.

"Everything is in order, master. They are changing the law to eighteen years old for a person to become a cabinet member."

"Excellent."

END OF VOLUME 2
TO BE CONTINUED…